# "You are very interesting, Anna…"

"Interesting?"

"I can't read people like you can, but I think I just read something about you."

"Really." Anna looked away at the room full of people having a terrific time, then she turned back to Ben. "It's a wonderful wedding," she said as she smiled at him.

Ben blinked. "That's it? You don't want to know what I think I've figured out about you?"

"I don't think I do, not right now," she said.

He came closer, his dark eyes holding hers. Then he took her hand. "Dance?" he asked in a low voice.

Anna had always thought that the idea of someone making your heart skip with a look or a smile was a silly romantic notion. But right then she knew it was a fact.

Maybe it was the whole wedding thing…or maybe it was Ben.

Dear Reader,

In the third story of the Eclipse Ridge Ranch series, Ben Arias comes home to the ranch where he knows he belongs. After a dark and broken childhood, Ben was assigned to the group foster home run on the ranch by a man named Sarge, who restored Ben's hope. As a teenager he thought he'd lost that forever.

Anna Watters arrives in town to change her own life—to get out of Chicago, where the grind of billable hours is robbing her of the hope of starting her own firm and practicing law like her father did until he passed. The more she's around Ben, helping his family with the summer camp they're creating on the ranch, the more she comes to know a man with a kind heart who wants to help foster kids. She knows she could fall in love with Ben if she lets herself.

Ben never planned on being more than temporary with anyone, until he meets Anna and all his plans for a life devoted to work start to crumble.

I've always been fascinated by a hero and heroine who don't know they're in love until they *know* they're in love. When Ben and Anna have their epiphany, they find themselves in a wonderfully scary world that neither one has ever entered before.

I hope you enjoy Ben and Anna's journey as much as I did writing it. Where there's hope, the most amazing things can happen to people who hold on to it tightly and open their hearts.

Best,
*Mary Anne Wilson*

# HEARTWARMING

## *A Cowboy's Hope*

—

*Mary Anne Wilson*

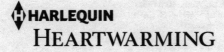

HARLEQUIN
HEARTWARMING

# HARLEQUIN®
# HEARTWARMING™

ISBN-13: 978-1-335-42644-4

A Cowboy's Hope

Harlequin Enterprises ULC
22 Adelaide St. West, 40th Floor
Toronto, Ontario M5H 4E3, Canada
www.Harlequin.com

**Printed in U.S.A.**

PLEASE RECYCLE • THIS PRODUCT IS RECYCLABLE

Recycling programs for this product may not exist in your area.

**Mary Anne Wilson** is a Canadian transplanted to California, where her life changed dramatically. She found her happily-ever-after with her husband, Tom, and their three children. She always loved writing, reading and has a passion for anything Jane Austen. She's had around fifty novels published, been nominated for a RITA® Award, won Reviewers' Choice Awards and received RWA's Career Achievement Award in Romantic Suspense.

### Books by Mary Anne Wilson

### Harlequin Heartwarming

#### *Eclipse Ridge Ranch*

*Her Wyoming Hero*
*Under a Christmas Moon*

#### *The Carsons of Wolf Lake*

*A Question of Honor*
*Flying Home*
*A Father's Stake*

Visit the Author Profile page
at Harlequin.com for more titles.

To Walker Scott Levin:
for being my constant inspiration
for kind, loving, handsome heroes,
since that wonderful day.
~October 19, 1993~
Love you more!

# *CHAPTER ONE*

*Eclipse, Wyoming*
*Mid-March*

ANNA WATTERS HAD never been a risk-taker. She'd been methodical and logical in her plans and life decisions during most of her twenty-eight years. She set goals, made lists, focused on work, and seldom veered off that path. But, in one weak moment, she'd stepped sideways out of Chicago and way out of her comfort zone, and ended up in a storefront firm in a small town in northern Wyoming.

She was sitting in a cluttered office looking across a large wooden desk at the only attorney in the Addison Law Firm, Burris "Burr" Addison. He was a patient man, from all she'd seen over her two-day visit, solidly built and maybe two or three inches over her five feet six inches. He looked to be in his midsixties, with thick gray hair and an impressive full mustache. Wearing jeans, flannel, Western boots, and with a black Stetson hanging on a hook by the door, he fit right in with the other people she'd seen around town.

As nice as Burr had been, she found herself in an awkward situation. She had to make a monumental decision about her future as an attorney before she left for the airport in one hour. The thing was, she didn't know what decision to make.

Burr fingered a gold-painted horseshoe that acted as a weight on a stack of papers in front of him while he made small talk. Obviously, he was trying to give her time to make up her mind about the partnership he'd offered her no more than half an hour ago.

"So, here we are," he said and sat back. "And you're flying out to Chicago soon."

"Yes, here we are," she echoed, buying time. "I don't suppose that horseshoe is solid gold, is it?"

"It's solid but not gold," he said with a smile that lifted the corners of his mustache. "I assume you know about cold winters, coming from Chicago. But if you decide to take the partnership, you're going to need enough warm clothes to carry you from September through

May to survive around here." He sat forward to rest his elbows on the desk, and his expression was a bit apologetic. "And boots, not heels."

Anna had always kept her professional wardrobe simple. Dark dress pants, two-inch black heels, a tailored shirt and her prized designer suede jacket, a gift to herself for passing the Illinois state bar exam. All she'd brought in her bag for her short stay in the town of Eclipse was two changes of the basics, both the same, except for the jacket. They had been appropriate for one of Chicago's top law firms, but not around a town where flannel and denim took front and center.

Maybe her hairstyle fit in, long and brown, pulled straight back from her face in a single braid that fell halfway down her back. It wasn't fancy. Her makeup was sparse; no mascara was needed on her dark lashes. None of that was a priority right now. Money and character were important—how much she could earn and the character of the people she'd be working with. She'd checked out this man and his business online and read great reviews from clients. That was probably the reason she'd agreed to fly out to Eclipse to discuss a partnership, along with the fact that Burr had paid for the trip.

"I do have warm clothes. I guess, if I were to stay here, I'd need to do the town uniform."

He crooked an eyebrow. "'Town uniform'?"

"You know, denim, flannel and boots, maybe thermals, too? Possibly a great Western hat. That's pretty much all I've seen in the past two days."

He chuckled at that, a deep, rich sound. "You're definitely right, but that's a minor concern compared to the huge steps you'd have to take to work here, both geographically and career-wise. I don't want to push, Anna, but I really need your answer before I take you to the airport."

"Of course," she said, hoping she sounded more confident than she felt about producing that answer for him by his deadline.

"Over the past two days, I've tried to give you my idea of what you'd gain by becoming my partner, but only you can evaluate your personal pros and cons."

Burr had done that, and he'd done it very well as he'd showed her around a laid-back town with hospitable people. There was a certain charm with its eclectic mixture of the old West, dude ranches and eclipse viewings. He'd said they even had meteor showers that were spectacular. The town was nothing like Chicago, and definitely nothing like what she was used to. But Burr seemed direct, thoughtful and honest. She decided that it was time to put all her cards on the table.

"After all the trouble you've gone to, paying my way here," she said, "and setting me up at that beautiful bed-and-breakfast, I won't play games with you."

He nodded. "I appreciate that."

"I came here because I've run out of options to get out of the firm I'm currently with. I signed on with them as soon as I passed the Illinois bar when they offered me a great bonus and an unreal salary. To get that, I had to commit to five years. At the time, I really needed what they were offering."

He listened silently, so she kept talking. "With my commitment up in another two weeks, I'm looking for a chance to walk away from that firm. But after I investigated my options in and around Chicago, reality hit me hard. The character and values of the firms interested in interviewing me aren't what I'm looking for. I want to help the clients, to deal with them personally and fairly, and not worry about the profit it means for the firm. I'm not stupid. Money's important when billable hours are the bottom line for every client. I can't keep doing that.

"I also can't afford to open my own office anytime soon, despite that being what I really want to do. So, right now, I'm stuck between a rock and a hard place."

She sighed. She'd begun to accept the fact that she'd have to stay at her firm and work to get her student loans down or pay them off. But that could take forever, the way things were going, and then Burr's unexpected offer had come in.

Anna's mother had moved to Colorado to be with Anna's aunt after her uncle died. Given Anna was an only child, there wasn't a whole lot tying her down to Chicago. Except memories, and they would be with her wherever she went.

Burr had kept stoic, without comment and without frowning even once at what she'd said. So she kept going. "I don't want you to think I see myself as a caped superhero, because all I want is to do right by my clients. That's what drew me to the law when I was a kid. It seemed so simple. A person needed help and my dad gave it to them. He took a burden off his client. So simple in theory, but not very easy to find in this world."

Burr finally spoke up.

"I understand what you're trying to do. I had ideas and dreams but not much money when I started out. I was lucky because I was in a small town and my first office was in my garage. I'm not surprised by your struggle, or that this position is your last option for the near future. We aren't fancy around here and most of our clients aren't wealthy. The money isn't nearly what you'd get where you are now, but we're the only option for legal help in the area, so we won't go broke, either."

"I didn't mean to offend you," she said quickly.

"I'm not offended. Truth is never offensive."

She took him at his word and laid out some basic truths. "Okay. I need to work some-where that won't suck the life out of me—where billable hours aren't the holy grail. That's not the atmosphere I want to work in."

"Okay, I know what you don't want in a firm but, specifically, what *do* you want?" Burr asked.

"This probably sounds a bit Pollyanna, but I want a law firm with a heart, that's fair, that's good at what they do, and when they talk about client care, they mean care, not how to offer clients a higher level of service to increase their billable hours, or talking about which restaurant is the best for client entertaining."

Burr stood unexpectedly. "Coffee?"

"Yes, thank you. Black."

Her dad had had a gift that had served him well when he'd practiced law. He'd been able to read people, to see them for what they really were, not what they wanted him to think they were. She wasn't as good at that as he had been, but he had taught her a lot.

After being around Burr for a few days, she could tell that he had a heart for the law, a real love for it. He was smart, kind and patient. Now she was starting to think that the man himself could tip the scales in favor of her taking his offer—if she did. She genuinely thought he was as close to any attorney she'd ever met who had the same character she'd admired so very much in her own father.

Burr came back with a steaming mug and set it down in front of her, then took his seat again. As she cautiously took a sip, he said, "I was hoping this town would appeal to you."

"I told you about my dad and how he worked, more with his heart than anything. He drove my mom nuts doing pro bono work or bartering for his fees. But Dad always did the right thing, and I loved him for that. He was my hero, and I wanted to be like him. I still do." She leaned slightly toward him. "You know I appreciate your offer so much and your help getting me here, and this town seems great, but I just don't know if I—"

"Oh boy," Burr said, cutting her off but surprising her with a smile that twitched his mustache. "Here comes the old brush-off line 'It's not you, it's me.' So, before you say something *I'll* regret, let me say a few more things for your consideration. Then you can tell me bluntly what you want to do. No hard feelings. I promise."

She liked him even more now. "Okay."

"You told me your plan had always been to work side by side with your dad at his law firm. I'm sorry that never happened for you, but you kept going after he passed away. I can tell you're passionate about the law, the way I bet he was. Here, the legal needs of my clients, no matter where I find them, are for honest, solid service, and for me to care for them and about their lives. But I understand that you're worth more than I can offer. You graduated law school second in your class. You could draw top money anywhere you want to go, but I have a gut feeling you'd fit in here perfectly."

"I'm not going to walk away from something good even if it means I need to stretch payments for my student loans further." She looked down at her hands cradling the warm mug, then back to Burr. "Dad didn't get wealthy from his practice, but he was a huge success."

Burr touched the gold horseshoe. "I understand that completely. That's why I contacted you about the partnership when I saw your query in the law magazine." He sat forward. "I did a full background check on you, just to see what would turn up. Do you want to hear something strange?"

Why not? "Sure."

"I went to the same law school in Chicago as your dad did, but I was a year ahead of him. So we may have crossed paths at one time or another. Smith Watters, right?"

Anna had never truly believed in "signs,"

but if this was genuine, maybe a very small sign had just hit her over her head. "Yes. Smith Watters was my dad. Law school's where he met my mom."

When he spoke, she could hear the sincerity in his voice. "I'm sorry you never had a chance to go into practice with him."

Her chest tightened. "That is the biggest regret of my life. I was only thirteen when he died."

"For what it's worth, from what you also told me about him, I think you're on the path to being a lot like him."

She felt the prick of tears behind her eyes and swallowed. This was not what she'd expected. "I'm not there yet, but thank you."

"Anna, I think you'd be a good fit in this town," Burr said again. "These people are mostly soul-deep good people, and I'm hoping that since you've seen it on our tours and met them, you're swinging toward taking me up on my offer."

Anna could feel things changing for her. The whole idea of being here, practicing law in this town with Burr, was something she was pretty sure her dad would have supported. Burr's honesty made that almost a certainty. "I like the town and the people I've met. But I'm not a small-town person. I'm not sure that I'd even understand where the people around here would be coming from."

"Anna, people are people. You're used to the big city, but believe me, this town is very easy to slip into and thrive."

She took a deep breath and, even though she still had some misgivings, she knew what she was going to do—or try to do. She'd given the firm in Chicago five years, and she'd been miserable. Maybe the least she could do was give herself time to see if she could make it work with Burr and the people of Eclipse.

Burr watched her across the desk.

"Okay, I think I should see if I could fit in here," she said before she could change her mind. "But the deal is, if I can't make it work, I will go back to Chicago."

Burr stood and came around the desk. "Is that a yes I hear?"

She looked up at the man in front of her who was starting to smile. Maybe working here with Burr was as close as she could ever get to what working alongside her dad might have been like.

"Yes, it is for now."

## CHAPTER TWO

ANNA LEFT CHICAGO two weeks later to move to Wyoming. By early April, she'd settled into her room over the carriage house at a beautiful Victorian bed-and-breakfast. She'd also set up her workspace off the reception area of the Addison Law Firm. The office was small, but it had a window that overlooked Clayton Drive, the town's main street. She could sit at her desk and watch the world of Eclipse go by.

With Burr's help, she'd managed to make the filing deadline to take the Wyoming bar exam in July. All she had in front of her until then was learning the ropes in the office, getting used to the town and studying every chance she could for the exam.

Footsteps sounded on the plank flooring and she turned as Burr stepped through her open office door. He was frowning, an expression that she'd learned was rare for him.

Another unusual thing was his pausing to close her office door behind him. They were the only two people there.

She rolled her chair back from the computer. "Is something wrong?"

"I don't know," he said, reaching for the only other chair in the room. He brought it close to her desk and sat on it to face her. He usually paced while they discussed work. But he took his time rolling up the sleeves of his brown flannel shirt then sat back. "I found out something that you might be able to help me with, something I can't do personally."

That surprised her. What couldn't Burr do at his own law firm? "I'm listening."

He exhaled then told her a story about a man on a huge ranch north of town who had once run a foster care group home for troubled teenage boys. His name was James Caine, but he went by Sarge. After his wife passed, Sarge had practically shut down his ranch. And with it had gone the dream the two of them had once had to move from the group home service and build a summer camp for foster kids.

Anna listened intently.

Burr, a storyteller, had her when he said,

"Sarge has been a good friend to me over the years, and I'd do anything for him." The big reveal, however, was Burr talking about three of Sarge's foster boys—now adults—setting out to make the dream of a summer camp on the ranch a reality.

Anna loved the idea of what the men were doing for Sarge, and how much Burr cared about his friend. "What do you need me for?"

He frowned at her. "Our mayor, Leo Getty, has heard about a development company trying to get Sarge's ranch land through the back door. Sarge has been very clear over the years that he'll never sell. It's his world. So, here comes a greedy developer who only sees dollar signs and who's looking for a glitch. A loophole that could challenge the rightful ownership of the property."

She really hated that some people were willing to destroy other people to get what they wanted. "But this is all a rumor?"

"For now. Though, sometimes around here, rumors end up being the truth. So we can't just dismiss this. I don't want Sarge or his family to be blindsided if it does turn out to be true. If it is, everything could be in jeopardy because of some obscure problem, and it could bring down the ranch itself in the process. Even if the developer can't find much, the minute the company files on anything, the camp development could be frozen for months, possibly for years."

He exhaled heavily as he shrugged. "They've already put so much into it, and not just financially—the boys set up a charitable foundation to take care of camp financials— but emotionally. Campsites are going up, older buildings have been repurposed for the kids. They're acquiring enough riding horses so each boy can have a horse for the week they'll be there. So much heart has gone into it... If it collapses, money isn't the problem. Hearts are the problem. Lost hope will crush them."

Anna didn't need to hear any more when she saw the stress etching deep lines at Burr's mouth and eyes. She was ready to do whatever it took to help. "Just tell me what you need me to do."

Burr stood and started to pace. "First, and most important, we don't want Sarge or the boys to have to worry about something that might amount to nothing. They have enough on them. So, no one around here can know about what we're doing because gossip has a way of getting around. This is just you, me and Leo for now."

"Agreed, but I have one question. The new foundation has to have strong financial backing, and an equally strong stable of attorneys who could blow any challengers out of the water."

Burr stopped pacing for a moment to look at her. "Smart girl. They do. But if we go to them, the family will have to be briefed on it, and that's not our plan. Leo and I agreed that if nothing is found, no one will ever have to know what we've done. But if something solid turns up, all bets are off and we hand everything over to the foundation's legal team out of Seattle."

"Agreed," she said.

Burr sat again and leaned toward her. "Technically, we're not working for anyone, just helping good friends if they need protecting."

"Good. No billable hours."

He smiled slightly at that. "None."

"Now, do we target the property records to see if anything's there and get to it before the bad guys do? Or do we concentrate on finding what company is involved and going after them?"

Burr nodded. "You can do public record searches and go back as far as you can. The town's been working on getting records online for public viewing, but so far, there's only about a tenth of them available. So you're going to have to go to the Annex by town hall where they have all the physical records stored in the basement. You have the perfect reason to be there. You're learning about the local laws for your exam."

She nodded, knowing that would work for her. "Okay, I can dig through the public records, but what about any personal records the family might have for the land?"

"I've done local work for the Caines over the years, but nothing that would explain my asking to look at ranch records now."

"Well, I'm a stranger, and who would let a stranger rifle through their personal business papers?"

"Excellent point. If you stand any chance of getting a look at those files, you'll have to meet and get to know the people staying out at the ranch." Burr, stroking his mustache smooth with his thumb and forefinger, was silent for a long moment. Then he glanced at her. "If I'm lucky, I might have an idea how to make you not such a stranger to at least one of the family."

He didn't wait for her response but reached for the landline by her computer and quickly dialed a number. "Hey, Elaine. It's Burr... No, no food order. I wanted to find out if anyone from Eclipse Ridge is in the diner or expected to be there sometime soon." He listened and smiled. "Perfect. What's he doing?" His smile grew. "I need a huge favor and, if you can do it, I'll tell Leo to buy your cookies for the next town hall potluck." He was nodding. "Can you give Ben a couple of boxes of your cookies and ask him to drop them off here before goes to Farley's?" He was nodding again. "Nice. Yes, that'll work... I'll explain later. Put the cookies on my tab."

When he hung up, he was smiling like the Cheshire cat in *Alice in Wonderland*. "Kiddo, we're going to have a visitor in five minutes, and if this works out, you're going to get an invitation from Ben to go out to see the ranch or as close to an invitation as we can manage. From there on, it's up to you to figure out a way to get access to the records."

"Who's Ben?" she asked as he moved to the window to look out toward the north end of town.

"Ben Arias is one of the three former foster kids who lives out on the ranch with Sarge. He's just finishing up lunch with our good doctor, Boone Williams— Ah, I think I hear his truck outside. Yes, there he is." Burr went past her into the reception area. "I'll be right back," he called over his shoulder just before the entry door opened.

Anna stayed where she was, hearing footsteps in reception and Burr speaking. She couldn't make out what he was saying at first but then his voice got louder. "Boy, I appreciate you bringing these by, Ben. Since you're here, I'd like you to meet my new partner."

"I never thought you'd have a partner," the other man said in a smooth, deep voice.

"These bones are getting too old to sit all day at a desk or stand in a courtroom for hours."

Anna had found out that Burr had turned sixty-five a few days before she'd met him the first time, so maybe he was speaking a truth.

"You're not that old," the visitor said.

"Old enough," Burr responded.

Then he was standing in her doorway, smiling at her and holding two pink pastry boxes in his hands. "Anna, I have a friend I'd like you to meet. Ben Arias from the Eclipse Ridge Ranch north of town. He's delivering our cookies from Over the Moon Diner."

Then Ben Arias came into view as he took off his beige Stetson. He looked to be thirty-something, with jet-black hair combed straight back from a tanned, clean-shaven face. She had the passing thought that he was striking-looking, maybe with some Hispanic or Native American heritage in his background. He was about six feet tall, and he was wearing a variation of the town's uniform: an unbuttoned denim jacket that showed a gray thermal shirt underneath. His jeans were faded, and his Western boots looked well used.

She stood to take his offered hand when he crossed to her while Burr hung back, out of the man's line of vision. "Ben, meet Anna Watters from Chicago." Burr accompanied his introduction with a thumbs-up sign only Anna could see after he'd put the cookie boxes on the nearest filing cabinet.

"Nice to meet you, Mr. Arias," she said, noting his handshake was firm but brief.

"Ben. I'm just Ben." His warm brown eyes echoed a touch of the smile on his lips. "Burr told me you're partnering with him."

"I am. What can I say, but he made me an offer I couldn't refuse."

Ben obviously got her movie reference and smiled. "I hope he didn't have to resort to any strong-arming."

"No, he used his charm," she said, smiling at Burr.

"Charming," Burr said, looking pleased. "And now I have a partner." He moved up on Ben's left side. "Anna's trying to get up to speed on local, county and state laws to prepare for the Wyoming bar. She's never been around open country like this. In fact, I was just telling her that your place is a prime example of what people do with larger plots of land." As if he'd just thought of it, he said, "You know what? How about if Anna takes a ride out to the ranch to look around?"

"Why?"

She knew Ben wasn't connecting the dots.

"Well, the local laws change with each district or county. She needs to get a real idea about land size and how it affects usage." Burr shrugged. "With the camp construction going on out there, she could see it firsthand. I mean, I can tell her about anything, but seeing it in person is better."

Anna almost felt sorry for Ben Arias, the way Burr had pretty much trapped him into either agreeing to his suggestion or making him look unfriendly. From what she could tell, friendly was the top virtue for the people around here.

It worked. Ben turned his dark eyes on her and gave her an easy smile. "Of course, you're welcome to come on out and take a look around."

"I wouldn't want to intrude."

"You wouldn't be. There's always someone at the place who can explain things to you. The gates are open for deliveries and workers all day."

"Thank you. I might drop by," she said and sat back down.

Burr looked at Anna, obviously expecting more from her, but he finally turned to Ben. "Tell Sarge I'll be swinging by sometime soon. I haven't seen him for a while."

"He'd like that." Ben glanced at Anna and a smile lingered, softening his strong features.

"Nice to meet you, Anna," he said as he put his hat back on and headed out of the office.

As soon as the entry door closed behind Ben, Burr spoke up.

"You should have asked if you could visit today or tomorrow."

"I didn't want to push and look like I was anxious to get on the ranch. Besides, I need to do some background work before I go out there, so I know what I'm looking at."

He nodded half-heartedly. "I guess that makes sense. I wish you could ride. That's a real conversation starter in these parts."

"Guess what? As a teen, I spent every summer at my aunt's ranch in Colorado, riding all day."

"That's fantastic!" Burr brightened considerably. "If you go out there, maybe you'll be offered a ride so you can see the land."

"If I get that offer, I'd do it in a heartbeat." Then she had an idea. "What would you think if I just plain offered a bit of legal help on day-to-day things that they're facing out there, the small things that can trip up people?"

Burr stopped her in her tracks. "No, Anna, you can't even hint at getting involved legally with the ranch."

She quickly walked that back. "Of course. That was a stupid idea."

Burr shook his head. "No, it wasn't stupid. I just can't imagine how you could ever do that without them thinking something's up. Just take everything real slow and easy."

"Absolutely," she said, then got up. "Now, I'm going over to the Annex to check out the plot maps for the Eclipse Ridge Ranch."

TWO DAYS LATER, Ben was ready to leave the ranch and head seventy miles southeast to Twin Horns, the county seat. He had a meeting with a code enforcement inspector and wanted to get it over with. It was, as far as he could tell, a check-in to make sure the foster camp conversion was on track for opening in July. Small things were always coming up, but so far they'd avoided any disasters with the construction. He looked forward to the camp being finished and showing it to Sarge.

After Maggie passed, the dream to build a summer camp for foster kids on the ranch had been lost. Then the accident. Sarge had broken his leg over a year ago and they'd found out about the Alzheimer's. Ben exhaled.

It was then that he, Seth Reagan and Jake

Bishop had set out to help Sarge any way they could. That included taking time for one of them to always be there for him at the ranch. After arriving at the group home sixteen years ago as foster teens, they'd become like sons to Maggie and Sarge. A family—even after they'd each left the ranch at eighteen.

Sarge and Maggie's lives had been devoted to giving boys like them a chance at a better life and showing them what it meant to be cared for. It was their gift to have foster boys leave the group home with something they'd lost in their shattered lives: hope, pure and simple.

Ben stepped out of the large log house onto the wraparound porch, then squinted up at the sun, which wasn't doing a whole lot to warm the air. Wearing jeans, a red flannel shirt, with his heavy denim jacket and boots, he put on his Stetson and tugged the brim down to shade his eyes. It was like the one Sarge had bought him when he'd first arrived at the ranch, and it felt very right wearing it again.

Seeing the dream of the summer camp come true would be a wonderful gift for Sarge, giving him hope this time—something he needed desperately. Creating the camp was all about him and for him. Jake, Seth and Ben were determined he'd be able to participate in the camp for a while before he got too sick, but with his Alzheimer's, the time where he would understand it all was finite.

Ben stopped on the top step to look out at the land that he'd first seen when he was fifteen years old and hated everything. Now he loved the place. He blinked when he heard a car engine. He waited as a white compact crested the rise halfway up the cement driveway and headed toward the house. He'd expected a truck of some sort bringing supplies for Seth and Quinn's wedding. His foster brother had proposed to Quinn Lake last year after she'd come out to work on the ranch. The wedding was getting close, but he was certain there was no delivery scheduled for today. Ben didn't want to miss anything, but he also didn't want to be late for the meeting in Twin Horns.

As the car came to a stop beside the ranch's old red pickup, which he'd been using to get around, sun glinted off the windshield. He couldn't tell who was behind the wheel until the driver's-side door opened and he was surprised when Burr's new partner stepped out.

She smiled up at him, and he remembered her name was Anna. He couldn't remember her last name.

"Hello, again. I was in the area and I thought I'd see if I could take a look around." She closed her door then came to the bottom of the steps and looked up at him. "Burr said this ranch sits on over six thousand acres. I can't even imagine that."

Ben slowly went down and stopped one step above Anna. He'd briefly taken stock of her when Burr had introduced them at the office. She'd seemed attractive enough, maybe five-five or five-six, her hair pulled straight back in a long braid. But now he noticed how the sun brought out streaks of gold in the deep brown locks. Her choice of clothes was similar to what she'd been wearing when they'd first been introduced: jeans, a heavy sweater and some sort of designer low-heeled boots. But this time her sweater was sky blue instead of white. He was surprised he remembered that.

"Welcome," he said. As her smile grew, matching dimples appeared, and he had the fleeting thought that he might have been premature thinking she'd just looked attractive at first.

"I probably should have called," she said, her smile beginning to fade when he took a moment too long to respond. Before he could fix that, she spoke quickly. "You know, I'm sorry for intruding. I'll come back later."

He thought about the meeting with the inspector and figured he could at least spare a few minutes to talk to her before he left. "No. It's not a problem. I'm on my way to a meeting, but I have some time. I just forgot you were going to stop by."

"I never gave you a day or time, so it's no big deal." She looked around then back at him. "This is quite a setup. Those boulders at the gates are spectacular, and I've never seen an honest-to-goodness log house before."

He watched her appraise the structure behind him. The center was the original home, two stories with a green-metal peaked roof. Single-story wings to the east and west, added over the span of ten years, blended perfectly with the look of the older log home. "Sarge built most of the buildings on this land from the timber he'd cleared for grazing pastures and trails."

"Hey, Ben," someone called from his left. He turned as Dwight Stockard, the ranch manager, came around the side of the east wing on a dappled gray horse Ben had never seen before. "Sorry to interrupt, but I wanted to show you what Josh Caldwell dropped off yesterday."

He rode over to where Ben stood with Anna. Dwight was in his forties, wearing a well-used, low-crown Stetson that partially covered his thinning brown hair. He wasn't all that tall, but he sat high in the saddle. "I was checking him out to see if he's got any problems that would disqualify him before I sign the papers on him. He's from an auction and not much information came with him."

Anna stepped closer to the man and the horse. "What would you be disqualifying him for?" she asked Dwight.

He smiled down at her. "Well, ma'am, it's for the kids, so we need to make sure he doesn't do things like bucking, trying to bite, or being too sensitive to sudden actions or noises."

She slowly raised a slender hand to stroke the animal's strong neck. "He'd pass the beauty test, that's for sure. He's very handsome." She looked down at his legs. "Strong, too, huh?"

"Yes, ma'am," Dwight said with an approving nod.

The horse snuffled as Anna ran her fingers down a white streak on his muzzle. Ben went closer. "A girl from Chicago who knows about horses. How did that happen?" he asked.

She gave him that smile that came with the dimples, and he saw the humor in her gray-blue eyes. "Because this girl from Chicago went to her aunt's ranch in Colorado for summer breaks from high school. If I could have slept on a horse, I'd never have gotten off."

"I didn't see that coming," Ben said.

She drew her hand back and her smile lingered. "I'll go and let you get to your meeting. Next time, I'll call first."

Ben made a snap decision. He'd rather go riding than sit in a stuffy office in the county buildings in Twin Horns. "Tell you what, since you're already here and you know horses, how about I take you for a ride to show you the boundaries of the ranch and give you an idea of its size?"

"Really?" she asked with an almost child-ish surprise that widened her eyes.

"Absolutely," he said.

"That would be great." She was obviously delighted for a moment then quickly looked concerned. "You can't. You have a meeting."

He didn't hesitate. "I can reschedule. I'd rather go for a ride than face some bureaucrat in planning and development at the county seat." Before she could protest any more, he took out his cell and said, "Hold on for a minute."

He moved away from them to make his call, and by the time he hung up, the meeting had been rescheduled for two o'clock the following afternoon. He turned and Anna was deep in conversation with Dwight, who had dismounted. "All taken care of," Ben said as he got close.

Both turned to him at the same time. "I don't want to cause problems for you with any bureaucrats," Anna said. "I've dealt with people like that, and they can make tidal waves out of ripples."

"That they can," he conceded and then looked at Dwight. "We'll be down at the sta-bles in five. I'd appreciate if you could get

Traveler ready for me and find an easy ride for Anna."

She spoke up. "If it's okay, I'd like to ride this horse."

"With Miss Watters being a seasoned rider, and you with her, I'd say he'd probably do fine for her, Ben."

Watters—that was her last name. She and Dwight must have introduced themselves while he'd been distracted moving the meeting time. "What's he called?" Ben asked.

"He's going by Punch, but his papers show him as Paul Bunyan."

"I'd like to ride Punch," Anna said to Ben. "If there's a problem, I can always get off and walk." She sounded as if she was talking about riding a bike that might get a flat tire.

He glanced down at her boots, which he thought looked more for show and style than for riding. "Are you okay with those boots?"

"Sure, they'll work."

"Do you have a jacket with you?"

"Absolutely," she said and quickly went to the compact to return with a suede jacket that she put on over her sweater. He could see it wasn't lined, and it was cropped short, so it wasn't even long enough to reach her waist.

It was all style and, he'd bet, not much protection against the cold. She did up the fancy buttons and then looked at him again. "There. I'm all set." He must have frowned at her because she added, "I've survived Chicago in the winter wearing this."

He wondered how she survived a real Chicago winter in that poor excuse for a jacket, but he wasn't going to argue with her. Cold was cold, and he would shorten the ride if she started turning blue. He looked at Dwight, who had remounted. "See you down there."

ANNA HAD NEVER really believed in luck the way some did, but right then she had to admit, it was kind of serendipitous that the ranch manager had showed up with Punch when he had. It had been a perfect lead-in for her to plant the seed for a possible ride in the future. But Ben had upped it with the invitation to ride that day. Then he'd mentioned a meeting with someone in county planning. That was the jackpot.

As they fell into step beside each other on the gravel drive heading away from the house, Anna said, "Burr mentioned your plans for the summer camp out here. I hope I'm not keeping you from something important."

"No, I wasn't even supposed to take the meeting, but Seth had to leave with his fiancée, Quinn, and their boy, leaving it in my lap. All I know is, we're close to the final sign-off. I haven't been here too much since this all started, so I'm running to catch up to speed on all things to do with the camp."

"You don't live here?" she asked to get more of his background than Burr had given her about the man.

"I have off and on in the past, but my job took more and more of my time away from the ranch. I came back to see Sarge and the others as much as I could. They're family to me, and Sarge has been a father to me. I'm off contract now, so I can stay with Sarge and be here for the camp's first season."

"Then you'll leave again?"

"I'll have to get some work in, but I'll be back all I can."

"Who's going to manage the camp?"

His eyes narrowed on her as he glanced at her. "You must be good in court."

She felt heat rise in her face and she knew exactly what he meant. She'd been that way all her life, needing details, exact answers, and she had to make herself stop. "I'm sorry. That's none of my business."

"No, that's a fair question. We're all in it for the first season, then we'll figure things out after that."

"Was it a camp when you were brought here?"

"No, not really, but it kind of was like camping in a way. We shared rooms in the big house, did all sorts of things outside, even swimming in a lake in the high foothills. We used tents, and drank out of streams, and rustled up cows." That brought a smile that softened the angles of his face. "That sounds better when I do it with a fake drawl." So he did it with an exaggerated twang. "I'm off to rustle them cows, pardner." He shook his head and finished in a low voice. "Coming here changed my life."

"How?" she asked.

He seemed confused for a second as if he hadn't realized he'd said the last sentence out loud. "Excuse me?"

"You said it changed your life. How did it?"

He pushed his hands into his jacket pockets and hunched his shoulders as he looked down at the gravel drive. "I was a city kid in every way I could have been. I'd never been anywhere like this, ever, and I was certain coming here would be even worse." He kept his eyes down, but she knew his smile was long gone as he spoke. "I found after I got past my anger and hate this was a home. A real home. When I left at eighteen, I went right to college."

His sigh was ragged before he said, "This is the only home I've ever known, and the people here are the only real family I've ever had. They mean everything to me, and when I speak about going home, this is the place."

Anna listened, trying to take in what he was saying. Until he came to the ranch, it sounded as if he'd been lost. She wouldn't dig into his past; that was a place she had no right to go. But she felt she understood more about him. She made a statement and didn't ask a question. "That's why you're doing all of this."

"I can never repay what I owe Sarge and Maggie. They gave me hope when it had been all but beaten out of me."

He stopped, exhaled roughly and kept walking as he changed the conversation abruptly. "All of the code demands from the county are covered, I think. Even the small things, but I'm still uneasy we might be missing something."

"How so?" she asked as they headed north toward a huge, two-story, log-walled building. Two men were busy unloading baled hay and bags of feed from a couple of large flatbed trucks parked along its eastern side.

As they kept walking in the direction of another building farther north, she knew the grouping had to be the stables. She waited for an answer from Ben about his worries about the meeting. "I always stress about not crossing a *t* or dotting an *i* and screwing things up."

She felt an opening coming, and if she played it right, she was beginning to think she might be able to do what Burr hadn't wanted her to even attempt. She'd be careful, but she hoped Burr would understand that she couldn't ignore the opportunity if it fell into her lap. "I understand. Just a wrong move can mess things up."

He chuckled roughly. "Tell me about it."

She filed that away for the moment as they approached the front of the stables, passing by a series of empty holding pens and a large oval training ring.

Dwight appeared at the open doors, leading Punch and a muscular chestnut quarter horse with a perfect white star between his eyes. She assumed this was Traveler. "Here they are."

"Anna, hold on, and I'll be right back," Ben said before he jogged off into the stables.

Dwight handed her the reins for Punch. "He seems good, but just be careful."

"I will be," she said.

Ben was back, carrying a pair of binoculars on a leather strap. He crossed to Traveler, looped the strap through a ring on the side of the saddle to secure them, then looked at Anna. "Ready to go?"

"I sure am," she said, then easily mounted Punch. She looked over at Ben, who was already in the saddle on Traveler. "Where to?"

He motioned ahead of them. "We're going west, then hooking northward in the higher open range area to a vantage point in the foothills where you can see the southern boundary meets up with the western boundary."

"What about the northern and eastern boundaries?" Anna asked.

He brushed that away. "We don't have enough time to do that, and riding near some boundaries higher up is impossible because of the configuration of the land."

With that, Ben led the way along the side of the oval ring, past the stalls, and headed up a wide access lane between fenced pastures. They rode west for quite a while in silence as Anna absorbed the beauty of the land and the sense of freedom she felt on the horse. When they came to the end of the fenced areas, they were on gently inclining grazing land dotted by stands of old trees. Ben drew Traveler to a stop and looked over at Anna.

With his Stetson shading his eyes, he really was handsome with those high cheekbones and strong jaw. "You're being very quiet," he said.

"Honestly, I'm trying to take this all in. It's overwhelmingly grand."

That brought a smile as he nudged at Traveler to get going again on the westward climb. "It certainly is grand. There's no place I've been that comes anywhere close to this land." Anna watched Ben gazing straight ahead as they rode side by side under clear skies.

"Did Burr tell you about Sarge's health problems?" he asked.

A light breeze was stirring the air. Anna felt its chill on her bare hands and face, then realized it found the place between her jacket and the waistband of her jeans. Her sweater did no good at all. Trying to ignore it, she said, "Yes. I was sorry to hear that."

"With the camp due to open the week after the Fourth of July, it's coming up soon, and we're all trying to keep Sarge as stress-free as possible, so he really won't be totally aware of what's being done until it's finished. There's also the wedding for Seth and Quinn, but he's already excited about that. He's smart, despite his problems, so it's hard to keep him in the dark about what's going on."

"He needs distractions," she said.

"He sure does."

"Not to be nosy, but who are Seth and Quinn again?" Anna asked. "I think you mentioned them earlier when you were talking about your meeting. He's apparently marrying someone named Quinn?" She was curious about the family.

"Yes, Seth Reagan came here when I did, with another boy named Jake Bishop, all of us foster kids. We got close, like brothers. Seth owns a tech company and is engaged to Quinn. They're adopting a seven-year-old boy named Tripp, who was also in foster care." He smiled. "And Jake married a woman named Liberty last year on Valentine's Day. They're around the ranch as much as they can be, but they travel for his work, setting up flight schools for future test pilots."

They got closer to a stand of slender, towering pines, some older ones with thick trunks and deciduous growth just starting to bud. Ben drew his horse to a stop again. He turned to Anna. "We need to ride parallel to these trees until we find the trail that cuts through them onto higher open land. It was widened recently for some surveying and, as soon as we get through, our destination is northward." He nudged Traveler to keep going. "Trust me, it's the best way to get an idea of the size and usage of the ranch."

# CHAPTER THREE

THEY FOUND THE newly cleared trail easily enough and started through the trees. The wind was building, blowing through Anna's jacket and sweater. She'd been so anxious to ride with Ben to secure a connection with him, she'd overlooked the fact that when she'd worn her prized suede jacket in Chicago, she'd barely been outside long enough to get cold. She'd step out of her house and directly into the garage, get into her car, then drive to work where she parked in the firm's heated garage. For long periods of time during the winter, she was never really outside in the snow and cold at all.

Ben glanced over at her. "Doing okay?"

"Great." She certainly wasn't going to tell him he'd been right to question her choice of boots and jacket. But, right then, being cold was worth being able to do what she was doing. "Punch seems to be a good ride, really instinctive."

"So, you're not going to call him Paul Bunyan?"

"No. It's better if he was named after a party drink than someone named Paul."

He glanced over at her. "Oh, now that sounds interesting."

They were deep into the trees and the world seemed muffled and removed. But the cold was right there. "It's really not. I had an unfortunate experience with someone with that name during my formative years."

"How unfortunate?"

"Leave it at unfortunate, and that I only say that name when I don't have any other option."

He reined Traveler and shifted in the saddle to look more directly at her. "Now I have to know what happened."

She couldn't remember the last time she'd even thought about Paul and certainly had no idea why she'd brought him up with Ben now. "No, you don't," she said, nudging Punch onward.

Ben was right beside her. "If you want me to show you the boundary lines, you're going to have to tell me."

She stopped and turned to find teasing humor in his midnight-dark eyes. It made him look younger. "What?"

"That's my price."

"That's extortion."

A smile played at the corners of his mouth. "I think of it as therapy for you to get it out."

Anna couldn't quite stop her own smile. "Okay, you asked for it. When I was a junior in high school, I had a major crush on a boy named you-know-what in my biology class." Ben nodded and motioned for her to keep talking. "We had to dissect a frog in science lab, and I was partnered with him. I was so nervous… He was so cute.

"For some reason, he went all macho as soon as he got the scalpel in his hand." She exhaled. "He looked at me, winked and jabbed it right into the frog's stomach. There was a strange popping sound and when fluid sprayed out, he turned green then fell forward into me. At the same time, he threw up all over everything, me included."

"Poor guy," Ben said with a shake of his head.

"He doesn't deserve your pity. He threw me under the bus. He said I was going to faint, and when he tried to catch me, I hit him in the stomach and that's why he threw up. He made me look like I was so girlie-girlie I couldn't bear seeing the frog impaled."

Ben was chuckling now. "What a jerk, huh?"

Anna was amazed at how things had fallen into place with Ben in such a short time. If Burr hadn't asked for her help, she would not have met Ben, never would have come out here and never would be riding Punch. Most important, she never would have found humor in one of her worst memories from high school. "Yes, a jerk," she agreed, still smiling.

"Did you ever speak to him after that?"

"My best friend, Maddy, told me that if I still liked him, she'd stop being my friend forever."

"Did you still like him?" Ben asked, his eyes narrowing slightly.

"Let's just say I'm still really good friends with Maddy."

He laughed, and the sound echoed faintly off the trees around them as he nudged his horse forward.

"How long have you been riding?" Anna

asked as the path widened and she could ride easily beside Seth and Traveler.

"Since I came here at fifteen. I wasn't sure at first that I wanted to after hearing about Jake overshooting the saddle and face-planting on his first try. Seth's horse spooked over a snake and he ended up being thrown off. Then there was me, a city kid who thought he was so tough and could do anything."

"What happened when you rode the first time?" she asked.

Ben motioned ahead of them where the trees began to thin out. "Come on. We're almost there," he said without answering her question.

A moment later, they broke out of the trees and Anna blinked, feeling as if she'd stepped into another world. The clearing was expansive, the rocky ground ahead of them gradually climbing higher. It looked as though it kept going right up into the sky. Farther to the north was a lake surrounded by massive trees that only partially concealed rough rock walls behind it. An old-fashioned tire swing dangled from a rope tied to the thick branch of a sturdy tree that arched out over the water.

"We're going straight ahead," Ben said, "But we'll leave the horses here."

He dismounted and led Traveler over to a low-growing tree and secured the horse's reins to a branch. Anna followed suit with Punch, then turned as Ben slipped the binoculars off the saddle loop. He stood beside an oxidized green pipe that was about ten inches in circumference and protruded three feet above the rough ground. A loop of wire had been threaded through a cap on top of it and there was a hole cut into its side. The wire ends had been pressed together with something red to secure them.

"What is that?" Anna asked.

Ben put the leather strap of the binoculars over his shoulder and glanced at the pipe. "An old well that ran dry years and years ago. A string of them dried up around the same time, and Sarge had to have them sealed so kids couldn't mess with them." He looked around, said, "Come on, it's not too far," and started up over rough ground littered with dried brush and rocks.

"Where it's staked out by the lake way over there, there are going to be camping sites and a gathering place for group meetings." Ben was speaking as the incline seemed sheerer with each step Anna took. "Farther north, there'll be more camping near a stream and waterfall on more level ground. But the lake's going to be the main area for fishing and swimming and protected fire rings. The rest of this is too rough for the younger campers."

"It's just beautiful up here," Anna said as she looked ahead. "It feels as if we're being drawn up into the sky."

He laughed. "It does, but we're going up to the lookout." He stopped and turned. "I should have asked if you have a problem with heights."

"No, but I've never wanted to rock climb."

"This isn't like that." He held out his hand to her. "Come on, I'll show you. It gets steeper from here on up." She reached toward him, and his hand closed around hers with warmth that was very welcome. Thankfully, he didn't comment on hers being cold as ice, but said, "Okay, let's do this."

They went higher, and she knew Ben was probably slowing his pace to accommodate her. Her calf muscles were starting to burn, and she was grateful for the adjustment to their speed. "So, you never answered how your first ride ended," she said. "Did you end up with a face-plant or broken bones?"

He kept on walking. "Neither. I got on and rode."

"Well, that's no story," she said on a scoffing exhale. "You could have made something up to keep me entertained."

He was smiling when he glanced at her, his eyes shaded from the bright sunlight overhead by the brim of his hat. "Sorry, next time I'll fake a broken arm or a cracked head, if it would make you happy."

"No, I'm quite happy knowing you stayed in one piece."

"Me, too." He motioned ahead at multiple huge boulders that were slowly coming into sight against the sweeping blue sky. "Just up there."

What she'd thought was to be a clear path forward between the massive rocks, was suddenly blocked by a ten-foot-tall, heavy iron fence that spanned a twelve-foot gap. The fence was anchored the same way she'd noted the gates at the ranch's entry had been: riveted into granite rocks. Here, though, more massive boulders spread out from north to south and strategic lengths of additional fencing filled any spaces between them. She couldn't see a gate anywhere.

"This is the place," Ben said as he stopped a few feet from the barrier.

"We came all this way only to be stopped by a fence that looks horribly out of place among giant rocks?" she asked.

"Sarge had the fencing put in years ago to satisfy the foster care program for the safety of the boys. We've had to do more work to pass the newer codes, but they accepted it. It costs a lot to safeguard kids against doing something stupid." He tugged her up closer to him and the fence. "There are sensors. I don't know how they work, but they'll let the counselors know when the kids are getting too close to trouble."

Then he let go of her hand so she could face the view through the iron rails. It was stunning. Barely six feet from the other side of the barrier, the ground plunged out of sight. In the distance of at least a hundred feet across a chasm, there were rugged rocks with stunted growth scattered among them. From there, the land climbed even higher. She felt a bit uneasy at the vastness of what was laid out before her.

Ben handed the binoculars to her. "Here. You'll need these."

She took them and stepped close enough to the fence to use them between the bars. "Look up, not down," she heard Ben say as she made a slight adjustment on the focus. Then she could see the other side of the chasm as clearly as if it had been no more than a few feet from her. She quickly lowered the binoculars when she saw a blur of something moving through the scrub bush.

"There's a wild animal or something over there."

"There could be, but it's probably just coyotes or a pronghorn looking for its herd. Most of the antelope stay on the government land to the west and north. That's their habitat, and they have good food access over there." His voice had a tinge of teasing as he said, "Although, to be honest, there is a stuffed head of a mountain lion hanging on the wall in the entry of the main ranch house. Sarge didn't have to go off his land to get it, but that was half a century ago."

She shivered slightly, only partly from the growing cold, but cautiously raised the binoculars again. Nothing moved across the chasm now except plants and trees being brushed by the wind. "Okay, what am I looking for, besides wild animals?"

"Look directly across the ravine to a thick stand of pines on the upward slope. Can you see them?"

Anna spotted the trees right away. "Yes."

He shifted to get behind her, so close she could feel the heat of his breath near her right ear when he spoke. "Okay, go slowly to your left until the ground starts to roll downward to the south. Watch for uneven four-strand barbed-wire fencing that follows the terrain."

She finally saw the barbed wire. "Got it," she said.

"Okay, that's the western boundary line. Now, keep following it south. It meets up with three-rail wood fencing."

She did as he said and just when she thought she'd messed up, she saw what he'd described. "Got the wood fence."

"That butts into more rail fencing that defines the southern border along the county road."

"Wow," she whispered. "How far away is it?"

"I don't know exactly, but it's a long ride on the county road to get there. Now, come back to the pines across from us and then go north. The land juts back this way farther up, and it's narrower and very irregular. It's hard to spot the demarcations because of the mixed elevations."

Anna did as he said, then eyed scrub growth and rock-roughened land climbing toward the northern foothills. At one point, she stopped. A slight dip in the terrain exposed a short run of barbed-wire fencing. "I can see barbed wire."

She felt his hands rest on her shoulders as he got closer and leaned toward her. "That's as much as you'll see."

She slowly lowered the binoculars. "I never would have thought it was this big. It's staggering." She turned to Ben as he moved back, taking his body heat with him. She felt the cold even more now. "That's all ranch property?"

"Yes. The eastern edge is right where you came off the highway onto the county road. The entrance to the camp is about a mile from the highway."

"Was the land for cattle or what?"

"Originally, Sarge ran cattle on it and did very well. Then he gradually brought in horses."

"You're using all of this land for the kids?"

"Not even close. The camp will be in this northwestern section where there's more water available, then it swings east toward the ranch's original mess hall and bunkhouse on the access road to the gates. They'll be used for registration, orientation, food prep and, on the first night, for sleeping. Then the kids will ride up to their assigned campsites and get to know their horses and counselors."

A ranch to Anna was a flat patch of land and some horses, like her aunt's place in Colorado. She could barely take this all in. "It's incredible that you're doing this for Sarge, but the kids are getting a special escape from their lives, too."

He squinted as he scanned the area around them. "Yes, it's a way of giving some healing and hope to them, even for a short time. That's why they're keeping the campers-to-counselor ratio at four-to-one to make the experience more personal. Every counselor has mental health training for dealing with teens and younger. It's going to be remarkable if we can make this all work."

Anna couldn't begin to explain to Ben how impressed she was by what he and the others were doing for one man. She had to swallow to ease the tightness in her throat. *Soul-deep good people*, Burr had said on the day she'd agreed to take him up on his partnership. She was standing with one of those people, and she wanted it all to work for him and the others, to get the camp up and going, and have Sarge there understanding what they'd done for him.

"What are you thinking?" Ben asked as his dark eyes came back to her.

That startled her and she shrugged. "This is overwhelming." But what she was really thinking was that maybe she'd found a way to at least make the odds better that the camp would become a reality, a place for kids to find the hope Ben had found at the ranch. She'd promised Burr she'd take it easy, but at the moment she had a strong feeling that Ben Arias was concerned about something happening, or maybe he was concerned about the meeting he'd rescheduled. She was going to follow her instincts and help, if she could. She braced herself and hoped Burr would understand.

"Can I ask you something?"

Ben's eyes narrowed. "Go ahead." He pushed his hands deep into his jacket pockets.

"You mentioned worrying about crossing the t's and dotting the i's with the county, and I'm sure with the money behind this project, there's a whole firm of top-tier attorneys to keep it all on track. They're in Cody or Cheyenne, right?"

"No. The foundation is out of Seattle."

Burr had already filled her in on that, but she'd wanted Ben to say it so she could ask a second question. "What do you do about things that come up on a day-to-day basis around here? Not big things, just annoying details and questions."

"We call Seattle, if we have to." She knew she'd given him the wrong impression when he continued. "Anna, we haven't pulled in Burr on the camp, or any other attorney from the area. The foundation is a world onto itself, with every legal mind needed to make things work."

She cringed inside. He thought she was working her way up to asking him about Burr representing the ranch locally. She couldn't let him think that was what she was trying to do, yet she couldn't make herself pull back and forget what she wanted to do. Pushing her cold hands into her pockets, she took a breath and tried to explain as clearly and concisely as she could.

"I understand that completely. What I wanted to do was offer you this personally, not as Burr's partner. I'm here, and I'm trying to learn Wyoming laws, so just by the nature of this area, land usage is probably one of the topics I need to explore. I was thinking I could make myself available to help with any minor questions or glitches you come across. I could be sort of like an insurance policy for watching those t's and i's. Believe me, I'm good at that, and I promise if I don't know something, or if I see something I believe could be problematic, I'll immediately hand it over to you for the foundation's legal team."

She could see the growing surprise in Ben's eyes just before some skepticism took over. "Why would you offer to do that when you barely know us?"

She told him the truth. "I'd like to see this all work out for you and the others, but especially for the boys and Sarge. The campers will be here for a week, but it might change their lives forever. Sarge deserves something good, too."

She watched Ben closely, saw his uncertainty, and had to force herself not to push. She felt she'd gone too far to just back out. Whatever happened was on her. As the wind brushed her ears, she wished she had a hat like Ben's with its fancy silver beading at the crown. But she endured the cold as she waited, just hoping she'd read him right.

WELL, THIS WAS a surprise Ben had to get his mind around. "That's quite a generous offer," he finally said.

"I understand you don't know me, but you know Burr, and he's a very good man who has great respect for Sarge. I'm not trying to muddy the waters or anything, just to help you and, in the process, maybe help myself get through the bar exam in July."

He exhaled. "You *are* Burr's partner. That speaks volumes about your ability and character."

"This will all be on me," she insisted. "Honestly, I need to do more than just sit behind a desk and study for the bar. If I can do other things, I'll be much happier, and this whole project is fascinating."

Anna Watters seemed to be a remarkable person making a remarkable offer. Ben knew he'd be a fool to refuse it. "You're quite sure you can manage it with everything else you're doing?"

"Yes. In all honesty, I really don't like bureaucratic involvement that can grind good, honest people down with rules and regulations. It annoys me, and I like triumphing over annoying bureaucrats." She stopped for a moment then added a caveat quickly. "But I'd never do or say anything that could cause trouble. I never have, and I won't. You have my word on that."

He almost smiled at her admission of enjoying a fight with the system and then trying to walk it back. As a child services consultant contracted out to fix broken systems in foster care centers, both public and private, he enjoyed that battle himself—at least when it all worked out in the kids' favor. But he wouldn't mind avoiding some of the battle he seemed to face every day if Anna could make some of that go away.

He glimpsed her slight shiver as she patiently waited for his answer. He finally said, "Okay, I would like to take you up on your offer. Name your retainer."

"Oh no. I told you I'm going to get as much

out of this as I hope you will. Whatever my time is worth, it's my gift to the foundation."

"Are you sure?"

"Yes, I'm very sure." She smiled, her eyes holding his for a moment, as if she had some other confession to make. But when she shivered again, he held out his hand to her. "Let's get back down." Obviously, the pockets of her suede jacket weren't any more protection than the jacket itself. Her hand was cold when he'd held it earlier.

"Thanks so much for showing me this," Anna said as they started down to where they'd left the horses.

"I've been wanting to come here myself," Ben said at the same time Anna's feet slipped out from under her. Even with his grip on her hand, she landed on the ground, pulling him down with her. He couldn't stop it. When he hit the dirt, he scrambled to get back on his feet and turned, surprised to see Anna sitting there, laughing up at him. Her dimples were back.

"Are you all right?" he asked, reaching to get his hat off the ground beside him and then crouching by Anna as he put it back on.

She answered a bit breathlessly. "Yes, I'm

fine. But you were right. This isn't Chicago." She reached out to him. "Please, get me up while I have a modicum of dignity left."

He took her hand again, leveraged her up, but kept his hold on her as she stood to face him. "You're sure you didn't get hurt?"

"No, I didn't," she said.

"What did you mean when you said I was right, this isn't Chicago? I don't think I ever said that to you."

She was brushing at her clothes with her free hand. "I knew when you saw my boots you were thinking that, and something like it about my jacket, too. You were right about both of them." She looked down at her worthless boots. "All glitz and no functionality," she murmured.

She'd pegged his thoughts perfectly, but he wouldn't do an "I told you so"—not when she was being such a good sport. He liked that a lot. There was no fussing.

"Okay, let's keep going, maybe more slowly this time."

"You've got it," she said and glanced down. "You've got something on your jeans."

He followed her gaze to the dirt and broken brush clinging to the denim. He shrugged.

"No one hits the ground here without taking some of it home," he murmured as he swiped his free hand at his leg.

"Good attitude. But I think you're living dangerously letting me still hold your hand."

He tightened his grip on her just a bit and smiled. "I like living dangerously."

That brought a soft chuckle. "Fool," he thought he heard her whisper, but kept going, still holding her hand for balance.

They walked in silence downward and were almost to the horses when Anna startled Ben by jerking free of his hold. She gasped, "Oh no," and hurried off down the trail. Ben, right behind her, saw the reason she'd panicked. Traveler was standing right where he'd left him, but Punch was nowhere in sight.

Ben caught up with Anna as she stopped by the limb of the tree that had once secured Punch but now lay splintered on the ground at her feet.

Anna turned to him. "How could he…? I mean, he destroyed that branch. I can't believe he could do that." She sighed as she looked around. "Wow, I guess I wasn't kidding about walking back."

"I won't let you walk," Ben said as he undid

Traveler's reins. "Not after I've seen how you walk in those boots." He swung up into the saddle then reached down to offer his hand to her. "Come on up. Traveler's okay with two on his back."

When she hesitated, he couldn't stop from saying, "You said I was right about your footwear before. I still am." He smiled at her. "I'm usually right about most everything."

She managed a slight smile before she put her foot in the stirrup, and Ben leveraged her up to sit behind him.

"I am so sorry about not tying him up right."

"Oh no, it had nothing to do with your skills. The horse obviously doesn't like being tied up at all and broke the limb."

"He shattered it," she said, and he felt the warmth of her breath on the back of his neck.

"I'd say so."

He felt her exhale before she asked, "How can you keep him tied up if he doesn't like it?"

"We probably can't. It's a shame, but he'll probably be off the safe list for the kids."

As they set off, Ben tried to concentrate on getting to the stables and not thinking about Anna pressed against his back.

"Oh," she said softly, "that's too bad."

"Yes, but safety's everything with the kids involved."

Silence hung between them until they were close to the riding ring. Ben spotted Dwight just outside the stable doors, Punch standing beside him. "Look ahead," he said and felt Anna shift to peer around him.

"He made it back!" she said with obvious joy.

Before Ben knew what was happening, she scrambled off Traveler and took off running toward Punch.

When Ben got to Anna, she was pressing her forehead to the horse's neck and crooning softly. "Good boy. Good boy. You're okay."

"I was just getting ready to ride out to see what was going on with the two of you," Dwight said.

Anna kissed Punch on his neck before she looked over at Ben. "It's pretty great that he knows where he belongs."

As Ben dismounted, Dwight asked, "So, what did he do, bolt or throw the lady?"

"He ripped the branch off the tree where he was tied while we hiked up to the smaller gorge."

"Dang." Dwight shook his head. "That's

a shame. I'll take him back tomorrow so he can make auction."

Anna looked at Dwight. "Back where?" she asked with none of the softness in her tone she'd had for the animal.

Ben answered quickly. "He means Punch can't be trusted around kids if he gets out of control. We'll have to send him back to the donor."

Anna looked stricken as she spoke to Ben. "Just like that. I thought you meant he couldn't be a ride for the boys, but he'd be okay for adults to ride. You won't give him another chance and try to figure out why he's scared of being tied up?"

Before Ben could respond, Dwight interjected, "Sorry, ma'am, but I sure didn't see this coming." Dwight shrugged and went to take Traveler's reins from Ben. "What do you want me to do about him, Ben?"

Ben looked at Anna then said, "Check him out to see if you can figure out what happened so you can tell his old owner when he goes back."

Dwight nodded then went off with both horses.

Anna turned to Ben. "He can figure out

something—can't he? Then Punch can stay here, right?"

Ben couldn't tell her that wasn't going to happen, so he avoided a direct answer. "If anyone can figure it out, Dwight can."

As if that settled things, at least for the moment, Anna seemed to relax. "Thank you so much for the ride. It was amazing, and I apologize again for making you fall."

He had enjoyed it a lot more than he'd expected to when they'd left, fall and all. "It was good to sit on a horse out under a blue sky instead of in a truck or in an office."

"Definitely," she said. "When did you reschedule your appointment for?"

"Tomorrow at two o'clock."

When she shivered, he started to walk toward the house and motioned her to come with him. "Let's walk while we talk."

She fell into step beside him. "There's one more thing I was thinking about, and I promise you I won't be offended no matter what you decide."

He wondered what was going to happen this time. "What have you been thinking about?"

"Would it be okay if I rode along with you

to your appointment to observe the county in action tomorrow? It's something that might come in handy for me in the future."

The woman never ceased to surprise him. He kind of liked that about her. "If you have the time, I'd be glad to have the company." The drive wouldn't be boring. So far, Anna had been anything but boring.

"Thank you. Count me in," she said.

As he kept walking, he glanced at her, and she was grinning, showing her dimples, as if he'd done her a huge favor. The thing was, Anna was the one doing all the favors since she'd showed up in her little white car. "I'll pick you up around twelve thirty. Will you be at the office?"

"No, I'm staying in the carriage house of a beautiful Victorian B and B, the Royal Lady Inn. It's over on—"

"On Riverview."

"Yes. Is the person you're meeting with an inspector or a planner or what?" she asked as they stopped by her car.

"He's the head man in Permits, Inspections and Code Compliance."

"Is he working from a list he provided to you, or is he doing a general update?"

"All Seth told me was that there were some questions that needed answers and a signature on some agreement that had to be notarized."

"You have power of attorney to sign?"

"Yeah, Jake, Ben and I all do."

"What's the man's name you're meeting with?"

"Norman Good."

"Have you met him before?"

He could see the lawyer in her again by the list of questions she asked without pausing. "Nope. First Jake and his wife, Liberty—most call her Libby—were dealing with him, then Seth and Quinn took over. It's my turn now."

"Too bad," Anna murmured. "It's always good to know something about the person you're going up against."

He frowned. "You're making it sound as if we're going to war."

"No, it's just good to be prepared."

She rubbed her hands together and Ben cut off the discussion. "You're cold, and we can talk about this on the drive tomorrow, okay?"

"Yes, I am and yes, we can," Anna said then got in behind the wheel of the compact and looked up at him with a smile. "Thanks again for everything."

Ben nodded as she closed the door.

He watched until the white car went over the rise and out of sight. The expression on Anna's face when she had turned to him after seeing the ranch's boundaries had been priceless. The fall, the horse taking off and the ride back, which could have all been disasters, hadn't been. He'd enjoyed every moment. He barely knew Anna Watters, but he looked forward to getting to know her better.

He was smiling when he turned to go into the house. "A very unexpectedly good day," he murmured to himself.

## CHAPTER FOUR

ANNA WAS ALL smiles on the way back from the ranch. When she got to the office and told Burr about her afternoon, he looked shocked at first, then he was smiling, too.

She'd been able to *read* Ben during their ride and conversations. She could see it in his eyes and body stance when he was uncertain or uncomfortable about what he was saying or doing, pretty much the way she could see those things in most people she interacted with. But she sensed there were things about Ben she hadn't picked up on. She'd been enjoying herself, not trying to figure him out the whole time. What mattered now was that he was honestly on board with her offer of help.

Anna was finally starting to feel halfway warm again as she sat in front of the computer studying Wyoming gun laws when Burr came into her office an hour later. He crossed to take the side chair to face her.

"I really am impressed," he said, taking his seat. "Honestly, I never thought you'd be able to pull off any of that without some deception. I was wrong."

"I'm so relieved you're okay with me doing it."

"Relieved? You worked a miracle as far as I'm concerned."

She could feel heat in her face but tried to ignore it. "I could tell Ben might need help, and it worked out the way I'd hoped it would," she said then shifted the conversation. "Have you ever dealt on the county level with anyone named Norman Good?"

Burr nodded. "Sure. That's who Ben has the meeting with?"

"Yes. What do you know about him?"

"I met Norm in court more than once when he was dealing with land usage. He's a rigid thinker with black-and-white views of everything."

"That's good to know," she said.

"When I got here twenty years ago, he was a real go-getter, bound and determined to do everything perfectly, even if he plowed other people under. I hope by now that he finally realizes that humans are imperfect beings, and sometimes that's their best feature."

"Great insight into your fellow man," she teased easily with him.

Humor twinkled in his blue eyes. "Yeah, I even surprise myself sometimes." As he got to his feet, his expression sobered. "I think the worst thing about Norm is—and remember this, Anna—he has no sense of humor, especially if he thinks he's the target."

She tucked that away. "I'll remember that."

"Are you going to be around here at all tomorrow?"

She stood. "For a bit in the morning." She reached to get her jacket off the nearest file cabinet. "Right now, I'm going over to check those plot maps again. That ranch is bigger than some small countries."

"Try taking pictures with your phone to save trips to the Annex cellar."

"Smart man," Anna said. The longer Anna was around Burr, the more she enjoyed being around him. She was starting to feel good about her decision to come to Eclipse.

THE TOWN'S RECORDS were kept in a jarringly characterless building called the Annex, next to the town hall. It was just off Clayton Drive at the southernmost end of town on Moonlight Drive, a romantic-sounding street that had nothing romantic on it. The Annex was a cement block, wood-shingled structure, where the full basement had been redone for the physical viewing and storage of the records with full climate control. The town might be working on putting those records online, but so far, the pickings were sadly lacking when she'd tried to hunt them down.

The town clerk, a balding older man who ignored the town's "dress code," always wore dark cardigans over his white shirts, partnered with slacks and loafers. He was simply called Bob. Even the name plate on his desk in reception read *Bob, Town Clerk*. He recognized Anna from her other visits and smiled. "If you know what you're after, Ms. Watters, go on down."

"I'm checking some plot maps."

"Section J12 against the south wall."

She already knew that from a previous visit but thanked him before she crossed to the cellar door and went down the stairs. Once in the basement, she retrieved what she needed and took the coded cardboard cylinder over to a large viewing table near the central aisle.

She slipped three maps out onto the table-top and carefully smoothed them flat.

One showed only the plot of land for the ranch. The second map was of that plot, plus immediately adjoining parcels. The third showed the ranch's land position in the county. She quickly took pictures with her phone before she put the maps all back in the tube and returned it to the shelf.

When she left the building, rather than head back to the office, she had something to do, and the sooner the better. She hadn't had many casual cold-weather clothes in Chicago, and what little she'd had, she'd brought with her. But she needed new boots and a jacket that could fight the Wyoming chill in April.

"Live and learn," she muttered to herself as she drove past stores on Clayton Drive, all fronted by raised walkways. Some were dedicated to the Western experience, some to astronomy, a tourist activity in the area, and some were providers for the dude ranches, along with the day-to-day necessities for life in Eclipse. Wood, brick and logs were the main building materials, some faux Old

West, some a bit more streamlined. But it all worked.

Four blocks north of the office was Garrett's General Store. It stood on the corner of the main street and Wylie Way, looking like a large barn with an exterior that seemed honestly aged from time, instead of by someone trying to give it fake character. She parked and hurried up the steps to go inside.

As the door swung shut behind her, she scanned the large interior that was filled with everything anyone could need from guns and rifles to clothes, to tons of boots and hats. There was even a coffee bar in the back corner, near a large potbelly stove, along with a sitting area that boasted rodeo posters.

A man approached her as the warning clang of a bell hanging over the entrance door died out. With thinning gray hair, a weathered face and a smile from ear to ear, he said, "Welcome, welcome." But it was what he was wearing that made Anna return his smile. A pink Western shirt with fringes that swayed as he walked, white jeans and gold boots with two-inch heels, all combined to make *garish* a mild term for his outfit. "I'm Farley Garrett and this is my store. How can I help ya?"

"I was looking for some clothes and boots that would be good for riding and walking."

"I have the boots for you," he said and led the way to the side wall that held shelves of footwear from floor to ceiling. One part was for men, the other for women and children. "I have a pair of beautiful purple boots."

"I'm just looking for simple boots that have good traction and will keep my feet warm," she said quickly.

"I know you're new in town but give yourself time and you'll be shopping for fancy boots sooner than you think. I promise I'll give a real deal to anyone who works with Burr." He was another stranger who someway had found out who she was, why she was in Eclipse and who she knew. At first that had been off-putting to her. Slowly, she was coming to like walking to work and having people she'd never met smile and nod to her. One couple had called her Madam Attorney. She knew she had never met them before.

An hour later, Anna left Garrett's with two pairs of boots, one for riding and one for casual wear. Neither pair was purple. She also had a great red jacket, some thermal tops and flannel shirts. By the time she arrived back at work, daylight was beginning to fail. Burr called out to her through the open door of his office behind the reception area. "Come on in here, Anna, please."

She dropped her bags by the door to her office then crossed over to Burr's, where he was seated behind his desk. "Who do you think called me about an hour ago?"

"Elvis?"

"Who?"

"Elvis Presley. You know, the singer, the King?"

He guffawed. "No, he seems to have lost my number. Ben Arias called."

That stopped her. "He isn't canceling, is he?"

"No, he actually wanted to talk about your offer. I told him it was your time, and how you used it was your choice. It turns out, he thinks you're pretty nice to make an offer like that."

"He didn't ask any awkward questions?"

He shook his head. "None."

"Good. I wonder why my ears weren't burning while I was getting fleeced at the general store by a cowboy wearing pink."

That brought a grin from Burr. "Farley is a character, isn't he?"

"He tried to sell me purple boots. I didn't buy them, but I did end up with a warm jacket and boots, even though it's April and it should be spring weather by now."

Burr chortled. "Heck, in these parts, at this altitude, we get snow in June."

"Then I'm prepared. Is that all you wanted to talk to me about?"

"That's it. I'm just tying up the settlement for Freeman Lee and heading out to get an early dinner at the diner. Want to come along?"

"I would, but I need to get some studying in, and your Wi-Fi doesn't cut on and off like it does at the carriage house."

"Can I drop something off for you before I head home?"

She smiled at him. "Yes, please. One of those burgers we had before—no onion, no bacon." She turned to go to her office. "Let me get money for it."

"No, no, it's my treat for what you accomplished today," he said then picked up his jacket and headed out.

Anna went to her office and pulled up the

last pages she'd been going over on the computer. When the office landline rang, she checked caller ID. It wasn't a local number. "Law offices of Addison and Watters," she said when she answered.

"Anna? It's Ben."

She sat back in her chair. "Oh. Hi."

"Glad I finally got ahold of you. I forgot to ask Burr for your cell number earlier."

"Is something wrong?"

"No, not at all. I just wanted to have your number in case something came up that I needed to talk to you about. I'm calling on my cell. Text me from your cell after, and I'll have your number."

"I'll do that. Thanks again for the ride. It was incredible."

"It was a good ride," he murmured. "No problems from your fall?"

"No. How about you?"

"I'm all good. I'll see you tomorrow. You're at the Royal Lady, the one Gabby Brookes runs, right?" he asked.

"Yes, that's the one."

"See you there," he said and was gone.

She quickly put his number in her cell and sent him a text.

Please promise that whatever Dwight does to figure out why Punch ran off won't be painful.

His response came almost immediately. Promise.

She was so hoping that Dwight could make things right for Punch. She could tell he was a good horse. She'd learned to really love horses at her aunt's ranch and had even once watched a foal being born. He'd been totally black with only a brush of gray on his muzzle, and she'd named him Magic. She'd been devastated when her aunt's breeder had rejected him because of his "lack of size and poor alignment." The breeder had recommended the "auction."

Anna had only been twelve when that happened, but she knew that when a horse wasn't physically what was wanted, the auction was to dispose of it, not find a new owner for it. Then her aunt had announced that Magic would stay with them, and it would be Anna's job to take care of him. That had been real magic for Anna during the summers, until the day she'd had to say goodbye to Magic when she went on to college. She'd made a promise that if she ever had a way to bring him to her, she'd do it. She'd never been able to do that.

Now Punch was there, a sweet horse, despite his display of striking chaos on the tree. She hoped against hope that Dwight could make magic and keep Punch on the ranch. Anna sighed, made a note to call her mother in Colorado and ask about Magic. But when she sat back, ready to get on with her studying, she felt tightness in her shoulders.

As she reached to tap the monitor screen, her muscles screamed in protest. The discomfort was not from the fall but from the ride. It had been so long since she'd been on a horse, her body wasn't used to it anymore. When Burr came back with her food, she'd head to the B and B and soak in a hot bath. While she waited, she transferred the map pictures from her phone to her computer and studied them.

Anna was thankful when she heard the outer door open and close, and Burr called, "Dinner!" She could smell the food as he came into the office and crossed to set the take-out bag down on the desk. "Thank you, thank you," she said.

"Elaine put in a cookie on the house. She also said for you to come with me next time.

That was right before she mentioned that you needed to get a good warm jacket and not the suede one that's totally useless here."

The lady who ran the diner seemed to have a "mothering" complex, and it made Anna smile. "Small towns, huh?" she asked.

"You'll get used to it."

"Well, she'll be happy. I now have a legitimate winter jacket to wear in April."

"That's good news," he said as he moved closer to look at her computer. "Is that the Eclipse Ridge Ranch?"

"Yes. It's huge, and the high northwest boundaries are incredibly irregular. It's crazy terrain up there, with some really impressive ravines and drop-offs. It took me forever to find what I think is the place Ben took me our boundary ride."

"It's God's country, that's for sure," he murmured. "Oh, I asked Leo, our mayor, about Norman Good. Seems his office has filed more complaints in the past few months than they have for most of last year. So, watch your back tomorrow, just in case."

"Thanks," she said and shut down her computer. "I appreciate you getting the food, but I'm going to have to take it back to the

B and B with me. I'm in misery," she said as she cautiously eased to her feet, a movement that she felt mostly in her thighs.

Burr frowned at her. "You hurt yourself?"

"No, it's from riding after so many years of not riding. My neck, my shoulders and my legs are all in a world of hurt."

His expression eased. "You'll get used to it."

"I guess so, if I go again," she said, reaching for her leather shoulder purse and the bag of food. Burr carried her shopping bags out to the car for her. Once she was inside with her purchases, she hesitated to close the door. "Burr, I could use your advice."

"Sure."

"Do you think it would be out of line for me to ask Ben if I could meet Sarge? I'd love to talk to him, get to know him a bit, so I can do a better job for him and the ranch. I'm curious about him, too, that he's done so much for Ben and the others. Ben makes him sound like some…I don't know…bigger-than-life person."

Burr let out a rough chuckle. "You should meet him. He's really something, even with the sickness. Ask Ben. All he can do is refuse."

"Okay, I will," she said. "Have a good night."

Anna drove to the B and B, an impressive three-story Victorian set among towering old trees on a side street named Riverview Drive. She hadn't noticed a river anywhere around, but the setting was lovely. The multihued pastel colors on the trim and the body of the house only added to its regal ambience. She turned onto the cobbled driveway that ran past the main house and back to the carriage house where she was staying in the room above an open double-car garage.

She parked her rental in her assigned spot by the stairs up to her room. After she retrieved her bags and turned to head up, she was stopped by someone calling out, "Anna? Hold up."

She turned as the owner of the bed-and-breakfast, Gabriella Brookes, came toward her. Anna held up the bags from Farley Garrett's store. "I've been shopping."

Gabby was maybe in her midtwenties, with a blond pixie cut that feathered around a cute face with freckles, blue eyes and an always bright smile. She dressed with a touch of Victorian style, mixing jeans and soft floral blouses with choker collars. "You're working late," Gabby said.

Anna wasn't surprised that Gabby had noticed. She knew everything about her guests. "Yes, and I'm ready to soak in a hot tub tonight. My muscles are really sore."

She frowned. "You're getting sick?"

"No, I went riding today for the first time in years." She sighed heavily. "I'm paying for it now."

"Where did you go riding?"

"At the Eclipse Ridge Ranch."

Gabby's eyes widened. "How did you get to ride out there?"

"Ben Arias was showing me the property lines." She slowly rotated her head to try to ease the growing discomfort in her shoulders. "I really overreached, but it was worth it."

"You and Ben Arias?" Gabby asked with slightly elevated eyebrows.

Now she understood the woman's surprise. "Oh no, I was just going out to see the ranch. I ran into Ben, and he offered to show me the boundary lines. I'm trying to learn the laws and codes for my bar exam, and I thought I should be more familiar with larger parcels."

"Oh," Gabby said. "I'm sorry I said that about Ben. It's just…he's available, you know, and good-looking. I just thought… I mean, he'd be a catch, that's for sure." She looked more than a bit embarrassed.

Maybe some women in town had their eyes on Ben. "That's okay. He's very nice."

"I just came out to let you know, the Wi-Fi is being upgraded in two weeks. Sorry it's taking so long," she said.

"Thanks for letting me know. For now, I can do that work at the office."

As Gabby headed off to the main house, Anna slowly took the stairs up. When she stepped into her space with its cabbage rose wallpaper in blues, greens and pinks, she smiled. The beautiful mahogany poster bed, which faced the back view through French doors, had been made up with a ruffle-trimmed spread in a soft green fabric that matched the canopy. Pastel-colored pillows were piled against the headboard, and a pink knit throw covered the foot of the bed.

It was cluttered and overdone, and Anna thought it was perfectly lovely. She had loved it since she'd walked in the first day. When Gabby had explained about the shower not working in the adjoining bathroom, Anna hadn't cared. There was a large oval bathtub that made up for any lack of her being able to take a shower.

She went in to start the bath then headed back to sit on the bed to eat the still slightly warm burger. It wasn't bad, and the cookie was delicious. All in all, despite the soreness in her body and the day going totally differently than she'd thought it might, she smiled. It had been a good day.

BEN PULLED THE old red pickup onto the cobbled driveway of the B and B at exactly twelve thirty the next day. Before he could drive around to the carriage house, he spotted Anna on the front porch with Gabby. He came to a stop by the side stairs as Anna hurried down the steps and went around to get in on the passenger side. She was wearing a bright red jacket that looked a whole lot warmer than her suede coat.

"Very punctual," she said as she did up her seat belt. "I'm impressed."

Her braid was gone in favor of a high ponytail, and he liked that. "Sarge taught us how to be a gentleman, bail hay, take care of horses and be punctual."

"A man with skills, huh?"

"Mad skills," Ben murmured, then added, "Nice jacket."

Her smile grew and it brought out her dimples. "I admit that I needed a sensible jacket, or I'd get sick from your crazy weather here."

He realized he was enjoying her admission that he'd been right without saying so directly. As they drove away from Gabby's he said, "Good idea. Actually, a genius idea."

"Okay, you were right. How's that, genius?"

"That's fine," he said, fighting the temptation to say something else, but he'd take his win while he had it. "Just fine. I'm surprised that no one else talked to you about your jacket. Sometimes the people around here are too involved, but once you get used to this way of life, you miss it like crazy when you're not here."

"Where have you gone that you missed it like crazy?" Anna asked.

"Where didn't I go?" Ben turned south on Clayton Drive, heading for the highway. "My work has taken me all over the country."

"If I did a search for you online, what would come up for your home address? The ranch?"

Another example of why she was an attorney. She was managing to pin him down to a specific response with almost admirable ease. "No, an address in Houston."

He picked up speed once they were on the highway heading south to Twin Horns. "I have an apartment there I use as a stopover between contracts." That sounded empty, even to him, so he added a rationale for it. "The ranch is out of the way and not usually practical for my schedule."

"What exactly are your contracts for?" Anna asked.

"Analyzing social services, child well-being centers, even private facilities for children." Ben hoped that generalizations would be enough for her. He hated talking about his work and having to explain the whys and the whats. He did that day in, day out under contract. But being in the truck with Anna, his work was not what he wanted to dwell on.

Yet she boxed him in when she asked directly, "Specifically, what are the contracts for?"

"You seriously want to know about that?" He gave her an out, and she didn't take it. "Yes, I do. Just as long as you're finished when we get to Twin Horns."

He gave up and started explaining. "As an unbiased party, I evaluate ongoing programs for child protection and welfare, to find any problems that aren't being addressed. The money that goes into the care of one child for a year in the system is staggering, but so much is being wasted, and the kids suffer because of it."

"So, you go in and tell them what they're doing wrong?" she asked.

"Not exactly. I go in to help them, not condemn them, and most of those involved are very thankful for the fresh eye, and really want the best for the kids. A few resent it, but I'm not working for them. I'm doing it for the kids.

"My last contract lasted for a year, an umbrella deal between cooperating agencies on the east coast. I went from Detroit to New York, down to West Virginia and back to Detroit for a final cleanup." He spoke a bit faster than usual, but he wanted to get to the end quickly. "I closed the whole thing out in February at an annual fundraiser for one of the finest charities to benefit needy kids in the

State of Louisiana, if not the country. I came right back here after the fundraiser. That's why I've gone off contract for now, so I can stay here as long as I need to."

"So, you do PR, too?" she asked.

"Not if I can help it." He cast her a quick glance and she was looking right at him. She really was interested in what he was saying, which, actually, was pretty unusual in the scheme of things. "I was talked into putting on a tux that cost more than a luxury car and wearing gold cufflinks that I know had enough diamonds on them to support a child center for a year. Then we went to a dinner held at one of the most extravagant hotels in New Orleans. It cost four thousand dollars a plate."

"I take it there was no rubber chicken?"

He glanced at her, catching her smiling. "As long as the kids got their money, they could have served hamburgers for four thousand a plate. My speech was my main concern at the time."

He felt her shift in her seat as if to look at him better. "What was your speech about?"

That was a request he'd never heard before. He wouldn't say she'd already heard part of it just now. "You're really interested?" he asked again.

"Absolutely," she said without hesitating.

"Okay. I talked about my foster care years, and how it changed me for the good and the bad."

"You didn't like making that speech, I take it?"

He wasn't aware he'd said that in any way that would have broadcast his dislike for the dinner or his past. But he admitted the truth to Anna. "I only did it because the organization is very well run and last year they hit a new high in donations. This year, after the donation of a beach house in the Florida Keys, they doubled last year's amount."

"Wow," Anna said. "That's incredible."

"It's going to make a difference in more than a few kids' lives. That's what my work is all about, making a difference as much as I can. Sarge was like that with every kid that was assigned to the ranch."

She shifted again. "You know, I've heard so much about Sarge, his life, and what he's done for everyone, that I'd really like to meet him sometime. If that would be possible? I mean, if it's not, I understand."

Ben wondered if he'd ever anticipate what Anna was going to ask him. "Well, with Seth and Quinn's wedding coming up next weekend, we're trying to keep Sarge calm and out of the craziness. Maybe a visit with you would keep him distracted while everyone else is running around like chickens with their heads cut off."

"I'd be happy to be a distraction anytime you need one."

She certainly made a good distraction for him without even trying. "You're a good sport, Anna," he said. "The wedding is going to be at the ranch, so it's kind of getting crazy out there. Seth and Quinn are loving the whole process of the wedding, though." He kept his eyes on the road as he said, "I'd just love to get it all over with."

"If it was your wedding, you'd probably love it, too."

He couldn't stop a scoffing laugh. "No, I'm not planning on anything like that."

"Oh, a real skeptic, huh?" she asked with a hint of teasing in her tone. "Not a believer in happily-ever-after?"

He chanced a glance and, surprisingly,

she wasn't smiling. "Not really," he admitted. "You a believer in all that stuff?"

"I don't know. Not now, for sure, not while I'm getting settled and building a career."

He could relate to that, except the part of her not knowing if she'd marry eventually. He knew he wouldn't. He'd made that promise to himself a long time ago—that he'd never have children. And that meant not marrying and dragging someone else into his decisions about kids and his work. That wouldn't be fair at all. His family at the ranch was all he needed. Anything more was off the table permanently. He never talked about it with anyone, just made it clear to the women he dated that nothing with him would be very long lived. He certainly wouldn't talk about it with a woman he barely knew, so he changed to a subject he knew Anna would jump at.

"By the way, Dwight, aka the horse whisperer, thinks he might have figured out something about Punch's bad habit."

He heard her take a sharp breath. "Oh my gosh! He can fix him?"

"He doesn't know yet. But he thinks he might have an answer shortly."

"That would be wonderful. Do you know what Dwight's doing?"

He had his eyes on the highway ahead of them but heard the excitement in her voice. She'd ridden the horse one time, yet he could tell she was getting all wrapped up in what would happen to the animal. He liked that in her, so he didn't tell her what Dwight had explained to him. Nothing was set yet. "I'll let him tell you when he's finished. Just know that if Dwight gets very lucky, you might not have to walk home next time you leave Punch somewhere."

"You'll keep him?" she asked with just a touch of caution in her tone now.

"If the problem's solved, he'll stay, and you can come out and ride him whenever you'd like to."

"I would love that, but what if it's not solved?"

She'd nailed him, and he hedged on that. "Let's wait to see what Dwight says."

She was quiet for a moment then launched into another conversation. "Was Sarge born around Eclipse?"

He was relieved and more than willing to take her mind off Punch's fate. "No, he came here from northern Montana with his parents when he was a kid. He met his wife, Maggie, right before he was deployed to Vietnam with the marines. He was older than Maggie and a rough rancher, and she was the only child of wealthy parents with land over by Jackson Hole. They did not approve at all."

"But they got married anyway."

"They sure did. After he returned from Vietnam, her family came around, but only after Maggie threatened to elope if her parents didn't accept him. They knew when to capitulate. Maggie was tiny, but a dynamo when she wanted something, especially anything to do with Sarge."

"The original happily-ever-after on the ranch?"

"Yes, I guess so," he said as he spotted a sign showing Twin Horns was thirty miles ahead.

"Does he remember much about his wife now?"

He tightened his grip on the steering wheel. "He remembers he loves her, the special things she did for him and things they did together. But sometimes he doesn't remember she's gone. That's okay, because he can't be sad about losing someone he can't remember losing. But when he does remember she died, it's very hard on him. I think he's always looking for her."

"I imagine he is," she said softly then cleared her throat. She offered another conversation switch without any lead-in. "How about we talk about Norman Good?"

Ben was all for that. "Go for it."

"Burr told me Norman Good has been around for quite a while, always pushing for advancement. He's driven by rules and sees everything in black-and-white, no subtleties, no shades of gray."

He'd dealt with tightly wound bureaucrats before in his work, and it was never easy. "Sounds like a peach of guy to discuss rules and regulations with," he said with a touch of sarcasm.

"It's not all that bad. I pulled up the calendar for civil actions at the courthouses in the county for the past five years. His name popped up all over code violations, but he's been in court only a handful of times in the past two years. So that means that he's been at a desk being a good little paper pusher. That explains why he's having you come to him instead of the other way around."

He slowed for scattered traffic ahead of them as they got closer to their destination. "That's everything?"

"One last but important fact. Norman Good has no sense of humor at all, according to Burr. So, he has no tolerance for anything funny, ironic or anything that would embarrass or minimize him. Self-deprecation isn't in his playbook."

# CHAPTER FIVE

"I NEED TO know that because…?" Ben asked.

"Never trust a man without a sense of humor," Anna said with no touch of humor in her voice.

Anna was bordering on being even more fascinating to Ben. "So how do we approach him?"

"Give him the benefit of the doubt, and you be a nice guy while you're in there. But if you see it starting to go south, ask me if I want to look at whatever you're studying or, if Norman Good's talking, ask if I have anything to add."

"Okay," Ben said, very glad that Burr had insisted he meet his new partner a few days ago.

The town of Twin Horns was one hundred percent bigger than Eclipse, but that still didn't mean it was large. It was a comfortable-looking place built around the main thoroughfare, and most of the county buildings were near its center. They found the public works building just beyond the central cross streets. It was a brick-and-wood, double-story structure with a parking area that ran along one side. Two white pickups with the county logo on their doors were parked near the entrance.

Ben checked his watch as he pulled off the street to park. "We're twenty minutes early."

"So, we'll go in there early and the worst that will happen is we wait in a reception area. The best that could happen is we get in to see him when he's not ready for us. It's a proven fact, my father told me, that when people are caught off guard, they're more honest than they might be if they're armed and ready for you."

He stopped the truck in a parking spot by the main doors and looked over at Anna. "Are you serious?"

"Yes. My dad also said to never let a bureaucrat get comfortable. Keep him a bit off balance, but not in a threatening way." She unsnapped her seat belt. "Oh, by the way, if I start to sound like some vapid little woman while we're in there, don't worry. Just go with the flow."

He was at a point where he wasn't too surprised by anything she said anymore. "Your dad's strategy again?"

"No, all mine. Dad would not approve."

Anna was fast, getting over to the glass entry doors before Ben was out of the truck. She was inside, reading the occupant list hanging in a hallway that had pale green walls and gray tiles by the time Ben was at her side. He spotted Norman Good's name on the list. "Second floor," he said, but had barely uttered the two words before Anna was on her way to the stairs. He hurried after her and caught up with her at the top, wondering when he'd signed on to play catch-up. "You really are going in early, aren't you?"

"I told you I was serious," she said as she looked around then crossed to a door to their left. He followed and she stopped to read the gold lettering on the panel: *Planning and Engineering—Norman B. Good.* She turned to look at Ben beside her and chuckled. "Really? Norman B. Good?"

He couldn't help but smile himself. "Makes you wonder what the *B* stands for, doesn't it?"

"I'll find out later." She reached for the door, but slowly drew back and shook her head slightly as color touched her cheeks. "Gosh, I'm really sorry. This is your appointment, and I'm just along to observe. I get a bit carried away sometimes. Do you want to go back downstairs and wait?"

He actually felt disappointed that Anna was backing down. "No, we're here. Let's do it and see how things go."

"Are you sure?" When he nodded, she pushed the door open and they stepped into a reception area that was surprisingly well appointed. With dark wood, thick carpeting and a bouquet of fresh flowers on a semicircular desk, it was a vivid contrast to the boring, industrialized green and gray of the hallways.

A woman coming out a side door stopped when she saw them approaching the desk. "Good afternoon. How may I help you?" The lady was middle-aged, wearing a simple navy dress with pearls, and her dark hair was cut short.

"Ben Arias. I have an appointment with Mr. Good."

She frowned slightly. "Oh yes. However, you're scheduled for two o'clock, I believe." She glanced at Anna. "You're together?"

"Yes," Ben said while Anna stood quietly beside him.

"I can inform Mr. Good that you're here, but he probably can't see you right away."

Anna spoke up as she slipped her arm in the crook of Ben's and leaned in to smile up at him. "Sweetie, I told you, Mr. Good is a very important man who obviously has to keep a tight schedule." She almost pouted as she glanced at the lady. "I'm so sorry, Ms. ....?"

"Janet Lund," the lady supplied.

"Well, Ben is just obsessed with not being late, and he ends up getting to appointments far too early. Don't bother Mr. Good. We can wait."

Janet hesitated then shrugged. "You know, let me check." She went back through the door and it closed behind her.

Ben looked at Anna and couldn't help himself. "Is this your vapid little woman act?" he asked in a whisper.

He didn't miss the flash of the dimple smile before Anna whispered, "Don't worry. No one around here knows me or you, so I can be as insipid as I want to and not ruin my reputation. Besides, if Norman Good will write me off as a tagalong, I can take in more when he's speaking to you."

He didn't get a chance to answer before Janet Lund returned. "Mr. Good appears to have some unexpected downtime at the moment and asked me to show you in."

Ben felt Anna squeeze his arm before she let go and preceded him to follow the receptionist into the private office of Norman B. Good.

The man standing behind an impressive antique desk looked to be fiftyish, with perfectly styled brown hair. His narrow face had sharp features, and a pencil-thin mustache occupied his upper lip. A slender build showed under a beige three-piece suit, and the man's red tie was the only splash of color around.

"Mr. Good, this is Mr. Arias and…"

When Janet glanced at her, Anna responded, "Anne," without supplying her last name, and Ben realized she wasn't about to give her full true name to the man. She was covering all her bases and he appreciated that.

Norman Good held his hand out across the desk to Ben. "Thank you for coming, Mr. Arias. So sorry you couldn't make it yesterday," he said in a deep voice as they shook hands. He glanced at Anna but barely acknowledged her with a nod before looking back at Ben. "Please, have a seat."

They sat on side-by-side leather chairs facing the desk. Norman Good took his seat but kept all his attention on Ben, as if Anna wasn't there. Ben took off his hat and rested it crown-down on the high-gloss top of the desk.

"Mr. Arias, it seems that there were forms filled out for land usage and safety measures that someone negligently forgot to get notarized. I do apologize for troubling you to come here, but it will only take a few minutes to rectify the matter." He sat forward, pressed a button on his phone and then looked back at Ben. With the tip of his forefinger, the man nudged some papers in Ben's direction. "Janet is bringing in her notary stamp and book," he said. "There are five pages, and I highlighted the signature that is required and also three spots for initials on the first and third pages. Your full signature is on the last page."

Ben felt Anna move slightly, leaning closer to him as if she were studying the first page of the document. She'd read his reaction, and he gladly put his hand over hers and asked, "Do you want to see the document?"

Norman Good pushed a pen toward him before Anna could respond. "It is a simple agreement to approve the conditions for the camp," he said.

Ben ignored the pen as he picked up the papers, scanned them quickly then turned to hand them to Anna.

She took them without saying anything, laid them side by side, in order, on the highly polished surface of the desk, then leaned forward and started to read both sides of each sheet.

Janet came in with her notary supplies and stood quietly off to one side. The man watched Anna unzip her jacket while she apparently read every word on all five pages.

When the inspector cleared his throat, Anna looked up, but not at him. Her eyes met Ben's gaze. "I'm not sure you should sign these."

"Excuse me?" Norman Good asked sharply. She turned the pages around and slid them toward the man so she could point out problems. "What am I looking at?" he asked, his voice tight.

When she spoke, Anna actually sounded sympathetic to the man. "I know good legal help is hard to come by, but I think whoever inserted conditions into your original document thought they knew more than you did." Norman Good was motionless, seemingly riveted to what Anna was showing him on the page. "I'm sorry, but Mr. Arias can't agree to the additions."

Ben still had no idea what Anna had found, but for some reason, he wasn't surprised and kept silent, letting her deal with the situation. Then she turned to him, motioned him closer, and he felt the fleeting brush of her lips on his ear as she whispered to him.

"They changed your safety inspections for compliance from once before the camp can open or in an emergency situation, to access anytime they want without prior notice. They wouldn't need any complaints, no accidents—they could just show up even while camp is open. They could go inside tents or the buildings, day or night, anytime they feel it necessary."

"Jake and Seth would have never agreed to anything like that," he whispered back to her.

"No one would. I can only imagine the

campers having the authorities enter the spaces they're sleeping or eating or swimming. That's excessive, intrusive and possibly dangerous. Insist on only signing the original version with one signature."

Ben trusted Anna completely in that moment as he whispered, "Okay."

She moved back then looked at Norman Good. She had his full attention now. "Mr. Arias would be happy to sign the original version of the documents, but the additions were not what has been agreed to." Then she gave Good an out. "Obviously, someone in Legal overstepped or got a bit power hungry and didn't count on the changes being noticed."

"Power hungry, indeed," the man muttered tightly as he reached to retrieve the papers. "I promise you this will not be tolerated." Then he turned on poor Janet. "How could you not have vetted these when Legal sent them down?" he demanded of her. "Inform Legal that I need a clean original as quickly as possible and warn the staff to never assume to add or subtract anything to documents coming out of my office."

"There might be a delay, since Legal is out for another half hour," Janet said.

"Get it to them the moment they show up," Norman Good said. The woman nodded and quietly left the office.

Anna stood and looked down at Ben. "Why don't we come back at a later date when it's ready for signing? I'm starving."

Before she finished talking, Norman Good was on his feet and speaking in a cajoling voice. "Oh no. Please, we can complete this in an hour, tops. No need for you to make that long trip twice. We can settle this by notarizing the clean documents today."

"I'm hungry. How about you?" Anna asked Ben, ignoring the man who was starting to tense up behind the desk.

Ben was very impressed at how Anna was playing this out and went along with her as he stood. "Absolutely starving."

Anna turned to the bureaucrat. "How about we come back tomorrow?"

"No," he said quickly, obviously wanting to forget about whatever he'd tried to pull with the changes. He didn't wait for Ben to agree or disagree before he threw out a bribe. "We have one of the best restaurants in the county just down the street. The Twin Horns Steak

House. By the time you've enjoyed a meal there, we'll be ready for signing."

Anna shrugged as she looked at Ben. "You know, steak houses can be really noisy, not much privacy."

"Oh," Norman Good said quickly, "there will be a quiet, private table waiting for you two."

Anna acted as if she didn't really care what they did. "It's up to you, Ben."

Ben didn't know who had made or approved the additions—the inspector or one of his minions in Legal—but he liked the way the man quickly upped the ante. "Private, quiet, with a view, and you'll be my guests, of course. That's the least I can do."

ANNA LOVED THE feeling of making the right thing happen for good people. But she restrained herself from celebrating until she and Ben were outside the building and walking to the restaurant. When she was certain no one who counted was around, she did a modified fist pump and whispered, "Yes!"

Ben stopped and turned to her. His expression was very serious, and it struck her that he might think she was being cocky. "Was that true about the papers?" he asked.

She allowed herself a smile. "Absolutely. Three added sentences, each at the end of an existing paragraph, and they changed the intent of those paragraphs completely. I mean… they'd have an open door to go to the ranch anytime to check on anything to do with camp security that they questioned. He put them there probably to get some future leverage with his superiors. Or someone put pressure on him." She startled herself with that idea, but let it go until she could think things through. "That's a game changer and not in your favor, no matter why he did it."

"How did you even recognize what he'd tried to do?"

"The additions were in a slightly tighter font in the printout to align them with the rest. And Good knew all about the alterations. He was ready to explode when I mentioned them. I think he believed he could slip it past whoever showed up."

Ben was still looking very intent. "You gave him a way out with that mention of a power grab in Legal. Why?"

"Because I didn't want you and the ranch

going into a war with the man, and I played to his bureaucratic ego."

Slowly, a smile spread on his face and a sense of victory grew in her. "I can see why Burr made you a partner." Ben lifted his right hand, palm toward her. "High five." She gave him an enthusiastic slap.

"That was fun," Anna said and meant it as they kept walking.

They were nearing the restaurant, a stand-alone brick building with an almost full parking lot, even in the middle of the afternoon. Ben chuckled. "I don't envy anyone who would have to face you in a courtroom."

She grinned at him. "A good guy like you would never be in that position. Shoot, you'll never even see the inside of a courtroom unless you're the plaintiff. Then I'd be at your table for sure. So, no worries." She was surprised when he responded by increasing his pace and keeping his head down.

ANNA'S WORDS HIT him like a gut punch in his middle. He'd seen the inside of a lot of juvenile courtrooms growing up, where he'd been labeled incorrigible at best, and unredeemable at worst. His dad had been arrested and his mother had disappeared. He'd never had a family, just parents who had wanted to be rid of him and had finally signed over parental rights to the court. He didn't want to tell Anna anything about what he was before he arrived at the ranch.

He kept quiet as he reached for the heavy wooden door to go inside what proved to be a good old-fashioned steak house. It was every bit as noisy as Anna had suggested back at Good's office. There was Western music playing over the buzz of conversation, laughter and the clank of dishes. As soon as the doors closed behind them, Ben took off his Stetson. A man wearing a black T-shirt with the silhouette of a cow's head in shimmering silver on it came directly over to them.

"Mr. Arias?" he asked and, as soon as Ben nodded, the man was on the move. "This way, please." He led them into a huge dining area decorated with everything cow and cowboy and bustling with servers and customers. He wound his way between the tables toward a set of sliding barn doors at the rear. Moving one aside to expose an unoccupied private dining area, he motioned them inside. "Sit anywhere you'd like."

Anna pointed to a spot by a window on the back wall. He could see it overlooked a small park with benches and beautiful old trees just starting to bud. "How about that one?"

"Excellent choice," the man said and crossed to help Anna out of her jacket to put it on an empty chair nearby while she took a seat facing the view. Ben laid his hat on the seat of an empty chair at their table, then took off his jacket and hung it on the back of the same chair. "I'm Beau," the man said and motioned to two menus on the table in front of them. "While you check our menu, I'll get you your drinks."

After taking their order for two coffees, the server left, sliding the door closed and shutting out almost all of the noise.

"Talk about privacy," Anna said as she glanced around at half a dozen unoccupied tables then picked up her menu and opened it.

"Were we really going to leave and come back tomorrow?" Ben asked.

He met her eyes as she glanced at him over the top of her menu. "It would have been your call, but I'd hoped we wouldn't have to. Besides, I had an ace in the hole."

"What was that?"

Ben thought her eyes looked more blue than gray right then. "Burr gave me a pretty good idea how that man does business. Norman Good wants to lead, not follow, and if he ever felt challenged in that regard, he'd be fierce. So, I mentioned someone overstepping their place in Legal, and his ego took care of the rest. I guarantee there has to be someone there who wants his scalp. That made him panic."

"He looked tense but controlled to me."

"He wasn't screaming, but his body language was. He's probably an okay person in real life, despite that awful mustache. But he's very afraid of being out of control, and he was bordering on that with the mistake he made. For now, he'll pull back, lick his wounds, and some heads in Legal might roll."

Ben frowned. "You saw all of that?"

"No, just made some educated guesses." She looked at the menu again. "Actually, I'd say he's the kind of man people wouldn't notice unless he's sitting behind a fancy nameplate or he was their boss." She nodded toward his untouched menu. "Check out this food."

Ben picked up the menu, thinking how impressed he was by Anna. "Are you always so good at reading people?"

"I am nowhere as good as my dad was with his people skills," she said, closing her menu and laying it on the table. "Dad could figure almost anyone out as soon as they shook hands and made eye contact." She smiled as she spoke of him.

"He once had a man come into the office for a consultation about low-income rentals he owned. I was about ten, and Dad let me sit in on the meeting. I thought they got along fine, even laughing over a stupid joke I didn't get. But when he left, Dad called in his secretary and told her to notify the man in three days that he was declining to represent him.

"When I asked why, Dad said, 'I don't deal with manipulative liars. It's in the eyes, Anna, and the handshake.'"

He could tell how much she admired her father by the way she spoke about him, something he'd never felt about his biological father. A touch of jealousy was there, surprising him. He'd much rather focus on the lady across from him.

"Norman Good resented even having to look at me, because I wasn't the one who could sign those papers and get him what he wanted."

"I bet you didn't get away with a lot when you were a kid," he said ruefully.

She shrugged. "I got away with a few things, but I was a pretty straight arrow. Now, what are you going to order?"

The door slid open and Beau appeared with their coffee and place settings. Within minutes, Ben had ordered rare prime rib and Anna had chosen barbecued ribs. As their server left, Anna sat back with a sigh. "What kind of kid were you?" she asked Ben.

He sat back and pressed his hands flat on the tabletop. He'd meant it moments ago outside. There was no way he'd ever tell her about the trouble he got into, the times he stole just to steal or the times he fought just because he wanted to hurt someone. When he thought about that, he was more convinced than ever that his decision never to bring a kid like him into the world was the right one.

He'd give up what he had to, to make sure that never happened. Marriage, he wouldn't miss. He still dated and walked away when he wanted to. He was making it work, and he'd keep making it work. But that didn't mean he couldn't enjoy himself from time to time, keeping that control in his life.

"I was just a kid," he said, then quickly pushed away more questions with one of his own. "Burr said you'd planned on going into practice with your dad when you grew up. Did you get to?"

It was a simple question, but it looked as if he had unwittingly hit a nerve when Anna's eyes didn't seem quite so bright.

"No. That was the plan, but Dad passed when I was thirteen and things changed." Her shoulders dropped on a soft sigh. "I thought I'd be in Chicago working with him now. But instead, I'm out here working with Burr, far from home, a move very much against most of my natural inclinations."

"But you did make the move."

"Yes. I wanted out of the firm I'd been working at for five years, but I didn't have the money to strike out on my own. Then, I received an email from Burr in answer to an ad I'd put in a legal journal about joining a firm. He offered me a clean fifty-fifty partnership, which I never expected, and I felt a connection with Burr right from the start. So,

I went against my cautious nature and took a chance."

"Are you happy you did it?"

As she appeared to consider that question, he watched her expression ease before she finally nodded. "So far, I think I am. I mean, I miss my dad always, but I decided to give myself time to see if Eclipse is the right place for me. Burr actually agreed to a clean exit if I can't do it. I never expected that, either, but he's more than fair and kind."

The door slid open again and the servers were back with their food. When they finally left and shut the door behind them, Ben watched Anna shake out her napkin and put it on her lap. Burr had told Ben that Anna's dad had passed, but he'd had no idea that she'd been a kid when it happened. It was obvious she'd loved him and her life in Chicago, probably as much as Ben hated his own past.

As he started to cut into his prime rib, he saw Anna begin to systematically slice the meat off her barbecued ribs. He couldn't resist saying, "FYI, Anna. People are not supposed to eat ribs with a knife and fork, especially in these parts."

She looked up at him with the hint of a

smile. "Thanks for the heads-up." She went right back to stripping the bones.

"So, you're doing good with Burr?"

"Better than good. He's easy to work with, and he knows what he's doing. I trusted him right from the start. That's not my usual reaction to a person when I meet them. But I felt that way right away with him." She shrugged. "I don't need to tell you that. You've known him for years."

"You probably know Burr better than I do, but I agree with your assessment."

"Thank you." She smiled and he found himself noticing a very small but unique thing about Anna Watters. Her dimples that showed when she *really* smiled were identical in every way, shape, size and location.

The door slid back and Beau stepped back in. "Sorry to interrupt, but Mr. Good asked me to inform you that everything's ready for you as soon as you can get back there. I can package your food to go, if you'd like."

"Thank you," Ben said, but Anna talked right over him.

"We'll finish our food then head back."

When the man left, Anna spoke quickly. "Sorry for that, but I really want to eat these when they're fresh. Reheating never works for me."

Ben shrugged. "No problem, you're right."

"Good, we need to finish this most excellent food," she said. "Then we'll take a leisurely stroll back to his office and see what Mr. Good has for you."

"Your game-playing is fascinating," he said and meant it, more than a bit pleased to be able to finish his prime rib and talk more with Anna.

"I wouldn't call it game-playing. I'd call it strategizing. Make them wait, even if it's just for fifteen minutes."

AN HOUR LATER, Ben and Anna were walking out of Norman Good's office with copies of the documents Ben had just signed, along with the papers that had first been presented to him for his signature. He'd asked to take them at Anna's suggestion on the way back from the restaurant. Although Norman Good didn't argue, he didn't look pleased, either. But he went on to assure Ben that he wouldn't need anything else for the camp before the final sign-off.

By the time they were back in the old truck

driving north out of Twin Horns, Ben admitted to himself that he'd had a good time, despite the reason they'd come to town. That made two good days in a row. If he'd gone yesterday by himself, he would have signed and walked away not even knowing what he'd done.

"Thank you for all you did today, Anna."

"I should be thanking you for such an entertaining day. Actually, practicing the law is a lot more fun than studying for the bar exam."

He sped up on the highway. "As hard as the testing is, it gets you where you want to go, right?"

"You sound as if you've been there."

"Nothing like the bar exam, but getting my masters was rough."

"What did you get your masters in?" Anna asked.

"Social Service Administration and a second in Child Advocacy and Policy."

She blew out a breath. "Wow, that sounds formidable and expensive."

"I had a lot of help from a grant, but you know how it goes."

"My mom helped me, and I had a partial

grant, but I still needed student loans to make it through. I just want to be able do half as well as my dad did helping people."

"What kind of law did he practice?"

"People law, that's what he'd say when anyone asked him. But he had a general practice, no specialty, just whoever needed his legal help, he'd take them on if he felt he could truly help them. I always admired that in him."

"He sounds as if he did what he felt was right."

"Oh, he did." He glanced at her as her voice grew flat, and he saw her bite her bottom lip before she said, "He had a lady come into his office, which was in our house at the time, and I was doing my homework in the kitchen right next to them. I heard her whole story.

"She had two kids and a husband who was taking them away from her. She didn't cry, but her voice shook, and Dad asked her a ton of questions. Then, finally, he said, 'I can help you and I will.'"

Anna sighed, a heavy sound. "You know, he did. He found out about her husband's criminal background and used it as leverage to get the guy to agree to her having full custody. And he even got support for the kids. I don't know how he did it, but we got a beautiful Christmas card from the lady that year with a 'Thank you' and a picture of her kids with her. My mom cried when that card came."

"He kept his word," Ben said in a low voice.

"Yeah, and every time a card like that showed up, I grew more certain I wanted to do that for someone. And when Dad…when he was gone, I knew I was going to, one way or the other."

He heard a soft sniff and didn't chance looking over at Anna. She was very special, a fighter with a heart. He knew she'd be as good or even better than her dad with law. "I think your dad would have been pretty proud of you today."

Her voice grew softer when she answered. "I hope he would be."

He couldn't let that pass, not after what she'd just told him. "I haven't known you very long, but I'm sure he would have been." He glanced away from the light traffic and over at Anna. She was very still, her eyes closed, her hands clasped tightly in her lap. "Are you okay?"

"Yeah," she said. "I'm sorry. There was just a ton of memories and promises there all of a sudden. I...I remembered so much that my dad did, and how people totally respected him, even some who went up against him in the courtroom."

He kept his eyes on the road ahead. "I'm glad you came today, and that you stopped me from signing those papers."

"It might have never come up," she said.

"Maybe, but now it won't come up at all."

Ben stared straight ahead. A simple ride to an appointment had turned out to be more fun and more consequential than he'd dreamed it would be. He'd learned more about Anna, too. She had her promise to herself and he had his. He understood that.

He chanced a quick glance at her again, and she was resting her head against the side window, her eyes still closed. He exhaled as he looked away and was glad that he wasn't leaving the ranch anytime soon. He didn't know how he'd ever leave for very long again. He'd have to figure out short-term contracts, one at a time. Family had been secondary to his work for so long, but by coming back to Wyoming, he'd found it was and always had been first. He'd just let it slip and he regretted the lost time.

Time was short, but he'd live every minute left with Sarge, and he'd never get far away from Jake and Seth again. Now Anna was getting in the mix, in a different way. He'd love to see how she flourished with Burr. He was sure she would, and she'd keep her promise.

When he slowed as they approached Eclipse, he turned, and Anna was looking at him. She had a soft smile on her lips. "I'm sorry, I'm not usually this quiet. I mean, I hardly ever stop talking."

"No problem," he said. "We're almost to Gabby's."

The town appeared tranquil as dusk started to gather around it, and the old-fashioned streetlamps were coming on. When he turned onto Riverview Drive, the grand old Victorian came into view, the glow from its interior lights spilling across the porch. He pulled onto the cobbled driveway and drove around back to the carriage house. Coming to a stop by the stairs that led up to her room, Ben spoke before she exited.

"Thanks again for all you did today, and I

promise to never say anything about the way you eat ribs again."

Anna chuckled softly. "Oh, you can say anything you like about the way I eat ribs. After all, an opinion is an opinion and not a law."

He nodded. "Agreed."

"Would it be all right for me to come out tomorrow to talk to Dwight about Punch?"

Ben would like that. "Come whenever you want."

"Thank you. You have a good night," Anna responded then got out. She closed the door, waved to Ben and then headed up the stairs to her room before he turned the truck around and drove off.

## CHAPTER SIX

ANNA ARRIVED AT work around nine the next morning in her new office attire—a pale pink sweater and jeans worn with her new boots. The ponytail was definitely taking over for the braid. Burr was already in his office with the door ajar, and she heard him laugh then say, "Absolutely, I am one lucky guy."

Anna caught a glimpse of him at his desk on his phone, and she turned to go into her office without bothering him.

"Well, well, well," she heard Burr say five minutes later. "You, my dear, are a solid hit around here." She glanced over at him standing in the doorway. He was wearing a blue flannel shirt along with jeans, and he leaned against the frame with his arms crossed on his chest.

"Guess who I was talking to when you came in?"

She shrugged. "I never guess right. Tell me."

"Ben."

She stopped moving her chair. "What did he want?"

"He was so impressed, he wanted me to know what you did yesterday and to tell me that I am a genius for bringing you out here. He also said that he sent the paperwork, both sets, to the big guns in Seattle, and they were blown away by what you found and how you handled it."

"Blown away?" she asked with a raised eyebrow.

"Okay, maybe he said they were impressed. Same thing."

She'd wanted to tell Burr about yesterday herself, but she was enjoying his version. "I just hope he doesn't tell anyone else about it. I'd hate to have it get back to Norman Good. He'd be pretty put off if he thought we were spreading the news of his attempted duplicity."

"You've got a point there. If I was you, I'd give Ben a quick call and explain that to him. Now, tell me, when did you realize what Norm was up to?"

She sat back. "I was uncomfortable when he barely acknowledged me, and the way he pushed the papers over to Ben—cautiously, as if they could bite him. I thought it wouldn't hurt to take a long look at the paperwork. It paid off, but one other thing's been bugging me since I met the man in person. Do you think he could be involved with any developers? I mean, he has a ton of power in his position to help them for pay under the table."

Burr rubbed his jaw roughly. "That's something I'd never think of, but he's pretty lethal when he wants something. It wouldn't hurt for Leo to quietly look into that possibility. He has people he could ask to check Good's records and complaints."

"It's probably my overactive imagination and my unease of the man, but it wouldn't hurt to check."

Burr straightened. "Yes, and you get ahold of Ben. If he starts talking to others, who knows who'll find out. Possibly someone connected to the development company, if there is one in Norman's life. I'll contact Leo after I keep my doctor's appointment."

That drew her up short. "Are you sick?"

"No, it's for my annual. Then I'll get the truck tires rotated. I should be back by noon."

"Okay, I'll be here."

As Burr headed off, Anna took out her cell

to call Ben. When it went to voice mail right away, she left a message for him to call her, and pulled up the court filings she'd promised Burr by one o'clock. When she looked up again, it was almost noon. Burr wasn't back, so she put in a call to Elaine's to have her lunch delivered and went back to work.

Right when she was sending some files to Burr, the outer door opened. She stood and stretched as she called out, "Your deadline's safe on the court order. I fixed it. I also ordered lunch, and I'm willing to share."

She was startled when she heard Ben say, "Thanks, but I just ate," before he showed up in the doorway.

"I thought you were Burr," she said with no idea why she sounded slightly breathless.

He smiled ruefully and shook his head. "Sorry, no mustache."

She thought he looked good clean-shaven. "Thank goodness," she said on a relieved sigh then caught herself. "Oh, I mean, mustaches are okay. Goodness knows, Burr rocks his, but…"

Ben came closer. "Just to put your mind at ease, I have never thought of growing a mustache." He held up a bag he was carrying. "I'm here delivering your order for Elaine."

"Really?" she asked. "I thought you were here because of the voice mail I left for you."

"That, too, but I just received it five minutes ago. I was at Elaine's having lunch with a friend, and when I mentioned I was going to stop by a store down this way, Elaine recruited me to drop this off."

"Thanks so much," she said and took the bag to set it down by her monitor. "I'm starving."

"You weren't specific on your message, so I assumed it's nothing horrible, like the second coming of Norman Good."

"It's about him but—"

"Do I need to sit down for this?" His smile fled.

"No, no, no, nothing horrible, but let's sit down anyway." She crossed the space to pull a chair over to her desk. Then she sat at the computer and waited until Ben was seated facing her. He took off his hat and set it by him on her desk. "Burr told me about your call to him this morning, and how we beat Norman Good."

He frowned. "I told him you were impressive and took him apart."

"No, he got caught, and I tried to pretend we understood. So, he's okay with us. But if he hears any gossip that makes him look bad, he's in a position of power to target us and the ranch. My dad used to say you never let your enemy know he's your enemy. I don't want that man to have an inkling that we think he's devious, self-serving and lower than a snail trail to boot."

Ben nodded. "You're right, snail trail and all, and I'll keep quiet. Seth and Jake know, and the attorneys in Seattle know. I'll talk to them."

She sank back in her chair with relief. "Thank you."

"You're welcome," he said. "By the way, the head attorney in Seattle said your work was very good." He stood. "Burr's pretty proud of you, too."

Anna hoped she wasn't blushing too much. "Thanks. That means a lot to me. Burr's made a real difference in my life in a very short time, and I've watched him interact with the people around him. He has such a good heart, a really good person."

"I never knew that really good people existed in this world until I met Sarge and Maggie and the people of this town. They changed everything." He exhaled, then reached for his hat. "I need to go."

"Can I ask you a question before you leave?"

"Sure."

"Why do you always set your hat down on the crown?"

He put the Stetson on as he said, "I guess, practically, it probably airs it out when you're not wearing it. But when Sarge handed me this, he told me that there's an old cowboy superstition that says all your luck will run out if you set the hat crown up."

She smiled up at him. "You believed that?"

"After ending up in Eclipse and finding Sarge and Maggie, I knew how lucky I'd been. I never want to take any chance of throwing that luck away." He sent her a smile as he tapped the brim of his hat. "Have a good day."

"You, too." She watched him leave and heard the door shut behind him, then realized she hadn't had a chance to ask about Punch. She wondered…if she bought a Western-style hat, would that superstition apply to wannabe cowgirls, too?

ANNA HAD JUST finished her lunch when Burr showed up. She hadn't heard the front door open before realizing he was looking in at her. "You ordered in?" he asked from her doorway.

"I sure did, and Ben delivered it for Elaine. I talked to him about keeping quiet, and he agreed."

"Good."

"How did it go at the doctor's?"

"He said I'm fine, and the tires have been officially rotated." He turned to go to his office, but she stopped him with a question she'd been thinking about since Ben had left.

"Do you know where Ben came from before he ended up at the ranch with Sarge and Maggie?"

"I don't think he was local. He might have been an out-of-area placement. Sarge and Maggie took kids in from all over the state. Why?"

"He said something about being a city kid, I think."

"Could have been. Most kids sent out to Eclipse Ridge were pretty messed up. You know, written off. I imagine Ben was the same, but you'd never know it now."

"On our way to Twin Horns, he told me about his work with kids. I thought that was kind of cool, to have gone through the system, and now he's trying to do what it takes to make it better for the kids."

"He had good examples. When the boys left the ranch, most of them were a whole lot better."

The more she heard about Maggie and Sarge, the more impressed she was. She thought Ben had been right about luck. His luck had been pretty good to end up there with the Caines. "Oh, I sent the court filing to you. Now I'm going to get more studying in before I head over to see Bob at Records. I might go back to the ranch later today or early tomorrow."

"You're going out to see Ben?"

She wasn't sure if she blushed slightly, but her face felt warm. "I'm actually hoping to see a man about a horse."

Anna started on a section of Wyoming constitutional law, intending to do some work before she went to see Bob at the Annex. But when she looked at the wall clock, it was half past three. She'd lost track of time again. Sitting back, she rotated her head to loosen muscles that still felt tight from the ride, then turned off her monitor. Putting on her new jacket, she went to tell Burr she was leaving, but his office door was shut, which meant he was with a client. So she quickly sent him a text, then headed out.

As she started walking to the Annex, her cell phone rang. She checked it while she paused in front of a gourmet chocolate shop, and it took her a moment to recognize Ben's number. She answered. "Ben?"

"That's me. Still studying hard?"

"No, I'm just leaving the office. I'm glad you called. I forgot to ask you about Punch when you were here." A couple she'd seen before passed by with a smile and nod. "I wanted to find out about what Dwight figured out."

"That's why I'm calling. Dwight said to get out here when you can so he can explain what's going on."

"Good or bad?" she asked cautiously.

"Come on out and see for yourself."

She made a quick decision to skip the Annex and head directly to the ranch. "I'll be there soon."

"Could you do me a favor?"

"Of course."

"Since you're going past Elaine's on the way out of town, could you bring a dozen cookies from the diner, half chocolate chip, half oatmeal? Julia, Sarge's live-in caregiver, had asked me to bring some back after lunch, but I totally forgot to get them."

"That's my bad. So, I'll get you out of the doghouse."

She heard a soft chuckle over the phone. "Much appreciated. See you when you get here."

Returning to the office, she went down the steps of the raised walkway and got into her car. When she arrived at the diner, she found Elaine, a petite lady with feathered gray hair and a huge smile, sitting at a table by the door doing paperwork. She looked up and the first thing she said was, "Nice jacket."

"Burr convinced me I needed something warmer. I didn't have a clue how cold it gets here in April."

She looked pleased. "Burr is one smart man, Anna. Now you have a good jacket you'll be wearing until June, then back to wearing it by early September."

"Really?"

"Yes, really," Elaine said with a chuckle.

She motioned around the nearly empty rustic dining area, done in red-and-white checks like a fifties' diner. The wall decor was split, with one section almost totally covered in sepia-toned pictures of the Old West, and the other section filled with photos of lunar and solar eclipses. Anna thought she noticed a couple that looked like a sky of falling stars. "Plenty of choices for seating, at least for now," Elaine said.

"I'm not staying. I came for the cookies Ben Arias forgot when he was here earlier."

"Oh yes. Chocolate chip and oatmeal?"

"Exactly. Also, could you get me a mixed dozen? Burr loves them, and I want to take some back to the office."

"I guess he needs cheering up, huh?" Elaine said as she motioned Anna to take a seat at the lunch counter while she went behind it. "Don't tell him I said anything, but he's a sweetheart and deserves better."

Burr had been to the doctor's, but he'd said he was fine. Anna swallowed then asked, "Is he sick?"

"Oh, dear, no. Not physically sick."

"Then what?"

Elaine leaned closer and lowered her voice to just above a whisper. "I heard Pearl Winslow from Wolf Bridge broke up with him, and right before the wedding, too."

"The wedding?" Anna asked with real shock. Burr was getting married and she hadn't had a clue.

"Shh. Jimmy's in the kitchen today and he's kind of a gossip. Yes, Seth and Quinn's wedding is at the Eclipse Ridge Ranch next Saturday. Pearl canceled going with Burr and word is she's seeing some guy out of Cody. Can you figure that one out?"

Anna didn't know what to think. "She broke it off?"

"Just like that." Elaine snapped her fingers. "I feel so bad for Burr." She moved back. "I'll get those cookies for him. That'll cheer him up." She went through a swinging door into the kitchen, returned in a few moments with two pink pastry boxes, then put them down on the counter. "I just made them an hour ago or so."

Before Anna could take out her wallet, Elaine said, "It's my gift to Sarge. Also, my gift to Burr to help cheer him up. Just don't let him know I told you about Pearl."

She wasn't about to admit to Burr she'd been talking to Elaine about his love life. "Thank you so much, and I won't mention Pearl to Burr," she said. "Are you going to the wedding?"

"You bet. I wouldn't miss it." She handed the pink boxes to Anna. "Make sure you tell Burr I'll be saving a dance for him."

The woman almost blushed, and Anna wondered if Pearl breaking up with Burr wouldn't be all that bad in the long run.

ANNA PULLED THROUGH the open gates of the ranch just after four thirty. The sun was starting to slip low in the west, but there was still enough daylight that she didn't have to put on her headlights yet. When she got to the top of the rise in the driveway, she could see the old red truck parked in front of the house alongside a jacked-up white pickup.

She braked to a stop by the vehicles.

Ben stepped out onto the porch then came down to meet her, stopping one step above, the way he had the first time she'd showed up at the ranch.

He was wearing his usual heavy denim jacket with jeans and boots, and he was just putting on his hat. "Glad you made it," he said. He really did have a great smile. "Are you ready to go see Dwight?"

"I'm not sure. I don't want him to say he can't do anything," she said.

"Dwight made me promise not to tell you before he could. So, all I'll say is, Dwight really is a horse whisperer."

She was almost giddy with relief. "Really, truly?"

"Yes," Ben said as he started down the drive to the stables, Anna beside him.

As the daylight faded, the cold was growing. "So, how's the studying going?" Ben asked.

"State constitutional law was never my favorite."

"So, you study, take the bar exam and that's that?"

"I wish. I study and study and study until July when I take the two-part exam. The first day you take a multiple-choice test with two hundred questions. The second day is for the essays. You have to score at least one-thirty on the first test, and seventy or greater on at least six of the essays."

"That sounds rough," Ben said as they passed the hay barn.

"It does take some people multiple attempts to pass."

"Burr said you were second from the top of your class when you graduated law school, so I imagine you aced the bar exam in Illinois."

She shrugged as they neared the stables. "I did okay." She wouldn't add that she'd passed on her first attempt.

"We have a welcoming party," Ben said as he looked ahead toward the riding ring.

Dwight was standing with Punch by his side at the open gate. "Ready to be amazed?" he called out to Anna.

"Yes, please," she said as she approached Punch and touched his muzzle. She felt the heat of his breath on her hand as he snuffled.

"I've got a second cousin, Sonny, who lives down on the Wind River Rez," Dwight said. "I explained everything to him, and he had an idea that Punch isn't headstrong or uncontrollable, because he hadn't showed none of that during transport or while being groomed or ridden. His guess was that Punch had had some specialty training at one time—maybe a rodeo show or something like it. Sonny figured it might be that when his reins are dropped on the ground, Punch holds to the spot without any physical constraints."

"What do you think?" Anna asked.

He didn't answer her question, just held out the reins to her. "Walk him out and around by the side of the ring, then go straight for fifty feet from the holding pens. Drop the reins and don't say a thing, just turn around and come back here slowly."

She glanced at Ben. He nodded. "Go ahead."

She led the docile horse away from the ring and farther from the holding pens, dropped the reins and returned to where Ben and Dwight stood. "Good, good," Dwight said in a low voice when she came close.

"Can I look at him now?" Anna whispered.

Dwight nodded. "Sure."

When Anna turned, Punch was right where she'd left him, patiently watching her. "But he can see me, and maybe he won't move if he has visual contact."

"Okay, let's get out of sight," Dwight said.

She wanted to argue but kept quiet when Ben said, "Even if he bolts, he won't get off the property."

As Anna walked with the two men into the

stables, her unease grew once they were out of sight of the horse. "When can I go back out?" she asked Dwight.

"I think you should come with me and let me show you around the tack room." He glanced at his watch. "Come on. Then you'll know where everything is for Punch."

Almost fifteen minutes later, and still out of sight of Punch, they approached the open stable doors.

Anna stepped out into the coming night, and squinted at the bright security lights illuminating the riding ring and the area around it. Punch was there, just at the edge of the glow from the lights. He hadn't moved but snuffled when he saw her.

She forced herself to walk slowly across to him then hugged his neck. "You did it, boy, you did it," she whispered and reached for his reins. As she led him back to Ben and Dwight, she had to ask, "We left him a lot longer tied to the tree. What if he just can't take a long waiting time?"

"Yesterday, I left him for almost an hour outside the ring, and he didn't move. Then I rode him up to the north earlier for a better test. I dropped the reins and walked away.

I didn't go back for two hours. He was still there."

"Wow, you really are a horse whisperer," she said to Dwight, dropping the reins to spontaneously hug the man. She drew back, grinning at him. "Thank you, and thank your cousin for me, please."

He was smiling right back at her. "I sure will." He reached for the reins. "I'll put him away."

"Thanks again," she said and turned to Ben. "He was just doing what he'd been trained to do. Being tied up was probably confusing and scary." She exhaled and then she had a thought that wiped away her smile. "He can stay here now that he's safe for the kids, right? You said he could."

"I'm not sure he's really suited for kids who have never ridden, but he's worth keeping, at least for now."

That wasn't the answer she'd wanted to hear, then she made a split-second decision with no time spent on the pros and cons of what she was about to do. She wouldn't let the horse dangle in the breeze until he made a mistake and was sent away. She'd never been able to take Magic with her, but she could try to protect Punch.

"Since Punch's staying here might not be permanent, would you give me the first chance to buy him if you ever think of getting rid of him?" She could see she'd surprised him almost as much as she'd surprised herself by the impulsive offer.

"You want to buy him?"

She had money coming from her mother when their house in Chicago sold, and she could use some of that to buy Punch. "Yes. I mean, when I get a place, and if you don't want him here any longer. I'd pay a fair price for him. I don't know what that would be, but you tell me, and I'll pay it for him. Please?"

ANNA WAS ASKING Ben to sell her a horse in the future that he would have gladly given to her for free right then. He knew they'd avoided a disaster with Norman Good. He owed her for that, and he knew how to pay her without money being exchanged. "When you get settled, he's yours."

Her blue-gray eyes widened. "Really?"

"Absolutely."

When her face lit up, Ben kind of thought

she might hug him the way she had Dwight. But a hug didn't come. Instead she started talking faster to make it clear how the deal for the horse would go down.

"Okay, okay, you let me know how much he's worth, and I'll get right on it. Maybe I could make payments while I'm looking for a place. I hadn't thought about a ranch here, but I could do that. A small one would be great, and Punch would be safe. I think it—"

"No, you can't." Ben cut her off abruptly.

Her eyes widened again then she looked stricken. "What?"

Ben quickly explained. "You can't buy him. He's yours right now."

He was surprised when she shook that off. "Oh no, I am not doing that. He's valuable, and I'll pay for him. I was asking you to allow me to buy him if you ever got rid of him, not to gift him to me."

He offered what he thought was the perfect reason not to take her money. "I won't sell him to you, because he was gifted to us. But I can regift him to you."

He realized his counteroffer wasn't close to perfect when she said, "Even if Punch was donated, he still has value. I won't take that value away from what you're doing here. Or I'll take him, but I'll donate what he's worth to your foundation as soon as I can."

Norman Good hadn't stood a chance with Anna, and right then Ben knew how the man had felt. She was boxing him in, all but forcing him to let her give him money. He tried again. "Listen to me. What you did for the camp by cutting Norman Good off at the pass would more than balance out any value Punch has monetarily. If you insist on paying me for Punch, I'll start paying you for your help with the camp."

She hesitated at that and looked down as if sorting through what he'd just said. He was prepared for at least one more pushback from her, but it didn't come. Instead she said, "Okay, have it your way, and thank you very much."

He'd won, but he didn't feel like a winner. Then he had an idea of what she was up to. "Is this a classic Anna Watters maneuver?"

She blinked at him. "What?"

"You know, letting Norman Good think that he'd won, and now you're letting me think I've convinced you to take the horse?"

"Why would I do that?" The suggestion of

a smile played around her lips. "Really, I'll argue with you some more, if you want me to, but I'll take the horse. How's that?"

He thought he might have been played, but he couldn't figure out how, or why he didn't mind if he had been played. He finally gave up with a slight directive. "Okay, it's a deal as long as you promise that you'll *never* try to give me money for the horse *or* send any money to the foundation."

He kind of thought he'd hit on exactly what she'd planned to do, when it took her more than a few seconds before she finally nodded.

"Promise."

"Good, he's yours now. Period. End of story," he said.

Dwight came up behind him right then. "Hey, boss. Do you need anything else before I head out?"

Ben didn't look away from Anna as he spoke to the man behind him. "Punch is now Anna's horse, Dwight, but he's going to be staying here until she has a place for him. She'll be coming around to ride him whenever she wants. Could you get the paperwork for the transfer started?"

"You got it," the man said then looked over

at Anna with a grin. "Have to say, Punch is one lucky horse. If you hadn't stepped in, he would have been heading back to the Old Dry Creek Ranch and going up for auction next week. Glad you stopped that from happening."

That brought a frown. "How could he be sold at auction if they knew what he did?" she asked Dwight. "Full disclosure mandates the provision of any negative information about a possible transaction."

"Well, ma'am," Dwight said, "that auction ain't for riding horses. It's a clearance auction."

Ben could see Anna considering his words and knew the exact moment she realized what Dwight had meant. "No. No, that isn't… Oh no, that's horrible."

"Anna, you knew Punch might not be staying here with the kids," Ben said quickly.

"Well, sure, that's why I wanted to buy him from you. I mean, I wouldn't have let him be sent to an auction, either. No way. That's horrible just because a horse isn't perfect. That's sick." She bit her bottom lip as she turned to Ben. "I didn't expect you'd ever do that. Now I'm glad he's mine—I mean, really glad."

Ben tried again. "Punch will be fine with you. That's all that matters."

She took a deep breath then released it. "Yes, and he'll be safe." She looked back at Dwight. "I'm sorry, but when I was a kid, I heard about horses that went to auctions and ended up being sold for dog food and to make glue from their hooves. There was one horse who was undersized, and his configuration wasn't just perfect, so the breeder wanted him at that kind of auction. I freaked out, and my aunt in Colorado ended up keeping Magic—that was his name. He turned into a wonderful horse. I don't know if all that glue and dog food stuff is real or just ways to scare kids, but I know they put down horses."

He got closer to her, fighting the urge to take her hand and get her out of there. He'd been gone so much, he'd never thought about some decisions Dwight would have to make as the manager. It was life on a ranch, animals coming and going, but he was thankful Dwight had come up with a solid explanation about Punch, and that Anna was smiling again.

Dwight said, "I'm going to close up now, if you don't need me any longer?"

"Take off," Ben told him.

Anna looked up at the darkening sky. "I guess I should get back to town."

When she turned to him, Ben barely stopped himself from saying, "No, don't go." Instead, he cut away from talk of her leaving and horses and glue-making, and asked, "Did you get the cookies?"

"They're in my car."

"Thanks. You got me off the hook with Julia. That's a relief," he said as they started back to the house.

When they neared where she'd parked, Ben asked, "So, is that car yours or is it a rental?"

"A rental. My car was so old, I sold it before I left Chicago and planned on replacing it when I got a chance."

"What are you going to get?"

She stopped and looked over at him. "I don't know. Something used, dependable, good gas mileage and not too expensive."

"Around here the gas mileage isn't as important as something that has weight and four-wheel drive to keep you on the road during the bad weather. Maybe an SUV or a truck, if you think you could handle one."

"I definitely could handle either one. I

drove an old pickup at my aunt's ranch. It was a four-on-the-floor stick shift, too."

He tipped his Stetson back with his forefinger. "How old were you?"

"Fourteen or so."

His eyebrows lifted at that "So, no driver's license, and here I thought you were a good kid, a straight arrow."

He liked the way she showed a slightly embarrassed smile. "I never said I was perfect. But I wasn't driving on public land, so it technically wasn't any sort of civil violation. I bet you drove around here before you had a license."

He shrugged. "You'd win that bet."

The door to the house opened and Cal Harris, Sarge's physical therapist, came out. The solidly built man with a shaved head was holding Julia Weston's hand. The caregiver was just a few inches shorter than Cal, blonde, with an athletic build, and she had a habit of wearing neon-colored running shoes when she worked.

"Hey, there, Ben," Julia said as she stopped at the bottom of the stairs with Cal. "I take it this is Anna?"

Ben nodded and introduced Anna to the two of them.

"Nice to meet you," Cal said. "Well, I'm heading back to Cody." He got into his truck, then pulled away.

"Is the big man awake?" Ben asked.

"Yes, very awake. He really is missing Seth and Quinn, but I think he understands how important the appointments in Casper are with the attorney working on Tripp's adoption." She sighed. "Honestly, I think he misses Tripp the most. No games of Go Fish or Old Maid to distract him."

Ben knew what to do. "I'll go in and make sure he's entertained."

"Great. Do that while I heat up the dinner Libby left for him. She and Jake left for his job meeting."

"Sounds like a plan," Ben said and looked at Anna. "The cookies?"

"Sure." She opened her car door, reached inside and came out with the pink box, which she held out to Ben. "Here you go. A present from Elaine to Sarge."

Julia intercepted her handoff and opened the top. "Chocolate chip and oatmeal." She smiled at Ben. "I take back everything I said about you earlier, Ben." She closed the box and passed it to him. "You take it in and make him happy."

When Julia went back into the house, Ben turned to Anna. "I'm taking you up on your offer."

Anna tilted her head slightly to one side. "Excuse me?"

"You promised me you could be a distraction for Sarge. You heard Julia. He needs one right about now."

Her smile came quickly. "I'd love to."

Her immediate agreement to stay longer pleased him a lot more than it should have. He deflected the thought, replacing it with the idea that he was sure that Sarge would like Anna, especially if he knew she was Burr's friend. "Great."

He led the way up onto the porch and when they stepped into the entry, Anna slipped off her jacket. Ben took it and put it, along with his hat and jacket, on the cowhide bench by an archway leading into the great room beyond.

Anna was wearing pretty much what most of the women in town did, a shirt in pink flannel along with jeans and her new boots.

His deflection of his thoughts didn't last long when he watched her brush at a few strands of hair that had come free of her ponytail. She more than intrigued him. He could own up to that, but he also decided to take a step back just to catch his breath and stop the foolish thoughts that came just at the sight of her.

## CHAPTER SEVEN

ANNA LOOKED AROUND the entryway that was unapologetically Old West while she thought about Ben making her another offer she couldn't refuse. From the ride, to going with him to Twin Horns, his giving her Punch and now inviting her in to meet Sarge. One thing after another just kept falling into place. Not just her plans to help the ranch legally...more than that was happening. She knew it, especially when she saw Ben come into a room or caught him looking at her when she didn't expect it.

She felt confused, intent on focusing on why she'd come to the ranch the first time, but she found that hard to do when she looked up and he was smiling at her. She couldn't remember saying anything funny. Quickly, she glanced away and froze. There, on the log wall, across from a staircase to the second level, was the head of a long-dead animal with yellow glass eyes that seemed to bore into her. "Is this the mountain lion you were talking about?"

"Yes, that is the legendary predator." She turned away and back to Ben, who looked amused at her uneasiness. "Sarge had quite a time tracking him down, but he got him."

Anna didn't look back at the trophy. "That's why the beast still looks angry," she murmured.

That brought a chuckle. "I guess he has every right." He picked up the box of cookies and walked over to where she still stood by the door. "Before we go in, I should explain a few things. Sarge is moving into the middle stages of Alzheimer's. He's really pretty good most of the time, but he gets emotional, good and bad, confused sometimes, and a bit scared. If he's not doing well, we'll quietly leave. Okay?"

"Of course."

He handed her the cookie box then led the way into a wide hallway opposite the staircase. He stopped at the second of two doors on their right and pushed it back slowly. "Are you up for a visitor?" Ben asked.

A man's slightly raspy voice came from

inside. "For you, any time is the right time. Get in here, son."

Anna followed Ben into a large bedroom where an adjustable bed was set up against the log wall directly opposite the door. A table by a window to her left had what looked like an unfinished card game on its surface, and shelves held linen and supplies on the opposite wall. A partially open door to the right exposed a large bathroom.

She didn't know what she'd expected of her first impression of James "Sarge" Caine, but she was surprised to see a tall man in jeans and a white T-shirt, semi-reclining on top of the covers of the bed. He looked to be in his late seventies, with thinning gray hair combed straight back from a face that showed traces of more outdoor than indoor living. Faded blue eyes turned to Anna, and she could see some confusion in them when she stopped at the foot of the bed. Ben went to the right side to get closer to the man.

"Sarge, I have someone who wants to meet you. Her name is Anna Watters."

He was very still as he stared at her. "Anna?" he questioned, obviously trying to figure out if he knew her.

She eased his puzzlement as quickly as she could. "Yes, I'm Anna. I know a friend of yours, Burr Addison."

The minute she mentioned Burr's name, Sarge's expression cleared. "How do you know Burr?"

"I'm his new partner at his law firm in town."

He looked skeptical. "No. You're too young to be a lawyer and way too pretty."

She felt heat brush her cheeks. "Oh, I've heard that before about my age, and I've also heard that no real lady should be a lawyer."

Sarge smiled at her. "I'd have a pretty lawyer like you any day, if I ever needed one." He looked at Ben. "I got to say, your taste in girls has improved since you brought that one home before."

Ben seemed to know exactly who Sarge was talking about. "Addie Plum asked me to the Sadie Hawkins dance at high school, and I was sixteen and didn't know how to get out of it."

The old man chuckled roughly. "You were something, son, and way over your head with that one." Then he spoke to Anna again. "So, you're Ben's girlfriend."

"I just met him, but I hope we can be friends," she said.

"Don't you like him?" Sarge asked bluntly.

She knew Ben was watching her. "Yes, of course I do." She remembered she was holding the pastry box. "I heard a rumor that what you like are cookies."

"Does a dog like bones?" Sarge asked without missing a beat.

She moved closer to Ben's side and opened the box to let Sarge see what was inside. "Which would you like, chocolate chip or oatmeal?"

He grinned at her. "Good old chocolate chip." She took one out and handed it to him.

"Thank you, darlin'," he said then took a bite.

There were two wooden chairs by the bedside. Ben motioned Anna to sit while he took the one closest to Sarge. "So, how are they?"

Sarge took another bite, chewed and then popped the last of the cookie into his mouth. Finally, he said, "The best ever."

"Do you want some milk?" Ben asked.

"Yes, please," Sarge said without hesitation. "And another cookie."

Ben glanced at Anna. "You're the cookie

person, so I'll get his milk." He stood and headed for the door.

Sarge took the second cookie Anna offered him but didn't take a bite. His pale eyes held hers, a touch of intensity in them that hadn't been there moments before. "That boy's a good one. He's a keeper. He…he's good and…" His voice faltered as he seemed to be searching for words. Then he sighed and said, "He's really good with kids."

She thought she knew what he was trying to tell her. "Yes, Ben seems to love kids and works so hard for them, doesn't he?"

His smile held a touch of relief. "Yes, exactly. He got nothing but bad when he was little, just awful, but he's grown up good. Real kind. Maggie and me are real proud of that boy."

Anna barely kept from flinching when she remembered something Ben had said before about having the hope beaten out of him, or something like that. To live through that and find himself in this place, with this man, had to have been a real miracle for the boy. "I am, too," she admitted softly without thinking about what she'd said.

Sarge was ignoring the cookie in his hand

as his smile faded into a faint frown. "It's wrong, you know. The way some people treat their kids. Shameful. To see someone blessed with a child and not love it, then just toss it away. Broke Maggie's heart, it did. Some of those poor kids didn't know nothing but hurting." He exhaled heavily. "Some never get over it. They're always expecting the hurt to come. I don't understand. I'll never understand it. No way."

He might have been diminished by his health problems, but she caught a glimpse of the heart of the man he had been when he'd taken in boys who'd had no one. "I've heard that you helped so many boys whose parents weren't there for them. As far as I can tell, you're the one who taught Ben how to care for kids by the way you cared for him."

He looked right at her with that touch of intensity lingering in his eyes. "He's worth it, darlin', you know. Really worth it. Don't you let go of him, even if he tries to get you to leave him alone. Promise me you won't." Then, out of the blue, he changed subjects and smiled. "Did you know he's a real good dancer? Do you dance?"

"I love to dance," she said.

"My Maggie could dance, but I was awful. But she still danced with me."

She loved the almost wistful expression that accompanied his last words. "What's your favorite song to dance to?"

He frowned, and she thought she'd confused him by asking for something specific, then his expression turned quizzical. "You know the song, the one part says 'memories of us are forever.'" He sighed softly. "That one." He didn't seem bothered to not remember the name of the song. "'Memories of us are forever...'" he repeated to himself in a whisper.

When he closed his eyes, a smile lingered on his lips. Slowly, the uneaten cookie slipped out of his fingers and onto the blanket. He murmured, "I'm real glad you're here."

"I'm glad I'm here, too," she said and meant it.

When Ben came back into the room Anna was pretty sure Sarge was asleep. She held her forefinger to her lips. He nodded and came over to put the glass of milk on the side table by the cookie box, then sat in the chair beside hers. "He had to be tired to not take a bite out of the cookie," he said in a low voice.

She reached to pick up the cookie and put it back in the box. "I guess so."

Julia looked into the bedroom, then motioned the two of them to come out into the hallway. Ben stood and bent over Sarge. "Sleep well," he said softly before walking to the door. Anna was by him as he stepped out into the hall.

"Thank you both," Julia said in a low voice. "Food's ready whenever you are, Ben. I'll be out in a bit."

"Thanks," he said as Julia slipped into Sarge's room. Ben started for the entryway and Anna went with him. At the cowhide bench, he turned to face her. "Was he okay?"

"He was fine. Thank you for bringing me in to visit him. He's pretty special," she said. So was the older man's asking her to promise never to leave Ben, even if he asked her to. She hadn't made that promise, but a part her thought whoever fell in love with Ben Arias could never leave him. He might even change his mind about happily-ever-after when he found the right lady.

"He's one of a kind." Ben exhaled. "How about staying for leftover meatloaf? I guarantee it's delicious."

"I'm sure it is, but I ate too many cookies in the car on the way here. Not yours, some Burr gave me out of his box. I snack when I'm trying to figure things out, and cookies are my favorite. It doesn't help much, but at least it tastes good."

She thought that might make him smile, but he didn't. "What were you trying to figure out?"

Once again, it happened. Ben gave her an opening for something she'd never thought she'd be able to do. "I got to thinking about the town records that they're trying to get online. Bob at the Annex said that some have come up missing or haven't been put back in the cellar yet."

He frowned slightly. "I'm guessing that's not good?"

"Some files I'd like to look at haven't been put up yet." That was honestly making her nervous. Leo was still hunting but hadn't found anything. "I'm a bit compulsive when it comes to knowing everything I can about people who could be a problem, and it makes me uneasy to not be able to see all of the files on Norman Good." She was becoming impatient with no way to track any more files just yet.

Ben shrugged. "Sarge kept every piece of paper, from the first payment on the land to the last horse sold for this place. And Libby keeps complete records. They're all in a pair of filing cabinets in the old office. You're welcome to look through them, if you think it's worth your time to search for Norman Good's signature on anything."

"That might be an idea," she said, trying to appear a lot calmer than she felt at the moment. Whatever coincidences of fate were at work since they'd met had revved up into overdrive. "I could come by tomorrow to look, if that's okay?"

"Actually, when the wedding's over, you can come and look through the files."

She'd have to be patient. "I understand, no problem."

"Too bad you need to get back to town now. You could take a cursory look at them to see if they might be of any use to you."

A perfect offer, but she took her time, as if thinking about it. "You know, I could put off studying for a while longer, I guess, and take a look at the files."

"If you're sure, follow me," he said and headed back into the hallway to stop at the first door on the right. He opened it for Anna to step past him. The space was pretty much overtaken by a large drafting table and a heavy wooden desk. Bookshelves on the side wall to the left were filled to capacity, and a wide window set in the back wall exposed the night view to the north.

Ben pointed to two waist-high filing cabinets by a second door on the wall to her right. "That's where any ranch files should be." He pulled a swivel chair away from the desk and closer to the cabinets for her. "If you need anything, you just come and ask. I'll be in the great room next door, through here," he said as he opened the second door. She could see into the large space with its massive fireplace and oversize leather furniture. A raised kitchen past a long dining table was at the far end. "Coffee?" he asked.

"Oh, no thanks."

"Come and get me if you need me," he said then went out, closing the door behind him.

Anna sat on the padded chair and, for a long moment, just stared at the closed door. She had what she'd been after: access to private ranch files. This might be the final step to her finding anything questionable and let her keep her promise to Burr. Then she wouldn't need to be here, except to ride Punch. There wouldn't be any long talks with Ben, or walks between the house and the stables. No rides to the higher ground to appreciate the vastness of the ranchland.

She felt a sadness that didn't make sense. She'd never been distracted by a man before. Dates had been casual and were never more than two or three before they ceased to exist. Work and school had demanded her time, and she'd given it all she'd had. But now, Ben distracted her with just a smile, a slight tip of his hat, his laughter and his dark eyes as he watched her. She couldn't read the expressions there and wished she could.

*That boy's a good one*, Sarge had told her.

"A good one," she repeated softly and closed her eyes. Ben was starting to matter to her—and that was scary. She had to stop whatever she was starting to feel now while it wasn't anything totally definable to her. She'd take a step back, maybe several, and keep things on a friendly basis.

She exhaled, opened her eyes and reached

to open the top drawer of the closest cabinet labeled *Lists/Forms*. Both were things she understood completely, and she turned her back on her confusion to do what she was there for.

An hour later, Anna was leafing through a file on the desk when Ben startled her by speaking. "Does it look like it might be worth your time?"

She hadn't heard the door open, and she swiveled the chair to look over at Ben standing in the hall doorway. She wished he wasn't smiling. "They're interesting," she said as she closed the file and laid it on top of others on the desk.

"You seem so serious," he said as he crossed to her.

She picked up the files, scooted her chair back to the open cabinet drawer, and put them away. "Just my thinking face," she said then looked up at him. "I do have a question. I checked both cabinets to see what order things were in and realized that you're right. There're a lot of old files, some decades old. I'd like to go through the rest to see if there are any sign-offs from the county. Would that be okay?"

"Sure, go for it," he said without hesitating.

She stood and pushed the chair back in place. "I should be going, but do you think I could come and see Punch during the week? I'd go straight to the stables and stay out of everyone's way. Then next week I can take another look at the files in here."

"Of course. When you come in the gates, there's a bladed service road to the left. It goes down then swings up to the hay barn and past that to the stables. You'll miss all the wedding service traffic."

"Thanks. I'll go that way."

Anna retrieved her jacket and put it on, then Ben walked her out to her car without bothering with his own coat. As they stopped by the small white rental, he said, "Try to check out something with four-wheel drive when you look for another ride."

"Thanks for the advice, even if it comes from a man who drives a truck that I'm certain doesn't have four-wheel drive."

"You got me," he said with a dry smile.

She slipped in behind the wheel and, before shutting the door, looked up at him. "Oh, just an FYI. Norman B. Good is also known as Norman Barry Good."

A boyish grin appeared on Ben's face. "Seriously?"

"Pretty funny, huh? Although, I doubt he's ever realized how funny it is." She didn't miss the way Ben crossed his arms at his chest. Without a coat, he had to be freezing, and she needed to let him go, no matter how much she'd love to just talk to him. "You get in where it's warm, but thanks again for Punch. He'll always have a home with me and be safe."

Ben nodded. "You're welcome. Drive carefully."

She started the car and Ben moved back to give her room to pull out. With a wave, she drove away. A glimpse in the rearview mirror showed Ben still standing there watching her leave.

As if he knew she'd seen him, he waved and then hurried into the house.

WHEN ANNA TOLD Burr the next day about the files, Punch, and Ben suggesting she buy a car that fit in the area, the purchase of a vehicle became his main interest. He told her he'd drive her up to Cody the next day to look around for a good used truck for her. He knew someone who knew someone whose brother knew a restaurant owner whose accountant worked for a dealer in Cody who gave great discounts on used trucks.

She'd thought she'd drive up there with Burr, look around and leave, but she'd ended up driving back alone the following afternoon in a three-year-old silver pickup that had four-wheel drive.

As she headed south, she had the satellite radio station blaring country music. If she could have driven and danced, she probably would have. She was in a very good mood. When she looked around and realized she was approaching the turnoff from the highway for the Eclipse Ridge Ranch, she made a snap decision. She was going to indulge herself with a ride on Punch before heading back to the office in her new truck.

When she drove between the boulders and through the open gates, she cut off onto the angled service road and took the soft curve to the north.

She saw the hay barn with a delivery truck out in front of it, then drove past to park by the stables. She got out and headed inside. Dwight was nowhere to be seen, so she walked down the middle of the wide central aisle and found Punch in a different stall near the closed back doors.

"Punch!" As soon as she said his name, the horse stuck his head over the open top of his stall gate. She wanted to think he remembered her, but it was more likely he was looking for someone to feed him.

"Hi, there, boy," she crooned to him as she stroked his muzzle. "It's just you and me today. Good news, I bought a fabulous truck, and I'm going to get a trailer hitch put on it so I can take you to live with me as soon as I find a place. Just know this, you are never going to auction, any auction, not ever."

"Hey, there!" someone called out sharply from the front doors. "What are you doing in here?"

"Dwight, it's me, Anna. I came to see Punch," she said quickly.

"Oh, sorry, Miss Watters," he said as he sauntered down the aisle toward her. "Didn't recognize the truck."

"I just bought it in Cody. I was on my way back to town and decided to come by for a short ride."

"It's good you're here, because there is a problem."

Her heart lurched as strange scenarios of Punch going crazy flashed through her mind. "What did he do?"

"It's what he's not doing. He isn't getting much exercise. I'm too busy with all this wedding stuff. And the new ranch hands I've been hiring to work with the horses and get ready for the cattle when they're shipped are being pulled into the wedding setup at the house, too. Afraid the horses are going to get a short shrift until after this weekend."

She was totally relieved. "Oh, I'll be sure to get him out as often as I can."

"Good. I'll show you how he likes to get ready."

Two hours later, Anna was riding back in from the north and heading toward the stables. She'd stayed on open land, a bit worried about running into some animals if she went up into the foothills, and she'd gone past what she'd been told were the old bunkhouse and the mess hall on her ride. Both were being transformed into sleeping quarters for the camp, to get the boys oriented on their first night and have a full breakfast the following day before heading up to the campsites.

As she approached the back of the stables, the doors were still firmly shut, so she rode around the south side to gain entry. As she passed her truck and circled the corner, she saw someone standing in the open doors. She smiled right away. Ben was there, his arms crossed over his denim jacket, his eyes shadowed by the brim of his Stetson.

When she dismounted, she dropped Punch's reins to the ground. "Hi, there."

Looking serious, he took a couple of steps toward her. "So, I was weaving lavender flowers into a lattice arch for the bride and groom to stand under when I got a call that a strange truck was parked by the stables."

"Sorry. It's mine. I bought it today," she said.

"You didn't do that because of what I said, did you?"

She had to think, then realized what he was asking. "Oh gosh, no. I needed it, and I felt safe transportation was a good investment. It's big, but it drives really well, and it's already set up for a heavy-duty trailer hitch."

"I'm impressed," he murmured. "And

thank you for getting me out of flower weaving. That was torture."

She laughed at that before she could stop herself. "You're welcome."

He motioned to where she'd parked. "It's a nice truck."

"I kept your recommendations in mind when I was looking." She liked that she could actually make out a touch of humor in his dark eyes.

"I think you did well," he said.

"Burr drove me up to Cody this morning to just look around, because he knows a guy."

"Of course he does," he said with another smile. "He knows everyone."

"I noticed," Anna said as she silently admitted to herself that she really liked talking with Ben and hadn't had to wait until after the wedding to see him again. "How's Sarge doing?" she asked.

"Pretty good. He had a couple of old friends drop by, and that was a success. I couldn't believe how engaged he was. He's just in a better mood most of the time recently. He loves Seth's fiancée and their little boy, and he's smiling more, you know. Everyone is smiling more lately."

She felt she was, too. "That's good, very good."

"Everything okay out here?" Dwight asked as he neared them.

"Oh yes, very good," Ben said without looking away from Anna.

"You want I should take care of Punch, Miss Watters?"

Ben still didn't look away, and Anna didn't understand what was happening right then. She had to force herself to turn to Dwight. "Call me Anna, and yes, I'd appreciate it if you took care of him. I'll do it next time, I promise."

Dwight moved to pick up the horse's reins, "Any surprises?"

She watched Dwight as he passed her to lead Punch into the stables. "None," she said.

"Good to hear," he said over his shoulder before he disappeared inside.

"Want to give me a ride up to the house in your brand-new truck?" Ben asked, drawing her attention back to him.

For her being reasonably good at reading people, she couldn't figure out Ben at all at the moment. The look in his eyes made her uneasy in some way, yet she could feel a slight heat creeping into her face. She was flustered and said the first thing that came to her as she ducked her head and went over to her truck. "It's used, but sure, get in."

She could sense him behind her, but never looked back as she settled into the driver's seat. He went around to the passenger's side and got in. Without thinking, she turned the truck on. Music blared out of the six speakers and she jumped, fumbling to find the radio. Before she could shut it off, Ben reached past her and pushed a button. The music was gone, but Ben's laughter didn't die.

She looked at him, knowing her face had to be bright red. "Wow, I'm sorry. I forgot about that."

Ben's laughter mellowed to a rough chuckle. "I never would have guessed that you liked Western music played that loudly."

She shrugged, his smile making it more fun to explain. "I'm eclectic in tastes," she said. "And the satellite radio was on that station when I turned it on."

"Oh, so that was accidental listening?"

"Sure, I guess so. I was feeling good coming back with the truck, and the music was sort of echoing that. And yes, before you ask, I was wishing I could dance to it."

"Could you?"

"Me? Dance to fast Western music? Of course. I got an A-plus in my college class, The Language of Dance, one semester."

He was still grinning at her. "You speak dance?"

She laughed this time. "Yes, I do and rather well," she said, then put the truck in gear and turned to head back up to the house.

As she drove, Anna felt tongue-tied suddenly and didn't know what to say. Ben didn't speak, either, but she felt his eyes on her. She finally spoke just to say something. Anything. "This dash has more dials and flashing lights than there are in a plane's cockpit." She took a breath. "It already has the mounting for a heavy-duty trailer hitch. Did I mention that?"

As she slowed to park in front of the house, he said, "I believe you did, right around the time you mentioned four-wheel drive."

Ben was making one of those teasing jokes that she liked, which he slipped in every so often. "So, how's it going with the wedding?" she asked, trying to sound a whole lot more casual than she felt.

"To me, it's total confusion, but everyone else seems to think that it's right on schedule. What do I know? All I've had to do whenever I went to a wedding was to show up with a gift."

She heard herself asking him something she'd wondered for a while. "Did you really mean it when you said you'd never marry?" When she thought of caring for someone else—someday—it meant forever. Not just for the moment. Yet he seemed to have made that a rule for his life.

"I won't," he said. "I don't need to ask you. Burr told me you've been so focused on your work, that you don't seem to have time for anything outside the office. In fact, he seems to be worried about your lack of dating or simply having fun."

She felt embarrassed that Burr had told Ben that. "I do what I have to do to get myself where I'm going in life, where I want to be." She didn't add that the last thing she wanted to do right then was to lose focus on her goals, on who she wanted to be for her father's memory, by getting tangled up in a relationship. "Burr is entitled to his opinion, but I know what I need. Actually, he's getting more than a bit like my dad. I've explained to him that I'm fine, that I need to be centered on my work." She stopped there, thinking she might be protesting too much.

"At least you penciled in time to ride."

"That's different. It's just a few hours when I can work it in, and it's worth it. I love it."

He frowned slightly. "Then you don't think you'd like a relationship?"

She hesitated for a moment before admitting an awkward fact.

"Truthfully, I don't really know. I haven't had time to ever be in a real relationship. I never wanted to, and I expect that won't change for the foreseeable future." Actually, that had been her life pattern for so long, she wasn't sure she could break it, even if she might want to. Right then, she wanted to change the focus from her lack of a romantic life to his romantic life. "You seem pretty work-centered—I mean, to be so adamant about never marrying. So, you don't have any relationships or don't you even date?"

He studied her for a moment then said, "Yes, I date. Yes, I've had relationships, but none of that equals any path to marriage."

"You sound as if you have it all worked out.

I don't have a clue where I'll end up. Maybe single—and that's okay. Maybe married—but far off in the future. For now, my life is what I want it to be."

She saw a smile coming from him right before he mimicked what she'd asked him. "So, you don't have any relationships or don't you even date?"

"No, and not right now. In the past, yes. And as I said before, I haven't been in anything you'd call a relationship."

"Hmm," he said.

"What does that mean?"

"I don't know." He reached for the door latch. "We can figure that out later. Right now, I'm sure they're ripping the house apart to try to find the missing flower weaver."

She was relieved to stop the conversation in its track. "Well, good luck with your weaving."

His dark eyes held hers, and she couldn't look away from him. Then he finally said, "On that note, I need to go into a house saturated with all things wedding."

"I wish you even more luck," she said.

He smiled ruefully at her. "I'll need it."

Then he got out and slowly jogged to the

steps and up to the entry. She almost drove away but hesitated as he turned to look over at her. He did that slight nod as he touched the brim of his hat with his forefinger, then went inside and closed the door.

As she drove out onto the county road, she had barely gone a half mile before a huge black truck came from the other direction. She hugged to the right as far as she could to let the behemoth pass her. Sun struck the windshield, and she couldn't make out the driver, but the window for the back seat of the king cab was down. A large black dog, with one ear up, one ear down and its tongue lolling, looked happy to be riding in that truck.

The dog looked as if he had no problems at all, no doubts, no confusion. "Lucky dog," she murmured as she tried to figure out what had happened with Ben and her back there. He was dead set on being alone with his work. She was starting to see that, as much as she loved what she was doing, she hadn't looked past her own work to a private life. She had people she cared about; but going beyond friends, all she could see was emptiness. Her dad had had her mother, and Sarge had

had Maggie. Their love still went on, even with one gone. That was what she wanted someday down the road, her own happily-ever-after.

By the time Anna was approaching the town limits, she realized she was becoming closer to accepting the fact that she might do very well in Eclipse, especially with Burr to work with and Punch on a ranch she owned. That appealed to her a lot, so much more than renting a boarding spot for Punch at a stable. She didn't want that, and the idea of her own place here—something she'd thrown out to Ben when she'd impulsively offered to buy the horse—had what she'd really wanted for both her and Punch. A home where they both belonged.

When she arrived at the office, she was surprised that Burr was still there, and it was almost five o'clock. He wasn't one to stick around later than he absolutely had to, but his door was shut, so he had to be in a late meeting with a client.

Anna veered off toward her office and went inside, closed the door, and sent Burr a text that she was there if he needed her. Fifteen minutes later, there was a knock on her door before Burr opened it. "Am I disturbing you?"

"Yes, and thank you," she said on a sigh as she sat back from her computer. The screen was filled with all she ever needed to know about the laws regarding vandalism in Wyoming.

"Mary Mable came in late and wanted to change one of her charities in her will."

Mary Mable Blaire, a slim lady with a brilliant smile, around sixty or so, was a ball of energy. She'd buried three husbands and, according to her, Larry was the best and the last. "She loves doing that, doesn't she?"

"Yes. It's kind of her hobby right now. She heard about a rescue center for wounded birds over near Sheridan and she might want to help fund it. Now, what took you so long to get back here from Cody?"

"I stopped to go for a ride at the ranch. There's a lot of action going on with the wedding getting close."

Burr finally stepped into the office but didn't sit. "Speaking of the wedding…" he said as he got closer.

"What about it?"

"I have a problem and I need your help on it."

## CHAPTER EIGHT

*OH, SHOOT.* Anna fought the urge to tell Burr she had forgotten an important appointment so she could get out of there before he wanted to talk about his love life. But she stayed put. "What problem?"

"It's a plus-one invitation, but my guest can't go."

He didn't look crushed, or depressed, but she still said, "I'm sorry."

"No, it's okay. I wanted to ask you if you'd come as my plus-one?"

She knew he had to see her surprise at his question. "Burr, I don't belong at a wedding for family and close friends."

"Why not. You're friends with Ben, and you'll be with me, an old friend of the family."

"I don't know."

"Okay, what's your excuse for not wanting to go to a wedding for two terrific people—actually, three if we include their boy, Tripp?

There'll be great barbecue, dancing and enough happiness to go around."

She was getting a bit too attached to Ben, and going to a private family wedding just seemed to be the wrong move for her. "Nothing, but I think it's kind of pushy."

"You think I'm pushy?" he asked with mock shock.

"Of course not. Insistent, but not pushy. Why don't you ask Mrs. Blaire to go with you? I bet she knows Sarge and the family."

"She does, but I won't ask her because I don't want to have to compete with Mary Mable's sainted husband, Larry."

"You must have someone else you'd like to take with you."

"I'd like you to be there with me."

He wasn't going to tell her about any broken relationship, and she was relieved, but she still didn't think it was a good idea to go. "How about Elaine?"

He colored slightly at her suggestion, and she wondered if she'd read Elaine right—that she was kind of sweet on Burr—and maybe vice versa? "Oh no, she's already going with someone. I really would like you to come with me. I hate going places like that alone."

She could see how much he wanted her there with him, and she decided it couldn't really hurt anything. The family would be completely taken up with the wedding, and she'd be on the sidelines. She could do this for Burr. "Okay. I'll be your plus-one as long as you don't ditch me as soon as we get there."

"Deal," he said with a smile. "It's on Saturday, and I'll meet you here at twelve thirty. I'll drive." With that said, he headed back to his office.

Anna returned to the computer and only looked up again when the clock read six and Burr was back in the doorway. "Just wanted to tell you that the invitation says 'casual dress' and in lieu of gifts they would appreciate donations being made to Sarge's Hope Foundation. They finally decided on a permanent name for it and for the camp. I think it was Ben's suggestion that won. Is it okay if I give money in both our names?"

"Sure, just let me know how much."

"It can be the bonus I was going to give you for not running back to Chicago before now." He didn't give her time to argue. "I'm taking off to meet Leo."

"Is it about the ranch?" she asked quickly.

"Partly to see if he's come across anything, but mostly it's about designer beers at One Pool Q, and about me beating Leo in a seniors' tournament. Why don't you leave, too? It's getting pretty late."

"I will. I need to figure out what qualifies as casual dress for a wedding in these parts."

"Jeans and fancy boots so you can dance," he said with a grin before he left.

WHEN BURR AND ANNA drove onto the ranch on the day of the wedding, cars and trucks crowded the cement parking area in front of the sprawling log house. Burr drove his huge dual-wheel pickup over to the edge of the space and stopped on the dirt. Dwight, in a pressed white shirt, leather vest and jeans, jogged over to them as Burr opened the driver's door.

"Hey, Burr," he said and then saw Anna. "Welcome, Anna."

"How's Punch doing?" she asked.

"He knew you weren't there yesterday, but I tried to explain to him that you'd be back. So, you two go on up and around to the back deck. It's warm there. Those heaters are amazing. I hear the food is going to be killer, too."

While Dwight hurried off as another truck approached, Burr turned to Anna. "Why not leave our jackets here so we don't have to carry them around or throw them in a pile on a bed somewhere?" He smiled encouragingly at her. "We'll survive if we keep moving until we get to the heat."

"Okay, let's get moving," Anna said as she slipped off her jacket, tossed it on the seat and got out into the cold.

Anna had found an outfit that she loved, a simple, midthigh, lightweight suede dress in a soft green with a scooped neckline and three-quarter-length sleeves. Her calf-high Western boots were a deep brown leather with two-inch heels and a simple flower design around the top. After settling on leaving her hair down in loose ringlets, she'd braided two side pieces and caught them together at the nape of her neck with a gold clip.

She met Burr at the front of the truck then headed quickly to the porch and up the stairs. She thought Burr was looking sharp in a light blue shirt, bolo tie, jeans and polished boots. As the inviting scent of barbecue and woodsmoke hung in the cold air, both hurried around the side of the house to get to the deck and the promised heat.

The mixture of music, laughter and voices got louder as they rounded the corner of the house. There were people milling around everywhere. A plethora of lavender flowers adorned the deck, and waves of blessedly warm air flowed through the space. Rows of white chairs faced a latticed arch, which she guessed was holding some of the purple flowers that Ben had helped weave through it. It sat on a large platform jutting out on the north side of the deck. With the backdrop of the land, the mountains and the big sky, the setting was stunning. Music seemed to come from all directions, the way the warmth did.

People approached Anna and Burr, some she knew, some she didn't, but everyone greeted her as if she truly belonged there. She spotted Sarge, who was all but surrounded by a group of people near the fireplace chimney on the back wall of the house. Some were crouched by his chair to get to eye level as they spoke, and some were standing. All were smiling. He was smiling right back, looking nice in a light purple Western shirt and dark jeans. The outfit was mirrored on a small boy with red hair, who stood right beside Sarge, leaning into his shoulder.

Burr touched her arm. "Do you want to come and see Sarge?"

"You go. I'll find us some seats when I figure out what side of the aisle friends of the groom are supposed to sit on."

Burr turned to a man by them, and Anna recognized Farley Garrett from the general store. He was in a surprisingly simple gray shirt and jeans, but he was wearing purple boots. "Farley, where do friends of the groom sit?" Burr asked him.

"They said you can sit anywhere, since we're all friends of both the groom and the bride."

While Burr went to see Sarge, Anna found seats in the last row of the section to the right of the aisle. As she settled, she was thankful that the heaters fighting the chill of the day were winning so far.

When Burr came back and slipped in beside Anna, she glanced past him. Of course, she knew Ben would be there, but at that moment, she was surprised to see him standing at the top of the center aisle. He was on one side of Sarge, their arms linked, and a tall, lanky man with ash-blond hair was on Sarge's other side. Someone called out to him, "Hey, Jake, good to see ya," and she knew who he was. Both Jake and Ben were wearing the apparent wedding outfit for the men in the bridal party: light purple shirts and dark jeans with boots.

As they moved slowly by toward the lattice, Burr murmured in a low voice, "Sarge is doing really well. Happiness is a remarkable medicine. He's crazy about his new grandson, and his boys are here. He's just thrilled."

She nodded as she watched the men make their way to the front row where Julia and the physical therapist, Cal, were saving an aisle seat for Sarge at the front. Another man, maybe forty, in jeans and a leather jacket, followed them, pausing by Sarge to say something. Then he went to be with Ben and Jake under the arch, standing to face the seated guests.

Burr leaned closer to her. "That's Zach Mc-Cloud, pastor at the church."

"Oh," she said, but her attention was on Ben. The pale lavender shirt set off his tanned skin, and the smile on his face never faded.

A moment later, the groom came in from

the left side in a black vest over a lavender shirt, black jeans and wearing fancy boots that really stood out. Seth crossed directly to Sarge, spoke to him, then kissed the man on his forehead before he went to stand beside the pastor with Jake and Ben.

As the music changed to a soft instrumental of strings and piano, two young women started down the white carpet, holding bouquets that matched their tea-length dresses in the color of the day, lavender. Then a petite woman with rich, coppery hair, came behind in an identical dress. She had to be Libby, Jake's wife, from what Ben had told her.

The little boy was next, seriously concentrating on carrying a satin pillow with two rings on it. Then the bride appeared on the arm of a tall, silver-haired man.

Quinn was beautiful in a simple ivory sheath, with lace sleeves and a slender knee-length skirt. Her blond hair was loose and framed her face, which glowed with happiness. She stopped by Sarge, whispered something and kissed his cheek. Then she turned to go to Seth, who held out his hand to receive her.

Anna was surprised at how touched she

was with the simple wedding ceremony. By the time the pastor announced, "Ladies and gentlemen, it is my distinct pleasure to present Mr. and Mrs. Seth Reagan," she was fighting back tears. A touch on her knee drew her attention, and Burr was offering her tissues.

"I came prepared," he whispered.

She took them gratefully. "Thank you."

Then everyone stood as Seth and Quinn walked back up the aisle with the little boy between them holding their hands. Jake and Libby followed, then Ben was there with the two bridesmaids, one on each arm. People were cheering and clapping.

When Ben glanced in Anna's direction, he almost did a double-take as their eyes met. She felt her heart catch when he smiled at her just before moving out of her sight. She'd been right to think she shouldn't have come, not when just seeing Ben left her feeling slightly unsteady.

Burr turned to Anna. "Glad you came as my plus-one?"

She took more tissues from him and nodded. "I'm glad you brought these. I did not expect to cry."

His mustache twitched. "I would have

cried, if I ever did cry, which I don't do, ever. Do you want to come with me and mingle?"

"No, you go and see your friends. I'm fine." She'd decided to stay on the sidelines until Burr was ready to leave.

He headed off while Anna followed the other guests who were slowly entering the house through two sets of sliding doors on either side of the fireplace chimney. Elaine came up beside her and took her arm as if they were old friends. "That was wonderful, wasn't it?"

"Yes, it sure was. That little boy was so serious with the rings."

"Yeah, Tripp is quite a kid," Elaine said. "Now, I can't wait to do some dancing."

When they stepped inside, the great room had changed from the brief glance she'd had a few days ago. The massive leather couch was still where it had been, but everything else in the middle of the room had been pushed to the sides and the braided rugs rolled up. A pool table was set up behind a row of leather pub chairs that faced the dance floor. Draped in lavender linen, the huge dining table near the kitchen held a three-tier wedding cake topped by what looked like, of all things, a small silver VW Beetle with bride and groom figures beside it. It made her smile.

Quinn and Seth took center stage for their first dance together. That was when Anna noticed a photographer taking pictures. An older song that Anna recognized as "Your Love Amazes Me" was playing, and the couple was lost in it. Guests took to the dance floor when the song changed, and the newlyweds went over to Sarge, who had settled on the sofa with Tripp attached to his side.

"Oh, there's Burr," Elaine announced and hurried off toward a group of men by the pub chairs.

Anna moved to her left, away from the doors, and glanced at the couch, which had been taken over for a photo shoot of Sarge with his boys. They were all smiling, and the obvious bond between the four of them was priceless. The little boy, still sitting by Sarge, looked overwhelmed with everything. They might not all be related biologically, but they were all, truly, Sarge's family.

She glanced away and saw Elaine dancing with Burr, who seemed to be enjoying every minute of it. Maybe he was forgetting about a woman named Pearl. As others joined them, Anna decided to find a chair and people-watch for a while. She stopped mid-step when she heard someone say her name, and looked to her right.

A man was smiling at her. She knew she'd never met him before, because she would have remembered him. He was a few inches over six feet, with dark hair, deep blue eyes and, despite wearing jeans and a black V-necked sweater along with Western boots, he looked better dressed than "casual."

"I'm sorry, were you speaking to me?"

He came closer. "Yes. Can I talk you into a dance?"

Anna hesitated then decided that dancing was way better than being alone watching the guests. "I guess so," she said, and he came closer, his hand held out to her as she studied him.

"No, you've never met me before," he said as he led her onto the dance floor.

When he turned to face her, she asked, "Then how did you know my name?"

"Burr talks about you a lot, and I saw you come in with him." He touched her waist, and she rested her hand on his shoulder as he took her other hand in his.

"I'm Dr. Williams, but I go by Boone," he said before she could ask.

As the music stopped and a faster country song started, he asked Anna, "Can you handle this music?"

"Sure. You lead and I'll follow."

The next thing she knew, they were in step perfectly. Enjoying the music, she never missed a move, despite constantly looking over at the couch to see what was going on. When the song ended, Boone asked, "Another dance?"

She would have agreed, except Ben stepped in. He'd been by the couch moments ago, but right then he was tapping Boone on the shoulder. "My turn," he said.

Boone nodded and smiled at Anna. "Thanks for the dance."

"My pleasure," she said. Then she was facing Ben, his hand taking hers in his, his other hand going around to rest at the small of her back. When slow music came over the speakers, Ben drew her close to him. She was quite certain he could feel her heart pounding in her chest.

"I didn't know you were coming," he said as they started to move together.

"I'm Burr's plus-one," she said, resting her left hand on his shoulder.

"You're what?"

"You know, on the invitation they always invite you to bring a 'plus-one.' Burr was going to come with a friend of his, and she couldn't make it, so he asked me. I hope that's okay?"

His hand moved higher on her back and slipped under her loose hair. "It's perfect," he murmured and then unexpectedly added, "I should have asked you myself."

"Oh no, I'm basically a stranger. Burr just didn't want to come alone."

"I thought he'd bring Pearl."

"You know her?" she asked, starting to feel a bit stupid that she hadn't even guessed Burr was seeing someone. Then again, she'd never guessed he'd be dancing a slow dance and beaming down at Elaine right then, either.

Ben chuckled. "I've never met Pearl, just heard about her." He twirled her out, then back against him, so close that she could feel each breath he took. When he spoke, his voice became a soft vibration between them. "He's got good taste."

"Burr only asked me because—"

"He didn't want to come alone," he finished for her then shook his head slightly. "Didn't you look in the mirror before you came?"

"What?"

His dark eyes held hers for a long moment before he said, "Because Burr brought the prettiest woman around."

She felt a flush of heat in her face and closed her eyes as she leaned in to touch her forehead to her hand where it rested on Ben's shoulder.

Anna felt his exhale and his hand move up on her back to lightly tangle his fingers in her loose hair. "You know, I've wondered what your hair would look like down," he whispered in her right ear.

She stumbled for a moment then steadied herself. She could barely catch her breath. Easing back, she looked up at Ben, and the tenderness in his dark eyes was more than she could deal with. "I...I need a cold drink," she managed to stammer.

Unfortunately, that only caused Ben to look at her as if he knew how confused she was right then. "Okay," he murmured and stopped dancing. She moved away from him, breaking their contact. But that didn't last long before Ben said, "Come on," and reached for her hand the way he had when they'd been hiking.

He led her through the dancers and over to the cake table. There was a silver punch bowl there, ringed with glasses of champagne. Crystal containers of candy sat nearby. Next to the table was a huge silver water tub holding bottled drinks pressed into shaved ice. "How about champagne?" he asked Anna.

She seldom drank, and now was definitely not the time. She slipped her hand out of his and moved closer to the silver tub. Before she could get a bottled water, the music stopped and someone announced, "Time to cut the cake."

She turned as Quinn and Seth came around to stand behind the table by the cake while the photographer snapped away. Their little boy was there with them, his eyes huge as he looked up at the fancy confection.

Sarge was making his way through the guests to the front of the table with help from Cal and Julia. Then Jake was there, taking Julia's place by the man, and Ben said, "I'll be right back," and crossed to replace Cal by Sarge.

People were passing out champagne flutes to the guests, and Anna found herself holding one. Then Sarge, Ben and Jake had theirs. Sarge held his glass up and a hush fell on the crowd.

"To Seth and Quinn," he said in a surprisingly strong voice. "What you two have found together is a priceless treasure to hold on to forever." His hand holding the flute was slightly unsteady. "To a wonderful future," he said as his voice broke. The guests lifted their glasses, too.

Seth and Quinn drank a sip then put down their flutes. Seth picked Tripp up and held him on one arm while he slipped his other around Quinn. "Today is the first day of the rest of our lives together," Seth began, and the guests grew silent. "We're proud and happy to announce that Tripp is part of our family and our new life. Yesterday it became official. Tripp is legally our son forever."

The guests clapped and raised their glasses again. Sarge stood very still and then a smile touched his face that didn't need translating. Tripp was hugging Seth's neck, and Quinn was brushing at tears. Finally, the three of them shared a slice of cake, then walked with

Sarge back to the couch amid more clapping and well wishes.

Anna wished Burr was close enough to give her more tissues as she sniffed softly. Then Ben was by her. "It couldn't be more perfect timing for the three of them."

Burr had mentioned about Seth and Quinn fostering Tripp and hoping to adopt him. "They look so happy," she murmured.

Ben glanced over at the couch where the photographer was taking shots of Sarge and Tripp together. Then he turned to Anna and smiled as he nodded at the untouched champagne she was still holding. "You wanted a drink, so don't waste it."

She looked away from his smile, her confusion about what was happening with him coming back full force. Then she glanced at her drink before she put it down on the table. "I'm fine."

Ben studied her for a long moment and smiled a knowing smile. "You are very interesting, Anna."

"Interesting?"

"I can't read people like you can, but I think I just read something about you."

"Really." She looked away at the room full

of people having a terrific time then turned back to Ben. "It's a wonderful wedding," she said as she smiled at him, not about to ask what he thought he'd read in her.

Ben blinked. "That's it? You don't want to know what I think I've figured out about you?"

"I don't think I do. Not right now," she said.

He came closer, his dark eyes holding hers. Then he took her hand. "Dance with me again?" he asked in a low voice.

Anna had always thought that the idea of someone making your heart skip a beat with a look or a smile was a silly romantic notion. But now she knew it was a fact. Maybe it was the whole wedding thing, or maybe it was Ben. Whatever it was, she let Ben lead her back to the dance floor. He drew her into his arms while the music flowed around them and everything else seemed to fade into the background.

She rested her head on his shoulder, her arms around his neck, and she closed her eyes to take the edge off an unsteadiness she felt being so close to him. They danced, although she couldn't remember thinking about the steps or the rhythm of the music. All she was conscious of was Ben, his hands at the small of her back, and the beat of his heart against hers.

"So, you seriously took a dancing class in college?" he asked.

The song they were dancing to was a slow ballad about new love, more jazzy blues than country. She eased back, slipping her hands to his shoulders to look up at him. "Yes, I did," she murmured. "I had to take two extra credits one semester and the only one that worked with my schedule was The Language of Dance. That involved actually dancing to participate in whatever emotion the particular dances fed into. Like country music—it's all about storytelling and concentrates on either rejoicing or being sad."

"Interesting." He studied her face, his gaze lingering on her lips for a second before he asked, "So, what does this dance say?"

She felt more heat in her face and looked down to somewhere near Ben's chin. "I'm not sure. I haven't heard it before, but it's slow and easy, not sad, more introspective."

She tried to breathe evenly but found that was impossible when she could almost hear her professor saying, *One of the main reasons for humans to dance together boils down to simple excuses for physical contact. I've used it a few times.* The professor had laughed at his own joke.

The music shifted and the new piece was upbeat and definitely for celebration. Ben stopped, and as Anna looked up at him, he took her by the hand and led her off the dance floor. When they were by the back doors, he turned, inches from her. His smile was slow and, yes, she had to admit to herself, probably added more color to her cheeks. "So, are you enjoying yourself?" he asked.

That brought a soft, slightly nervous laugh from her. "I think I am."

# CHAPTER NINE

ANNA REALLY WAS a beautiful woman, and an unexpected presence at the wedding. "When you figure it out, let me know."

Ben wasn't sure about the last time he'd been with a woman who actually blushed, and he was pretty certain Anna had no idea how appealing that was to him. "You'll be the first to know," she said.

Unexpectedly, Burr came up to them and nodded to Ben, but spoke to Anna. "Winslow Hart, from the old Echo Creek Ranch, is on his way to the office to meet with me."

"Did you tell him you're at a wedding and it's Saturday?" Anna asked.

Ben couldn't tell if Anna was relieved or annoyed that Burr had broken into their conversation.

"He thinks it's an emergency," Burr said. "I couldn't talk him down. So, I have to get back."

"Okay," she said. "Let's go."

"Oh no, you don't have to leave. I'll pick you up when you're done. Just give me a call."

Ben didn't hesitate to offer an alternative. "I'll drive Anna back when she's ready to leave. You don't have to make the double trip."

"Thanks, Ben," Burr said. "Now, where are Seth and Quinn? I want to say goodbye to them and Tripp."

Ben looked around. He'd lost track of them when he'd been dancing with Anna, but he spotted the trio near the entry. "Over there," he said.

As Burr headed in that direction, Ben turned to Anna. "I need to talk to Seth and Quinn, too. Do you want to come with me?"

"Oh, I don't want to intrude on family, but I'd love to meet them and their son."

"Good." He led the way over to the couch and all of the family that Ben had. Sarge and Maggie had given him his life when he thought he'd lost it forever. They'd handed him hope and he'd finally lost his attitude and been smart enough to take what they'd offered him. Sarge was his father. Some punk in prison meant nothing to him, neither did the mother who'd walked away and disappeared.

Thinking about his biological parents brought a need in him for Anna to meet his forever family, the people he loved and respected.

As they approached, Sarge looked up from the couch and said, "Anna, it's you, right?"

Ben was shocked he could pick her out and remember her name.

Anna smiled at Sarge, a sweet expression. "Yes, and I'm so happy to be here," she said, crouching to come to eye level with Tripp, who was retreating shyly against Sarge's side. "You must be Tripp. I've heard so much about you from your uncle Ben."

The boy looked up at Sarge then back at her. "I'm Tripp Allan Reagan now. That's my new name. Do you like it?"

"I sure do. It's a great name."

That made the boy smile. "Thank you, ma'am."

"Call me Anna, please."

"Anna," Tripp said with a glance at Seth and Quinn. "Them are my mom and dad."

Ben watched Anna turn toward the couple.

"Oh, it's so great to finally meet you and to be here when you start your new life."

Quinn looked ready to cry, and Seth held her against him. "Thank you. Ben's told us about you, and I'm so glad you got to come." Quinn smiled at her. "Don't leave without tasting the wedding cake. It's pretty special."

"I'll try not to miss it," she said, and Ben was entranced by how easily she fit in.

Jake was there, leaning toward Anna. "So, I finally meet the famous Anna who most likely saved our skin down the road."

Libby reached to touch her arm. "We all owe you a great deal of thanks."

Ben could tell the praise was embarrassing Anna, and he was glad when Tripp scooted on the couch to get closer to his new mother, Quinn. The little boy piped up. "My mom and my dad—" he proceeded to push himself between them "—they like you, Anna. I heard them talking about stuff and they said you were really, really smart. You're a good person, they said, too."

Quinn looked down at her son. "Little pitchers have big ears."

"No, I don't have big ears," Tripp said.

Those close to the conversation laughed,

and Seth ruffled Tripp's hair. "No, son, you have perfect ears."

Tripp grinned at his mom. "See, told you so."

"You sure did," Quinn said and looked up at Anna. "We won't forget what you did for us."

As Ben watched the interaction, his throat tightened. As new as Anna was to the rest of them, he could see a connection that was between them all. He guessed he wasn't the only one who'd liked her from the first. "We need to get some food," he said. "Tripp, do you want to come and eat with us?"

"Nah, I'm eating with my mom and dad, then with Grandpa when we play cards later on. He's got chocolate ice cream."

"Sure do, Tripp," Sarge said.

"That sounds perfect, Tripp." Ben smiled at his family. "Love you all," he said. After hugs for everyone, including Sarge, he took Anna by the hand and started across the dance floor.

When they stepped outside onto the deck, the area had been cleared of the chairs and the white carpet, but the heaters were still doing a great job. The flower arch was the only reminder of the wedding and evidence of his participation in the decorating. Individual tables had been set up for dining, and the guests were being served near the grills.

Ben led Anna over to a table along the back rail and off to one side, a bit more private than the others. Anna took the chair that Ben pulled out for her, and he heard her sigh. "Isn't it beautiful out here?"

"Yes," he said, barely looking at the backdrop of the ranchland flowing up toward the foothills, or the pure blue of the late-afternoon Wyoming sky. His eyes were on Anna as he took the chair opposite hers. "You hungry?"

"Yes," she said.

"Okay, just tell me what you want to eat and I'll get it."

"Ribs, please, and maybe coleslaw, if they have it, and a roll, too."

He glanced over at the grills and the long food table. "Anything else?"

"No thanks. That's plenty."

"You aren't going to use a knife and fork to eat your meat, are you?"

She nodded and her loose hair drifted around her shoulders. "Of course I am."

"I thought so," he said before he stood and took off toward the grills.

When he returned with food for both of them, two bottles of water were sitting in the middle of the table along with a single flute of champagne. "You've been busy," he said as he sat and pushed her plate in front of her.

"I told you I was hungry," she said with a smile then reached for her knife and fork and started stripping the ribs of meat. He wouldn't argue with her method at all.

And in that dress and boots, with her hair falling down her back, he couldn't think of one thing he'd change about her.

She must have felt him staring at her because she raised her blue-gray eyes to his. "You think I can't eat ribs with my fingers? Is that it?"

Not even close to what he was thinking, but he found himself saying, "I haven't thought that once since I got your food for you."

"Look," she said and picked up the smallest rib on her plate. She kept her eyes on him while she took a bite of meat off the bone, chewed, swallowed, then lifted her hands to show the barbecue sauce on her fingertips.

"I can eat it that way but look at the mess it makes."

He reached into his pocket and took out several small packets of hand wipes he'd picked up by the grills and dropped them in the middle of the table. "Knock yourself out," he said as Anna quickly picked up one, tore it open and studiously cleaned her hands.

She sat back. "Thank you. Now, can I eat the way I want to without you staring at me?"

He laughed at that. Probably not, because he had trouble not staring at her. "Sure," he lied and picked up his knife and fork to attack his steak.

Minutes later, Anna set her knife and fork down on her plate. "Thank you for introducing me to your family. I can see that you were right when you said you were lucky to come here and become part of this family."

Her words took him back. "I know how lucky I've been."

She studied him for a moment. "They're really nice people, and I love it when good things happen to good people. Tripp is great. A lucky boy, too. And Sarge—he's got family around him who love him and will be there for him always."

She'd read them perfectly. "Tripp said you're a really, really smart lady, and I know they all like you." He grinned at her. "What's not to like?"

"Plenty, but I'm not going to tell you what," she said and flicked her fingers at him. "Eat while your food's hot." Then she methodically finished stripping her ribs and started eating. After some silence, she asked Ben, "When will Quinn and Seth and Tripp be leaving?"

"They've left quietly already, so it wouldn't upset Sarge. They're taking Tripp with them for the first half of their honeymoon, kind of a bonding time for their new family. Jake and Libby are going to meet them in Seattle and pick Tripp up to fly to Texas with them after. Jake's reviewing a place for another flight school for pilots who want to get into testing. It's near Houston."

"I bet Tripp will be fascinated by the planes."

"No doubt."

"Burr told me that Tripp was a runaway."

Ben explained about the boy running away from a foster home and ending up in the ranch's hay barn on a cold October day, where Quinn found him. "All three went through a lot before they found each other. They're happy, and Sarge is doing fine. So, all in all, today's been a huge success."

Ben was enjoying his food, the company and the conversation on a day that was one of the best he could remember.

Then Anna's eyes widened slightly as she looked past him. "Where did everyone go?"

Ben glanced back to see the last of the guests were leaving by the sliding-glass doors. Men were wire-brushing the grills while others stacked tables and chairs off to one side. He'd honestly lost track of his surroundings.

It was probably time to take Anna back to town, but he didn't want the day to end just yet. He made a suggestion he was pretty sure she'd agree to. "How about heading down to the stables to see Punch before I take you home?"

Her eyes widened and he knew he'd hit the nail on the head. "Yes, please," she said and ignored the rest of her food as she stood.

Ben didn't hesitate to get up, too. "Okay, let's go."

Anna hesitated. "Oh, shoot, I left my jacket in Burr's truck."

Ben wouldn't be done out of going to the

stables with her just because of a missing coat. "Not a problem," he said and motioned her to follow him inside.

Once he'd donned his denim jacket and Stetson, he found what he'd wanted for Anna.

"This should work for you," he said as he held out a leather aviator jacket he kept at the ranch as a backup. It was lined with sheared lamb's wool, and he knew it would be too big for her, but definitely warm enough.

Anna took the jacket and slipped it on, flipped her hair free of the collar to let it fall down her back. She smiled up at him. "This is great. Thank you."

As they made their way to his truck, he couldn't help but enjoy the picture she made. All that showed at the cuffed wrists were the tips of her fingers, and the stitched seam at the shoulder slipped down onto her upper arms. It worked.

When Ben parked the truck by the closed doors to the stables, security lights flashed on, almost blinding him for a minute. He could see that the doors weren't locked, so he got out and slid one open. When Anna joined him, they quietly slipped inside. Lower-watt overhead security lights illuminated the main aisle as they walked to the dappled gray's stall.

"Punch," Anna said, and in less than a minute, the horse was pushing his head out over the half door. When she came nearer, he stretched to get closer to her.

She stroked his neck and the horse snuffled, obviously pleased with the attention. "I missed you," she said softly, kissing him on his muzzle.

"Have you figured out where you might try to relocate near town?" Ben asked as he watched the woman with the large animal.

"I haven't had a chance to look at anything yet," she said, running her slender fingers lightly through Punch's forelock.

"What are you looking for?"

She shrugged. "I intended to buy a small ranch, but when I put it all down on paper, it sure didn't work out, at least not yet. Realistically, I have to plan on renting for a while."

"How long was your list before you came to that conclusion?"

She turned and gave him an eye roll. "One page of pros and cons and two pages for options and monetary totals."

He chuckled. "How many hours did that take?"

"Oh, two, maybe three. It was late, and I was getting sleepy, but I wanted to get it done so I knew where I could go around here and where I couldn't go."

"You're welcome to come here whenever you want to ride Punch, so don't feel rushed about finding a place."

Punch nudged her shoulder, demanding attention. She reached to stroke his forehead. "Thank you, but I don't want to intrude, especially now with family around or while the cleanup from the wedding is going on."

Ben wanted to see her more often than once in a while, but he wasn't sure that was a good idea. He didn't want to get too involved when there was nowhere to go with her, yet she pulled at him by just being close. "Everyone is pretty much gone for at least the next week or longer, so it might be a good time for you to go through the files. It'll just be me, Julia and Sarge at the house, so it should be pretty quiet."

She considered that then said, "Burr isn't very busy right now, so that works for me." The horse pushed at Anna's shoulder again.

"Do you think it would be okay for me to get him a carrot before we leave?"

"Sure, go for it."

She turned and went to the center cross-aisle and out of view toward the expanded tack room. The horse looked at Ben, but when he went to pat him, he shifted away from his hand. "I get it," Ben said. "I'm not her and you like her. Well, so do I, buddy." His own words settled in him and he wouldn't fight them. Right then, he didn't want to.

Ben smiled at his making that confession to a horse. But it was true. The time they'd been dancing had been something special for him. Then the meal had been so easy and enjoyable. Selfishly, he wanted more of all of that, and if she came out to see the horse or to read the files often, that worked for him.

"No carrots, but there were apples," Anna said when she came back to Punch's stall. She had an apple in her hand and proceeded to bite a chunk out of it. "I couldn't find a knife, but my aunt always did it this way," she said as she held the apple piece flat on her palm and offered it to Punch.

He looked at it, rolled his eyes, but made no effort to take it. "Okay, okay, no apple."

She'd barely uttered the words when Punch dipped his head and neatly snatched the piece off her hand. She looked up at Ben, her eyes wide with disbelief. "What just happened?"

"Offer him another piece."

She repeated the process, and Punch didn't make a move to take it. Ben moved closer to Anna and leaned in to whisper in her ear, very aware of the soft scent of flowers he'd noticed while they'd been dancing. "Look at him and say, 'Okay, okay,' just the way you did the first time."

As Ben stepped back, Anna said, "Okay, okay," and the horse retrieved the piece of apple in a flash.

"Oh my gosh." Surprise was written all over her face. "How did you figure that out?"

"We know he was trained to stay in place untied, so it made sense he might do other things on cue. Now, the trick is to find out what other triggers he has."

She looked excited. "I wonder if he counts with his foot. Or maybe he can bow or dance or something."

Ben loved her enthusiasm, but he didn't want her to get her hopes up too high. "Give him the rest but say the word just once."

Anna held out what was left of the apple, and said, "Okay." Punch did nothing.

She said it twice and the horse snatched the fruit out of her hand.

She clapped with obvious delight and before Ben knew what she was going to do, she reached out and hugged him. "You're right! He's really, really smart!" She was almost bouncing up and down as she held on to him and he surrounded her with his arms. He definitely liked it when she was happy.

Then she was moving back. As she looked up at him, he thought her eyes seemed more blue right then than gray. "That was such a good surprise," she said. "I mean, he just gets better and better, doesn't he?"

The horse was a surprise, but not half as much as Anna when she'd walked into his world from out of nowhere. And surprises kept coming with her. "Maybe he's only a two-trick pony—or horse, at least," he said.

"Even if he is, that's so great." Her face was slightly flushed, and she paused before she said, "Thank you for giving him to me. I really owe—"

He cut her off. "No, Punch owes you. You're the one who kept him from going to auction."

She let out a sigh then moved closer to him. "However it worked, it's because of you telling Dwight to try to figure it all out. I thank you so much for that kindness," she said softly.

"You're very welcome." He touched her chin with his forefinger to gently tip her face up to his. "Do you know your eyes change color with your moods?"

She blushed slightly. "My mom told me they look bluer when I'm happy, but I never could really catch that myself."

His hand shifted and gently cupped her chin. "If that's true, you must be happy right now."

She closed her eyes for a moment before she looked up at him again. "I am. Very happy."

Ben leaned toward Anna for a kiss, something he wanted very much right then. But Punch had other ideas. The animal bumped his muzzle into Anna's shoulder, jarring her sideways, and she grabbed the top rail of his stall to steady herself on her feet.

"Take it easy," she said, smiling fondly at Punch.

Ben wasn't feeling quite so kindly toward

the beast, but whatever had been happening in that moment was gone.

"I didn't forget about you. I couldn't," Anna said softly.

Punch had bonded with her quickly and completely. Ben kind of understood. He couldn't remember a woman like her becoming so interesting for him in such a short time. Just the way she explained things, the way she talked to others when she wasn't caring who was there, the kindness that came from her in the most unexpected situations. And the horse and the woman seemed to understand each other. He could almost believe that Punch knew that she'd probably saved his life. Over and over again, she caught Ben's attention and wouldn't let go.

Anna had said herself that she had no time for relationships in her life—at least, not anytime soon. He matched her on that. The fewer complications in his life, the better. But that didn't mean he didn't want to be around her, to laugh with her, to ride with her, to get to know her more and let life happen within reason. Then they could both walk away without regrets when the time came.

He watched as Anna stroked the horse's

muzzle and whispered, "I'll be back soon." With a quick glance at Ben, she said, "I guess it's time to go."

He didn't want to leave, but he nodded, and they headed out to the truck.

With the heater going, he drove up the service road and toward the gates. They were both quiet until they were on the country road heading east to the highway.

He was the one who broke the silence. "I'm glad you came with Burr," he said honestly.

He thought Anna said, "Me, too," but she'd spoken so softly that he wasn't sure he'd heard her right.

What he knew for sure was that they were both on the same page about not wanting to get serious. She'd said her focus for now was on her career. He thought he might sound calculating, but the realization was actually liberating for him. He wanted to enjoy his time with her until it was over.

"It all turned out better than I ever expected," he said.

Silence fell in the cab of the old truck and there was something about the empty road in front and behind that gave Ben a sense that the two of them were isolated from the rest of the world. He kind of liked the feeling. Then he heard Anna sigh softly. "Tired?" he asked as they approached the highway.

"Pardon me?"

"You sighed."

"Oh, I was thinking that this place is so quiet and peaceful. It's almost like its own world."

He darted a look at her then back to the road. It was as if she had paraphrased what he'd been thinking.

"When I first stepped foot onto the ranch, I remember thinking it smelled." He could bring that memory up so easily now. "It was noisy with crickets and birds and howling animals. I couldn't think straight. It took me weeks to finally figure out why Sarge and Maggie went up to the original house, an old cabin on the road to the mess hall and bunkhouse, where they lived while Sarge built the big house for them. They went up there just to sit on the porch during the evenings."

"Why would they do that?" she asked.

"First, they needed some time away from us boys. But mostly I think they just went to be together, to look out into the night and know that everything they could see in any direction was theirs and always would be." He hoped against hope that would never change, that this land would always be Sarge's land.

Anna was quiet for a moment then asked, "What about the smell?"

He almost laughed at that. "Oh, it smells like home to me now."

Once on the highway going south, he glanced at Anna again, the faint bluish light from the dash not enough for him to really see her expression. He shifted slightly in the seat and gripped the steering wheel as he turned to look ahead down the almost empty highway.

"I do appreciate the ride back to town," Anna said.

He checked the plain wristwatch that Maggie and Sarge had given him when he'd graduated high school and left for college. Six o'clock. He thought about the almost kiss at the stables. The horse had won. He must have chuckled or something, because Anna asked, "What's so funny?"

"We missed getting a piece of the wedding cake. Seth told me before that he'd had it specially made from stacking those sponge snack cakes with cream filling. Quinn is addicted to them, and it seems Tripp is, too."

"He sure seems to love Sarge."

"Yeah, he's the grandson Sarge and Maggie always wanted, and Tripp never knew what a grandpa was until Sarge was in his life. Sarge, one of the best Stud Poker players around, is on a terrible losing streak with Go Fish."

Ben looked over at her, her dimples showing, and they laughed at the same time. She got his joke about Sarge just being a good grandfather and letting the boy win at the game. The day just got better and better. It had become the best wedding he'd ever attended. It was so easy to talk with Anna and to laugh with her, and to tell her things he'd honestly never wanted to tell anyone but had ended up telling her.

As he slowed to turn off the highway onto the town's main street. He wished the drive wasn't almost over. "Where should I drop you off, Gabby's or the office?"

"The office, please. My truck's parked there."

As he approached the building and slowed, he slipped into the parking spot by her new truck. He got out and went around to the passenger side. When he opened her door and looked up at her, the shadows of the gathering night blurred her expression until she stepped down and into the glow from the streetlamp.

"Thank you for everything, especially driving me back," she said. "I really had a good time."

"So did I," he said in a low voice as he reached without thinking about it to brush back an errant strand of her long hair and tuck it behind her ear. His fingertips skimmed lightly over the silky warmth of her cheek before he drew back. "I never expected to see you there."

"I didn't expect to be there until Burr asked me."

"Remind me to thank him for bringing you," Ben said, knowing it was time to go. "Sleep well." He went around the truck to get back in behind the wheel, then watched Anna safely get in her vehicle, start it, then back out with a wave to him through the window. He pulled out after her, but drove in the opposite direction by himself.

## *CHAPTER TEN*

ANNA WAS UP at dawn after a restless night in which she'd gone over and over her time with Ben the day before. It was exciting and a bit frightening to have such an immediate response to being held while they'd danced. Then just his light touch on her chin at the stables had almost made her stop breathing. She thought she hadn't been looking for anything like that, until Ben Arias had stepped into her world.

It wasn't just the fact he was so attractive, amazingly easy to be with, or the way he laughed, but his interaction with his family had touched her heart in another way. He loved them and wasn't afraid to show it. They were his world.

She was on her way to take an early ride on Punch, and by the time she drove off the highway onto the country road, she was still thinking about the day before. The wedding had been perfect. Meeting Ben's family had been very special, and the time at the stable with Punch and Ben made her sigh.

She was going to go riding, enjoy the crisp air of Sunday morning and the brush of pastels lingering from the break of dawn in the clear sky. Halfway to the entry, she saw someone walking on the side of the road in the direction she was heading. When she realized that someone was Ben, she was happier than was reasonable for her to be at just seeing him again. She stopped and slid the passenger window down. "Good morning," she said.

He looked in at her. "Good morning to you."

Anna had dressed quickly before heading up to the ranch. Her pink flannel shirt and jeans, along with her boots, were pretty much her new normal. She'd braided her hair. Now she kind of wished she'd dressed up a bit, and maybe done something better with her hair. She thought Ben looked tired. "You're up early."

"I didn't get much sleep last night, and I'd rather be moving than lying there pretending to sleep."

"Is something wrong?"

"Sarge had a bad night and it was just me and Julia, so we took turns sitting with him. I think the wedding, as wonderful as it was, might have been too much for him."

He opened her truck's passenger door and climbed into the cab. "Did Dwight give you the code for the entry gates?"

"No, I didn't even think about that."

"I just happen to know it," he said as he shut the door and buckled up.

"My lucky day," she responded as she put the truck in gear.

THE DAY WAS BEAUTIFUL, and Anna felt as free riding Punch, next to Ben on Traveler, as she ever had doing anything in her life. It was perfect. Ben hadn't had to ask twice if she'd like company on her ride. They'd started toward the west but shifted north the way they had on that first ride, slowly heading farther up into the foothills. The sun was climbing in the sky, and the cold didn't seem quite so sharp, but she made a mental note to get a hat as soon as she could.

They went past the trees they'd cut through to get to the lookout, then passed scatterings of tangled brush and bushes. Then the land was more open, and Ben led the way west, heading toward an impressive stand of old trees. When they got closer, she saw a wide swath freshly cut through the trees and tangled brush to give access to whatever was beyond. It was more than wide enough for them to ride side by side.

"Sarge had this passage cut years ago when he was harvesting trees for construction for the mess hall and bunkhouse," Ben said. "Now it's been enlarged for an easier trail to the main camping area."

"I went by the mess hall and bunkhouse the other day," she said. "You'd told me they've been partially repurposed, but they look as if they'd been sitting right there for years and years."

"They have been. Libby did new interior configurations. Between the two buildings there's now a registration area and small office, a lounge for the kids, sleeping quarters, and the kitchen's been redone to look more like a restaurant kitchen. I'll take you for a tour one of these days when you have time."

"I'd like that." She inhaled the scent of earth and pine mingled with the freshness of the morning as they went higher. She thought she heard a faint humming in the air. "What's that sound?" she asked.

"You'll see when we get there. I want to show you where some of the camping sites are going to be."

Another sound of splashing water began to blend with the persistent humming, accompanied by a growing dampness in the air. As they broke out into a vast clearing, Anna finally saw what she'd only heard and felt up until then.

A waterfall tumbled down over the middle section of a rough stone bluff a few hundred feet to their right. It splashed into a small lake that flowed into a shallow creek and disappeared from sight to the south. Punch snorted and shifted uneasily as they neared the water, something he hadn't done before. She soothed him by leaning forward to stroke his neck.

As the horse calmed, she looked over at Ben. "The hum, what's that from?"

"It's something to do with a rock formation at the top of the falls. Most folks call this spot Singing Falls, although it actually only has one tone, so it's more like Humming Falls."

Anna was awestruck by the setting, the trees and bushes showing the fresh green of their spring buds and the waterfall that had to be over thirty feet high. The land beyond it climbed even higher. Mist rose when the water hit the rocks at the bottom and hovered low to the ground in the early-morning air. "How far does the creek go?" she asked.

"Into the gorge we saw last time, then another side gorge, where it disappears off into a rock basin and drops underground."

"The Magical Disappearing Singing Rock Falls Creek or something like that?"

He chuckled softly and the sound echoed off the rocky bluffs as he dismounted and turned to look up at her. "We can't get up to where the water and the humming all originate," he said, "but I'll show you the next best thing."

She dismounted and dropped Punch's reins to the ground. It seemed natural for her to take Ben's hand when he offered it to her before they started off to the north on rocky ground that took them higher.

They walked in silence. Anna sensed they were angling away from the falls and wondered where this hike would lead. Then there was level ground where the mist was heavier. She could almost feel the humming vibrating on her face and heard the sound of crashing water echoing from below.

"Okay, now for the second best way to show you what's going on," Ben said, looking pleased with himself. He let go of her to shift around behind her and then rested one hand on her shoulder as he pointed up, seemingly at the sky. "There it is," he said, the warmth of his breath brushing her cheek as she looked up. "Between the jutting rocks on the left and the tangle of brush to the right."

Anna raised her hand to block the sun's brilliance from getting in her eyes. Then Ben moved and the next thing she knew, he'd put his Stetson on her. "The brim cuts down on the glare," he said, and she looked back up. He was right, and she knew she must have gasped. There was a crazy cluster of massive rocks high above their position at the top of the falls. Water ran around them, over them and through gaps in spots where they seemed partially fused together. Above was no water, just more rock, dry brush and scrub trees.

"It hums just from going over those rocks?" she asked.

"Mostly it's to do with the shape of the rocks and the amount of force as the water pushes through and around them. That's as close to an explanation for all of this as anyone's come up with so far."

"Good. I don't think anyone should really know how it works," she said.

He shifted back to look at her. "Why not?"

"It's more fun to make up fantasies about what could make it hum. If you prove it, it's reality."

"I thought you were a realist, a by-the-book person, a compulsive list maker," he said as she met his dark eyes.

She sighed then smiled. "Even I think I sound dull when you say it like that."

"No, you're not dull," he said softly. "But the dampness makes it even colder here. We need to go back down."

Anna exhaled and looked one last time at the high bluff where the waterworn rocks continued to hum. "Thanks for showing me this," she said.

"We'll come back in the middle of summer when the days are hot and this all becomes a natural misting system. You'll love camping up here. It's great." They headed down the trail. When there was a whinny from below, Ben said, "Come on," and picked up their pace.

As the horses came into view, both where they'd been left, they seemed to be shifting nervously. "It's time to go," he said as he moved to untie Traveler.

Anna picked up Punch's reins. "When we got here, it felt like Punch got spooked, but he settled. What do you think's going on?"

"He probably sensed other animals going for the water."

"Like that mountain lion who lost his head to Sarge?"

"No, probably just coyotes. Come on, let's leave the water to them."

"What about kids coming here? Is it safe?"

"Yes. We have a contract with a scouting service to do sweeps up here when the camp is in use. They have the sensor system to keep track of each boy inside the perimeter, and any other unusual stirring or activity."

They started riding back the way they'd come. "It must have been wonderful living here, even with the animals," she said.

"It was." His gaze lingered on her. "You look good in that hat."

She'd almost forgotten she was wearing it. "Oh, here." She took it off and handed it back to him. She really would like to get one for herself as soon as she could. She'd actually felt warmer wearing it.

His eyes narrowed as he put it on and asked, "What was your 'normal' as a kid?"

"It wasn't peace and quiet and humming waterfalls," Anna said, remembering her childhood clearly. "It was noise, and people, with snow in the winter and sweltering heat in the summers. Sometimes the lake was the best place to be with my mom and dad. Christmas lights reflected off the water and made the holidays seem so special. But, honestly, I spent more time in my dad's office than I did anywhere else. I loved being there with him."

"A lake and lights and noise and heat or cold—was that good or bad?" Ben asked.

She shrugged. "I thought it was pretty great. Besides, I never had anything like this to compare it to, except my aunt's ranch, and that isn't exactly like this."

The silence in the trees was broken only by the cry of a bird. "I measure every other place I go against here," Ben said. "I've never found any that came close."

"It must be hard to leave when you have to. I mean, you have a career where you're doing great, and I'm sure it's really important for you to stay involved."

"Very important. But right now, it's more important for me to be here. I'll take off when I need to, and Seth's planning on living here now with Quinn and Tripp in the big house. Jake and Libby are drawing up plans to build a place beyond the original cabin, so they'll always be close. I can fit my work around them." He glanced over at Anna. "It's about eight o'clock. Jake and Libby are taking off soon for Montana, but they won't leave until I'm back."

"You never looked at your watch this whole time. Do you have some superhuman DNA that allows you to read the sky or something like that?"

Anna knew as soon as she'd spoken, intending to tease Ben, that she'd said something wrong—very wrong. Ben's features grew taut as he answered. "As far as my DNA goes, no superhuman powers, and even if I had it tested, I only know about the character that runs in my blood."

That seemed an odd choice of words. "Character?"

He exhaled. "The temperament that's

stamped in my DNA is a mix of my biological parents—one of worthless character from both, even dangerous character."

The more she heard him speak, the more it hurt her heart to think of what he must have gone through. "I'm sorry for—"

"Don't feel sorry for me," he said abruptly. Then he laughed, a harsh humorless sound in the still air. "That kid didn't deserve sympathy. He was a mess."

He stared at her hard, a look of disgust on his face that she knew was directed at his younger self when he spoke again. "You know, I actually hated Sarge and Maggie at first. Two of the best people I'd ever meet in my life, and I was told they were going to be the people who won me over and put me on the right track. I hated that. I didn't want to be fixed, I just wanted to survive. Then this big guy, an ex-marine, and his wife thought they understood me and could help me. It turned out I was wrong about Sarge and Maggie, and I owe everything that I am now to them never giving up."

Shrugging, he nudged his horse forward, and Anna rode beside him. She kept silent, unable to think of what to say. Any words that came to her wouldn't be right, because she had no idea what he'd really gone through, just what she imagined he had. She respected him so much, what he tried to do for kids, working from the pain he'd lived through to try to keep them safe and away from that agony.

Silence between them lasted until they neared the stock fencing that marked the transition from open grazing land to contained pastures. She couldn't take it anymore.

"Ben, I just want to say that what you're doing and why you're doing it is life-changing for the kids you connect with. You *are* the son of Sarge and Maggie."

Ben looked over at her, his eyes narrowed as if he was absorbing something hard for him to handle, then he looked away and kept going.

"I am Sarge's son. Luis Arias and Marcella Arias are nothing to me now."

Anna felt her chest tighten even more, but she kept quiet. So did Ben. Anna could hardly wrap her mind around what he'd said about his biological parents' character. She saw none of that in Ben. "I have to say, from what I know about you, Ben, you broke the cycle. You ended it."

He glanced at her. "What?"

"Look what you've become despite your past."

He looked away and spoke in a flat voice. "Thanks for trying, but it's not that simple." He took off at a slow gallop away from her.

BEN RODE, his breathing tight, keeping his head down, only glancing at Anna once to make sure she was still there. He didn't know why he'd done that, telling this woman more about the ugly side of his life. But he'd heard himself saying things he hated he'd said to her. Words had been coming before he even thought about them. He'd felt a heaviness on him, a weight he'd needed to get rid of. It was still there, and he knew if he looked at Anna right then, there would be sympathy or pity in her eyes.

Traveler slowed and whinnied as he flicked his head to one side. Punch did the same. Ben drew Traveler to a stop again, and Anna was right beside him. He scanned the land around them. "I think there might be something ahead they don't like," he said with intentional vagueness. "Why don't we cut farther south and ride nearer to the southern property line?"

Anna agreed without argument, and they shifted south onto cleared land with only a scattering of trees. Ben was pretty sure the area wouldn't hold a problem for them. He finally stopped to look ahead across the relatively level ground and couldn't see a thing. There was no movement, no flock of birds taking sudden flight or any animal cries. "I think we're fine," he said.

He dismounted to check the cinch on Traveler then turned to look up at Anna, but she'd dismounted, too. She was scanning the land and pointing to the south. "Is that the county road way down there?"

He scanned the area she pointed to. "Yes, that's it."

"This section looks pretty level," Anna said.

"We kids thought it would have been great for racing, but Sarge was always rotating crops, so it got too soft."

"It looks great for racing now," she said as he looked back at her.

He saw the hint of a smile play at the corners of her mouth. "Are you challenging me to a race, Ms. Watters?"

Her eyes widened with a perfect expression of feigned innocence. "Who, me?"

She was coming to his rescue again, not even knowing she was doing it. She was bringing an easing of the heaviness that all his words hadn't been able to ease at all. Now she was doing it for him.

"I don't know what to think about you," he admitted honestly.

That brought a real smile accompanied by her dimples. "What I think is, we should get back as quickly as possible so Jake and Libby can take off soon."

He thought he knew what she was thinking. "Okay," he said and turned to get back in the saddle.

Anna followed suit, then looked across at him. "We need to go quickly, as in flying like the wind," she said, adding, "Oh, and by the way, that was a challenge, unless you're afraid of losing?"

He'd been right. "Not even a thought of it," he said.

Anna nudged Punch, and the horse took off, strong and intent. Traveler was on it right away, and as he drew up alongside Anna and Punch, Ben called, "We have to stop at the new hay lean-to way up there."

She glanced into the distance, then called, "You got it," and urged Punch on.

The feeling of almost flying was wonderful for Ben, and he kept his eyes on the goal. "We've got this, boy," he told Traveler, and the horse exploded with speed. They were at the empty lean-to mere seconds before Anna and Punch, just in time for him to tease her. "What took you so long?"

"You think you're so tough, don't you?"

It wasn't her fault that her words jarred him. It wasn't her fault that he actually felt like a fraud most of the time. Even with someone he was interested in, he'd have to push past who he knew he was, to be who he knew he should be.

His past was too close to the present again, a past that he knew had robbed him of the ability to do more than not just trust people. Maybe it also blocked him from whatever answered for love in this world. He'd exposed enough to Anna, and he wondered if she'd walk away after they got back from the ride and never look back. Most people had walked away. "Traveler's tough, for sure," he murmured. "But we do need to get back."

When they arrived at the stables, they left the horses to be cared for by two new ranch hands, then went up to the house.

Half an hour later, he left Anna in the office going over more files. She said she'd come back the next day, too, and he felt his stomach clench. Maybe there would be a quick call that she was busy and she wouldn't have time to come out to the ranch again. That would be the politest way he'd been brushed off.

Ben went in to sit with Sarge while Julia took a rest. He trusted Sarge. That was the one permanent thing in his life now, the one thing he knew would never change. Sarge had accepted all of him, the good, the bad and the ugly, never calling up his past. He loved the man for that. He was a safe place in Ben's world.

Ben sat by the bed just watching Sarge sleep peacefully. He might be diminished somewhat mentally but in Ben's mind, he was still the huge man with the huge voice, with a heart just as big as everything else about him.

The phrase *A life well lived* came to Ben to describe Sarge's life. Ben hoped that at least the second half of his own life might be encapsulated by that phrase someday.

Hopefully, it wouldn't be defined by the all too familiar phrase that Anna had inadvertently said to him after the race. *You think you're so tough, don't you?* He'd heard that often in his first fifteen years, spoken by police or social workers or teachers, or other boys, even his parents. Sometimes it was uttered sadly, sometimes tauntingly, sometimes to hurt and sometimes to shame, but it was always accompanied by annoyance or anger.

He stayed very still, concentrating on the man in front of him, and on thoughts of the wife who should still be there with him. He had to make very sure the camp was a huge success, that the boys who came took only good back with them. He wanted them to take hope with them. Sarge and Maggie's hope.

Ben didn't know how long he'd sat there before he finally stood, reached for the monitor that Julia used to keep track of Sarge when she left the room, clipped it to his belt and stepped out into the hallway. He went to the closed office door, but before he could knock, he heard Anna behind the barrier muttering, "Oh, shoot, shoot, shoot!"

Ben quickly knocked and went in to find her crouched on the floor with papers scattered all around her. "What happened?" he asked as he crossed to hunker down beside her.

Her eyes were on the mess. "Oh, I'm such a klutz. I dropped some folders, and now they're one big mess," she said as she began picking up the loose sheets.

Ben started doing the same and, when the floor was cleared, they both stood and set everything on the desk. The tabs on the years-old folders were labeled Horse Sales, Land Clearing, Heavy Equipment and Water. Anna and Ben got busy sorting the papers and putting them back in the right folders. When they'd finished, Anna tucked them all back into the bottom drawer of the cabinet.

"I didn't get any breakfast or coffee this morning, and I get cranky when I'm hungry and caffeine deprived," Ben said. "How about you?"

"Coffee would be great," she said. Ben headed out the door that opened into the great room. All the furniture was back in place.

He crossed to the kitchen, but when he turned, Anna wasn't with him. He looked back and saw that she'd stopped by the old pool table. "Are you coming?"

She started slightly, as if she'd forgotten he was even there. "Oh...sure. I was just... This table is beautiful," she said as she headed toward him.

"Do you play pool?"

She stepped up to where he stood by the kitchen island that overlooked the great room. "No, I have no talent for playing pool, but my mom and dad used to play all the time. Talk about a ringer," she said.

"Your dad, the attorney, suckered people into pool games?"

She shook her head. "My dad could hold his own, but my mom is like a pool savant. She's as tiny as Libby, but she can bring big old bikers to tears."

She seemed proud of her mother's talents. "And the bikers accept losing to her?" he asked.

Her eyes widened. "They have to. How would it look for a six-foot-five, three-hundred-pound biker with a tattoo that says *Meet Doctor Pain*, to cry over a ninety-pound woman beating him?"

He laughed at that. "Doctor Pain?"

Anna's eyes looked a lot bluer right then. "Yes. And, just for the record, I love to watch her, but I stay away from pool games."

"Is that true, or are you just trying to draw me into a game and beat the stuffing out of me?"

She shrugged noncommittally. "What do you think?"

He loved that she never gave him the satisfaction of admitting what she was up to. "I don't know what to think," he said truthfully. "Except your parents sound like they would have been fun to be around."

"You hit that nail on the head." She looked a bit wistful. "They had such fun together, no matter what they were doing. And Christmas... well, that was just plain fantastic, especially for me as a kid."

He thought her eyes looked a bit overly bright, as if she was holding tears back despite her smile. She'd had everything he'd never had in his early life, and it made him uneasy that he was quite certain he could never live up to what she'd expect from him, even in a short-term relationship. He heard himself speak without realizing that his words were touched by some sarcasm.

"Santa, the Easter bunny, Thanksgiving turkeys? I bet you even had the tooth fairy show up at your house."

She lost some of the glow from her expression and seemed to be trying to figure out why he was talking like that. He wished he'd kept quiet. It wasn't her fault that he could barely imagine the life she'd had. "I got a silver dollar from the tooth fairy twice," she said, almost daring him to contradict her.

"I'm impressed. You really scored," he said, making sure his tone didn't hold even a touch of sarcasm. Then he crossed to the intricate coffee maker by the double ovens. "Coffee in a few minutes," he said. "Now, how do you feel about food?"

He watched her dimples show up. "My feelings about food are ambiguous. Do you eat food to live, or do you live to eat? I personally don't know."

"Okay, okay," he said, raising his hands in surrender. "What do you like to eat—and don't say food."

She giggled. A real giggle. He liked that. "Not to put too fine a point on this, Ben, but I am known to be easy when it comes to food. No allergies, so everything is fair game."

He enjoyed the information on her uncomplicated eating habits. "That was quite a succinct summation, Your Honor."

"You call a judge 'Your Honor,' Mr. Arias, but a lowly attorney is usually called 'Counselor.'"

"I'll remember that," he said and figured he'd better lay out what was available for breakfast. "Let's keep this simple. We have eggs, bacon, toast and cold cereal. Any or all?"

She didn't hesitate. "Eggs over easy with toast. Is that okay?"

"Great," he said.

When they eventually sat down at the large dining table facing each other over their plates of food and full coffee mugs, Ben almost sighed. The food smelled great, and with Anna sitting across from him, life was very good at that moment. He could almost imagine doing the same thing every morning, laughing at silly jokes and talking about anything either one thought of. He could almost imagine it, but not quite.

## CHAPTER ELEVEN

On Monday, Anna went into the office, planning to leave at noon to go to the ranch for a ride and to see if she could look at the private files again. Leo had turned up some signatures by Norman Good, but nothing out of the usual regarding development in his files. She was getting impatient and couldn't wait to get into the ranch files again. She barely had time to boot up her computer before a call came in on her cell. She glanced at the screen and her heart skipped slightly.

"Good morning, Ben."

"I'm not interrupting anything?"

"No, not at all. I just got to the office."

"I needed to let you know, I'm going to be gone for two or three days. I'll most likely be back Wednesday or Thursday."

She sank back in the chair, knowing she should be relieved to have a few days to concentrate on work instead of being disappointed that she wouldn't be riding with Ben again for a while. Hoping that didn't show in her voice, she asked, "Oh, is everything okay?"

"Yes. Sarge is going to Cody for some therapy and a complete checkup at Wicker Pines, the rehab center there. Julia is going with him, and I want to be there, too."

"So, it's just routine?"

"Yes, he does it every six months, and I want to see how it's all done, and learn what I can do to help when he gets back here."

"I hope it all goes well," she said.

There was silence for a few moments then Ben asked, "Have you been up to Cody or to Yellowstone area yet?"

"No, I don't have time. You know me and my work ethic." She said that as a joke of sorts but didn't smile. Her disappointment was lingering, and she tried to push it away. At least she could get some work at the office tied up, and maybe have a meeting with Leo and Burr to see where they all stood on what to do next.

"Yes, I do. Well, at least make time to go riding while I'm gone. Dwight will be here."

"Thanks, I will."

"Anna, do you remember when I told you I think I figured out something I could read about you?"

She did. "I think so."

"You never asked me what it was."

Anna closed her eyes, not certain she wanted to know. "No, I didn't, did I?"

"Do you want to know?"

She was cornered and finally said, "Okay, what do you think you can read about me?"

Ben made a pronouncement. "You feel guilty about having fun."

"What? I don't. I do have fun, really. The wedding was fun, and riding Punch is fun."

His low laughter seemed to surround her. "A great start, but maybe we can work on the finer points about having fun when I get back."

She knew she should make some comeback and laugh, but her throat felt tight. "I…I probably won't have time for much more than the rides. I'm really kind of busy…for now." The truth was, she was feeling more pressure to keep her promise to Burr, and her own promise to herself, to study and to do the right thing and help the ranch. Getting tangled up in Ben's life in a way that was starting to go past that unsettled in her. She had to get some space, and Ben had handed it to her with him leaving for a while.

"For now?" he asked in a tone that had shifted and it caught her attention. It was the same suggestion of tightness his voice had taken on at the end of their ride. She hadn't understood it then, but now she felt as if he was distancing himself from her, too.

"Ben, I…"

"I have to go," he said, the edge still there.

"Oh, of course."

She opened her eyes and sat straighter. "Have a safe trip."

The call was over, and Anna just sat there swiveling slowly back and forth in her chair. She had a sinking feeling, whatever she'd thought might be happening with Ben had vanished, and she had no idea why.

OVER THE NEXT few days, Burr, Anna and Leo had two meetings about the ranch and discussed the idea that Norman Good could be on the side of whatever development company might be trying to take over the land. But nothing specific came up, and that only left Anna with a hunch that wouldn't go away.

She had no idea what that might be, or even if Norman Good was involved; still, an uneasiness about him persisted.

By Thursday, she had no idea if Ben was back or not, and she couldn't make herself call to find out. What he did, or where he was, wasn't her business. She had to step back. Dwight had been evasive when she'd gone out to ride Punch, telling her he hadn't seen Ben and word was he was still out of town.

On Friday, she was ready to leave the office when her cell rang. When she saw Ben's number on the screen, her heart did it again, and she swallowed hard before answering.

"Hello?"

"Hi, Anna. It's Ben." She heard him sigh. "I'm back, but I'm not going to be free to do anything."

She hated that sinking feeling at his flat tone and lack of any suggestion he'd want to go riding later. "Is Sarge okay?"

"We got back late yesterday, and Sarge had a really bad night after doing so well in Cody. They say it's expected when he's had too much stimulation. It's hard on his focus and…" His words faded away. Then he said, "It's been rough."

From the exhaustion in his voice, she knew it was bad, and all she wanted to do was to help in some way. Worrying about her own scrambled feelings just seemed selfish. "I'm so sorry."

"Go ahead and enjoy your ride." She heard Julia's voice in the background just before Ben said, "Gotta go," and the call was over. She sat by the computer for a long moment before she let Burr know she was leaving for the ranch.

When she arrived at the gates, she put in the code and drove through. Ignoring the service road, she headed up to the ranch house, parked and got out of the truck. She'd barely taken a single step up to the porch when the entry door opened.

Ben was there, and she realized too late that coming out here might have been her worst decision in a while. He looked exhausted. His chambray shirt was untucked and creased, as if he'd slept in it, and his jaw was shadowed by the beginning of a beard. No hat, and his dark hair was mussed.

It was too late to get in her truck and leave without him knowing she'd been there. Honestly, she didn't want to leave, even though she knew she probably should. "How's Sarge?" she asked, a bit surprised at the intense concern she felt for the elderly man, but also for the man standing just above her.

"He's finally sleeping," he said, shaking his head. "It's over, I hope."

"Did you get any sleep?"

"Here and there." He closed his eyes momentarily and then exhaled as he looked at her again. "He was so good on the ride home. He even asked to go in the original gates and past the old cabin. But when we got him in the house, everything changed."

When he tucked his fingertips in his jeans' pockets, he hunched his shoulders as if into the wind. But there wasn't any wind.

"What can I do?" she asked without hesitation as she slowly climbed the steps to stop just below where he stood. Fine lines she hadn't noticed before showed at his dark eyes.

"I'm not asking you to—"

"I can sit with him while he sleeps, or if he wakes up, I'd be glad to read to him. I could play cards with him. I'm pretty good at poker or even Old Maid. Or I can visit with him so you and Julia can take a break."

"Anna, it's not—"

She cut him off but kept her tone as soft as possible. "Just say 'thank you, Anna.'"

He ran both hands roughly over his face and met her eyes. "Thank you, Anna."

"Now, show me the way."

After she'd left her boots and jacket at the cowhide bench, they met up with Julia at Sarge's bedroom door. Ben quickly explained Anna's offer, and before Julia could put up any argument, Anna said, "Please, let me do this. But I could use a cup of coffee, if you have some made?"

Ben headed to the kitchen while Julia settled Anna in one of the two chairs by the bed. Sarge was restless, his hands worrying the hem of his blanket, but his eyes were closed. Julia whispered to Anna, "My room is right across the hall if you need me."

When the woman left, Anna reached for a book on the bedside table. It was a well-used copy of Zane Grey's *The Border Legion*. She opened it and found the corner of the page that started the fourth chapter turned down. As she moved to put it back on the nightstand, the bedroom door swung open and Ben was there with a mug in his hand. He crossed to Anna, put the coffee down where the book had been, then crouched by her chair. "Thanks again," he whispered, laying his hand briefly on her forearm. "I'll be in the great room." Then he stood and went out, leaving the door ajar.

As Anna turned to put the book back, Sarge surprised her when he spoke in a low voice. "Are you gonna read or what?"

So, he wasn't asleep, and he probably thought she was Julia. "Of course. I'd love to read."

"Go ahead," he said, keeping his eyes shut.

After each chapter was read, she'd ask Sarge, "Another chapter?" After chapters four and five were finished, he'd asked for more without her prompting him to. But at the end of the sixth chapter, when she asked in a low voice, "How about another chapter, Sarge?" there was no response. Now it appeared he really was asleep.

Anna finally sat back and glanced over at the wall clock on the far side of the room. She was surprised that it was almost three o'clock. She'd enjoyed the story that had taken her back to her childhood readings with her father. He'd loved Zane Grey and other Old West writers. She missed those days so much at the moment. What she wouldn't give to be able to go back to that time and sit listening to her dad's animated reading. She hugged the memories to herself the way she knew Ben was holding on to all the memories he was making with Sarge.

Putting the book on the side table, she looked at a picture someone had propped on a chair close to the other side of the bed. She recognized the young man as Sarge, with his arm around a tiny woman she had no doubt was Maggie. They were holding on to each other, smiling brightly. It had to be when the couple was just starting on their journey together that led to the boys coming to their home. They'd made such a difference during their life together. She hoped, in her own way through the law, she could make a difference like that in the lives of others.

When she caught movement out of the corner of her eye, she glanced toward the door and saw Julia peeking inside. As quietly as she could, Anna got up and crossed to step out into the hallway. "He's asleep," she whispered.

Julia stretched her arms and rotated her head slowly. "Thank you so much," she said on a soft exhale. "I needed that nap. I've got this now. Jake and Libby called and are worried. They're coming back for tonight to make sure things are okay before they fly out to Seattle tomorrow to pick up Tripp. With them here for the night, we'll have reserves in the wings."

"That's good. Have you seen Ben?"

"Last I saw, he was asleep on the couch in the great room."

"Okay, I'm going to check out more files in the office." She wasn't certain what she was even looking for, but she thought she'd recognize a red flag if she saw one. At least she hoped she would.

"Do you need more coffee or anything?" Julia asked.

"Thanks, I'm fine."

Julia glanced at the door that was ajar. "I know a caregiver isn't supposed to be emotionally involved with their patient, but I'm way past simply being involved. Sarge is like family to me. They all are." Unexpectedly, Julia turned and hugged Anna. "Thank you. You're a lifesaver," she said, then slipped quietly into Sarge's room.

Anna headed for the great room. Ben was

on the leather couch, stretched out with his head against the back cushions. His feet rested on a large ottoman in front of him, and he seemed to be sound asleep.

She quietly closed the office door, then turned to the filing cabinets and opened the bottom drawer. It held the older paperwork that had scattered on the floor when she'd dropped it before. They were dated from at least thirty years ago. She took five files out.

When she finally sat back after going through three folders, she knew she wasn't going to ride today. She didn't want to do it alone, and she suspected she and Ben wouldn't be riding together again soon. She also had things she should sort out at the office. A ride could wait. Protecting the ranch had to come first for her. She picked up the remaining two files she hadn't checked so she could take them back to town with her and read them over the weekend.

She quietly opened the door to the great room and was surprised to find Ben sitting up and combing his fingers through his mussed hair. Anna almost backed into the office and closed the door, but he turned and saw her. "What's going on?" he asked as she approached him, his dark eyes holding lingering traces of sleep.

"Julia's with Sarge. I read to him, and he finally fell asleep."

Ben checked the time. "I owe you for this."

"No, you don't," she said. "I'm taking some files back to the office to go through them there."

"They're important?"

"I haven't really looked at them yet. They're all older, but I have a dread of missing something because I didn't check everything. Maybe it's a mild form of obsession."

"You're free to obsess if it makes you feel better," Ben said as he flicked the tabs of the files on her lap.

She needed to not be there, taking in the touches of exhaustion that still showed on his face. There was nothing else she could do for him—other than try to make sure the camp would open as planned.

She stood and looked down at Ben. He probably wanted her gone but was too polite to tell her to leave now. "I hope you have a good weekend."

"You haven't found anything?" he asked as he stood to face her.

"So far, everything looks okay. I only have these files and half a dozen more, then I'm done," she said as she started for the entry. Ben unexpectedly fell into step by her side.

She set the files on the cowhide bench and reached for her jacket. But Ben beat her to it and held it up so she could put it on. She turned her back to him then slipped her arms into the sleeves and shrugged it up. "Thanks," she said as she sat on the bench to put on her boots.

When she stood, Ben was barely a foot from her. He still looked so tired. She didn't plan to do it, but she found herself reaching up to touch his cheek, feeling the bristle of the beard shadow under her fingers. "Please, try to get some more sleep."

"I will eventually," he said in a husky voice, his dark eyes holding hers. Then he smiled slowly and, unexpectedly, he leaned toward her. She knew he was going to kiss her, and she knew she shouldn't let him, but truth be told, she wanted him to.

"He's sleeping," Julia announced.

Both Ben and Anna jumped back like guilty teenagers. Julia either hadn't noticed or wasn't about to comment on what had almost happened. "I'm going to start dinner." She looked at Anna. "Would you like to stay? I know Jake and Libby would love to see you again."

"No, uh…no thanks," she said, slightly uncertain what to do, before adding a generic excuse. "I have things I need to do."

"Okay, but you're welcome anytime."

Anna nodded. "Thank you so much." Before Ben could say or do anything, Anna headed to the door and stepped out into cold air. Quickly, she went down to her truck and got inside.

As she drove toward the gates, she stared straight ahead. All she could think of was the kiss that hadn't been. The kiss she'd wanted. It all confused her, and she didn't know how to figure it out. She hadn't been able to figure out the change in Ben again. That tenderness was back, and she didn't know how to handle it. She hadn't been seriously interested in any man before, too focused on keeping her promise to herself about what she wanted to do with law. It had overwhelmed her day-to-day life. She'd had a date here, a date there, but nothing she remembered being special. Nothing that scrambled her common sense and robbed her of her focus as much as being around Ben did.

That scared her to admit it to herself, but he stirred emotions in her she'd never experienced before. She had to learn how to balance her feelings, and to keep her promise. That was a whole lot easier when Ben wasn't anywhere around.

When she drove onto Clayton Drive, she spotted Burr's truck parked in front of the office. She pulled up beside it, then hurried inside. His office door was shut, but she could hear his voice and another man's muffled tones from behind the wooden barrier.

She went into her office and quietly closed the door. Before she could settle at her computer and send Burr a text telling him she was back, she heard him say something in the reception area that she couldn't understand. When the entry door finally opened and shut, she called out to Burr.

Her door swung open. "I didn't know you were back," Burr said. "But I'm glad you are. Guess who just left here? The mayor of this lovely town."

She swiveled her chair around to face him

more directly. "Did Leo find out anything about Norman Good?"

He came into the room, retrieved the wooden chair and set it to face her. Once he was seated, he rolled up the sleeves on his brown flannel shirt.

"Burr, did he or didn't he have something new about anything to do with the ranch?" she asked a bit impatiently, even though she knew she couldn't push Burr to make him hurry up and answer her.

"He might have or might have not," he finally said, continuing with some ambiguity. "Two men came up from Cheyenne two days ago. They're staying at a private ranch about eight miles south of here. It was sold last year to the president of an international land development business, which happens to have corporate offices based in Denver. The men have been in town drinking, mostly at the Lucky Golden Fleece Saloon. They're loud, talkative jerks, apparently."

"What are they saying?"

He shrugged. "Nothing much so far."

This was more frustrating than informative for Anna. "Then why is Leo taking note of two obnoxious drunks?"

"He wasn't. Not until he ran into Bob Roberts from the Annex and he asked him how his day was going. Bob never complains, but he did complain about a man who called to have him pull tax records and plot maps for four totally unrelated parcels of land. He told Bob he'd be in to pick them up around four-thirty this afternoon and take them with him. When the guy found out that original documents can't leave the Annex cellar, he went ballistic."

Anna kept quiet, wanting Burr to get to the end of his story quickly.

"Seems he's some big wheeler from Denver," Burr added. "He's temporarily in an office out of Cheyenne, and some deal depends on him getting those documents tonight. Bob being Bob, told him it isn't against the law to take pictures of any documents, or he could pay for Bob to make him copies. The man refused the offer, said he'd take care of it himself and wanted everything ready when he arrived. His time is valuable."

"Wow," Anna breathed. "He does sound like a jerk, but that isn't against the law."

"True, but one of the ranches on his demand list is Eclipse Ridge."

Anna exhaled. "Do you have any names of anyone or anything we can run checks on?"

"Leo did find out on a quick search that there are two land development companies that have corporate offices in Denver, with satellite offices in Cheyenne, and both have international connections." He took out a slip of paper from his shirt pocket and handed it to Anna. She read the names: Stag's Leap Development, and Triumph Land and Development.

"So, Leo can check them out, right?" she asked.

"Yeah, he could and will. I can, too, but no one reads people like you do. What Leo suggested was that you go to the Annex and be there when the guy shows up. You could watch him and see what you can figure out about him. We're not asking you to make any contact. Just watch and listen. Then we'll meet with you to figure out if it's all a dead end or who we're looking for."

Anna didn't hesitate. "Okay, you do what you need to do, and I'll run a quick check on these companies for my own information before I head over to see who shows up."

"Thanks," Burr said and stood. "Oh, did anything happen at the ranch today?"

A kiss that didn't. She shrugged and said, "I read to Sarge."

"I bet he loved that," Burr said then left.

Anna quickly put in the names that Burr had given her and searched their websites for departments that dealt in large-parcel acquisitions. Both companies had branch offices in Cheyenne, and each had a two-man team overseeing their large-acquisitions division. But when she contacted each company to ask for an appointment to discuss selling her property right away, only Triumph had available agents to meet with her. Stag's Leap wanted to push the meeting to next week or have her meet with an assistant. She was pretty sure their Cheyenne agents weren't in the office—probably because they were here in Eclipse.

Back online, she took a breath, then searched for the name of the person in charge of large acquisitions at Stag's Leap in Denver. Bruno Tyson headed it, but the main team that worked under him in Cheyenne was comprised of William Finnegan and Brody Lanier. She found their photos. Lanier was a pale, slender man with thinning blond hair. Finnegan was overweight, with a round face and unrealistically jet-black hair. Both looked to be in their fifties.

Anna sat back, feeling a degree of excitement at the thought she might be lucky enough to find one of those two men in the basement of the Annex.

She called Burr in and asked him if Leo had done any tracing on the ranch where the drunks were staying. Leo had put in a request for the escrow paperwork for the ranch, but nothing had turned up so far.

Finally, Anna drove to the Annex. When she arrived at the building next to the town hall at four twenty, there were three trucks and one car in the parking area. She went inside and Bob, in his usual dark cardigan and white shirt, looked up from behind his desk.

"Hello, there, Miss Watters." He glanced at the wall clock then back to her. "You've got just over half an hour, but if you need a bit longer, I might be here past five."

"Thanks, Bob, but I shouldn't be too long. I just need to look at some old census records for the Clayton family."

"Section C-15 and C-16," he said and went back to his computer.

She'd hoped that one of the four vehicles in front of the building belonged to Finnegan or Lanier. But when she got down into the climate-controlled basement and the door automatically swooshed shut behind her, she was alone in the cavernous space.

As she crossed to where the census records were kept, she spotted three cardboard cylinders and three thick file folders neatly stacked on the long table near the map section close to the aisle. She quickly crossed to glance at a sticky note on the top file. All it said was "Pulled for W. Finnegan." Bingo! "Nailed it," she whispered.

She looked around and found a spot where she would have full view of the table with the files and also be able to see anyone coming down the stairs. She pulled a binder of the census records from 1900 through 1910 before she settled at the table to wait for the man to show up.

For ten minutes, Anna read about the Claytons, the founding family of the town, but she was aware of every sound from the offices above her. Then she heard voices as the cellar door opened, followed by footsteps on the stairs and the door swooshing shut. She looked along the middle aisle and saw fancy cowboy boots come into sight on the stairs. Then she eyed jeans, a red Western shirt tight across a beer belly and, finally, the face of William Finnegan. She upped his age to early sixties. Then, right behind him, she recognized Brody Lanier dressed all in black.

She was pretty sure the two men had no idea they weren't alone in the basement. So, she sat very quietly with her head down, as if reading the binder, just in case they spotted her.

They went directly to the large table and sat on opposite sides. Despite the hum of the climate-control equipment, she could hear what they were saying without any distortion.

"Should have been able to take these with us," Finnegan said, a slight twang in his voice. "These stupid small-town hicks always have their rules that make it tough on us."

"I'll take shots of the pages we need," Lanier said as he opened the top folder.

"Yeah, yeah," Finnegan muttered as he started to flip through the second folder.

After watching them in action and hearing their chatter for ten minutes, Anna knew that Finnegan was the dominant personality and that Lanier was riding the man's coat-tails. Both men seemed to be, as her dad used to say, full of themselves. She had a sense that Finnegan could have a pretty explosive temper, too, but Lanier would quietly follow Finnegan anywhere he went.

Finnegan sat back finally. "Okay, once I get these cleared and can connect the dots in our favor, we need to meet up with Blanchard and his guy to get it settled. We're close. So freaking close, I can feel it."

Lanier's voice, more nasal than his friend's, had a snarky tone. "Gotta love these good old boys who can barely read and can't count beyond ten without taking off their boots. They won't know what hit them until it's over."

They both laughed roughly at that. "Yeah, we just need to settle with Blanchard, and if it turns out all right, we're finally on our way back to Denver. The big dogs are coming back to town."

They both guffawed, though it left Lanier's pale face flushed. "Yeah, and look out, Triumph Land and Development."

Finnegan passed another sheet to Lanier.

"Capture this and the map shots to have enlarged for the presentation. We just need that last piece of this puzzle and then we're kings."

Anna was relieved that they didn't appear to have found the magical key they needed to challenge ownership, but they apparently weren't going to give up.

Lanier did as he was told then reached for the largest cylinder, opened it and took out rolled maps. He carelessly pushed aside the papers he and Finnegan had been going through then smoothed each map flat. "When we're finished here, we can find that other bar the guy told you about," Finnegan said. "I need something cold and loaded." He flicked the corner of the map. "It's hard work trying to rustle up over six thousand acres of heaven."

Anna had no idea what they had already found to make them so cocky about getting this done. One thing was for sure, Ben had to know, and she'd promised to tell him. She hated to have to do that, but at least he would be on offense instead of defense. The Hope Foundation's attorneys could level Finnegan and Lanier, along with Bruno Tyson.

Anna quietly got to her feet and turned to

slide the census book back on the shelf. She then reached to pick up her leather shoulder bag, intending to just leave. But that didn't happen. Finnegan was staring right at her across the space that separated them. He was smiling, an expression she'd have to describe as smarmy. It made her skin crawl.

"Hey, there, pretty lady," he drawled.

She made a quick decision, willing to speak to the man if she might be able to get more information. So, she braced herself, took a breath and said, "Sorry if I disturbed you."

"Not at all, sweetheart. We're just getting ready to find the closest watering hole and grab a cold one."

Lanier smiled a bit stupidly at her as he added, "We're in a mood to do some precelebration," he said. "You want to come help us?"

Anna couldn't imagine they'd get too many women with those lines. She knew she should walk away, but she had a feeling that she might be able to pick up some pertinent information if she was very careful. She wanted to try. "Thanks, but I'm not in the mood. I came all the way here to look up some records, and they don't have them."

"So, you're not local?"

She made up her responses as she went along. "No, not anymore. I left here as fast as I could."

"Well, well, well," Finnegan said as he stood and sauntered closer to her, his oily smile intact. "Where're you from?"

"Denver," she lied.

"Whoa, babe, me, too. I'm very close to heading back there."

"Good for you. It might cost a fortune to live in Denver, but it's worth it to not be here anymore."

He brushed that aside. "Well, babe, money's not an issue for me. I've got a huge deal going, and I'm going to be up to my neck in gold when I put it all together."

She challenged him, knowing he'd defend his words at all costs. He had an ego the size of the Grand Canyon. "I can't imagine any deal around here that would be that lucrative."

He and his friend were totally ignoring the mess they'd made with the maps and scattered files. "Let me tell you something…" Finnegan stepped nearer and spoke in a low voice as he leaned within inches of her face. "I'm brokering the biggest land deal this area's ever seen."

She could smell stale beer on his breath. That could work for her. "Jackson Hole is where the expensive land is." She hoped she sounded dubious enough for him to explain further.

"Forget about Jackson Hole, babe." He dismissed that with a flip of his hand. "This is better than anything over there."

She pushed him further with a sarcastic, "Okay, sure, go tell that to the rich and famous there."

That got to him, as his ego and alcohol collided to force him to prove himself to her. "Okay, I'll tell you something just because you're pretty—but it's between us. Okay, doll?"

She nodded, thankful he'd stopped calling her "babe," and waited for him to speak again.

"There's land up north of here, a huge parcel, and it's just about the best thing I've ever seen. The owner's sitting on a pure gold mine. If it's done right, subdivided perfectly, it will be the go-to place for a lot of very rich people and it'll knock Jackson Hole right off the map."

Finnegan was so predictable; he was making it almost too easy for her. "Why would anyone around here want to sell a gold mine like that?"

He laughed. "The guy who's sitting on it won't have a choice but to sell it when we're done. Besides, he's an old coot, been there for years, and never did anything with it except use it for a kid care thing. What a fool to waste all that land on some snot-faced brats."

Anna barely restrained the honest urge to slap the man across his smug face. But she had to ask one important question. "How can you force him to let go of his own land?"

"By making it useless to him but gold for us, and we're getting close to figuring it all out." He exhaled, and she barely stopped a grimace at the lingering smell of his breath. "We're close. Real close."

She was finished. "I need to go," she said, ready to get out of there and into fresh air.

Finnegan reached for her, and she quickly evaded his hand. "Hey, come on, babe," he said. "We're connecting."

Babe again. She hated that. Out of his reach, she got some satisfaction saying, "Yeah, but I've got to get back to my snot-faced brats."

He looked stunned. "You got kids?"

She pulled up a lie that she enjoyed handing to him. "Five, all boys, and I'm here trying to hunt their daddy down. Well, at least the daddy of two of them. I'm not sure about the other three, never have been. But kids need a daddy."

That stopped Finnegan in his tracks. "Well, good luck with that. We gotta go," he said and turned away, done with her. Lanier was frowning as he stood to follow Finnegan to the stairs.

They left their mess behind, so Anna crossed to sort through the papers and put them neatly back in the folders before she looked down at the plot maps for Eclipse Ridge Ranch. They hadn't opened the other cylinders.

# *CHAPTER TWELVE*

ONCE ANNA WAS out in her truck and driving away from the Annex, she called Burr at the office. "I'm on my way back."

He met up with her when she stepped into the reception area and then followed her into her office. As soon as they were both seated, Anna quickly went over what had happened.

When she finished, Burr was smiling. "You never cease to amaze me."

"Well, you can tell Leo that the enemy is known, but that's just the tip of the iceberg. Do you know someone named Blanchard around this area?"

"No, but I'll ask Leo."

"Well, it seems Blanchard has a part in what they're doing with someone they referred to as 'his guy.' From the way Finnegan was talking, they don't quite have a clear idea of what they need to actually challenge Sarge for the land. But if something's there to find, they *will* find it sooner or later. They aren't going to walk away empty-handed."

The landline rang and Burr took the call. "Hey, Leo, just talking about you. Anna's back and it appears we've found the developers." He repeated what she'd told him, then put Leo on speaker and asked, "Hey, do you know anyone named Blanchard around here?"

"Anna, you hit pay dirt," Leo said. "Blanchard is the name on the deed for the place those two are staying—James Kawani Blanchard. I went over the sales papers and deed, and do you want to know who walked that all through the county to get it closed fast without any hitches?"

She knew she'd probably spoil his surprise. "Norman Good."

"Boy, you're dead right."

"I don't suppose you can prove any wrongdoing on his part?" Burr asked.

"Not sure, but if money changed hands instead of just helping a wealthy man with his land purchase, it could trip Norman Good up. I'll pull the rest of the records on the purchase, then hand it over to an attorney I've worked with at the county seat. He's very discreet. He'll keep it quiet until we want it known."

When they hung up, the three had agreed to let things settle over the weekend then call Ben on Monday to arrange a meeting with him and the others at the ranch, either in person or on a conference call.

Anna felt so good. She'd been right. But there was no fist bump yet, because the real problem with the land, if there was one, could rear its ugly head anytime. They still had to protect the land at all costs.

Burr stood and grinned at her. "Great work, Anna, plain great work." He patted her on her shoulder. "I'm so proud of you."

He had no idea what that last sentence meant to her.

When Anna finally went back to the B and B, night had fallen, and she was surprised to find Ben leaning against the fender of his old truck, which was parked beside the carriage house steps. She'd never get used to the way her heart did its own thing when Ben smiled at her as she pulled to a stop by him. He straightened as she got out and she noticed he was holding the files she'd walked away without taking home earlier because he'd almost kissed her.

"You forgot these on the bench when you left," he said and reached around her to lay them on the hood of her truck. "I thought you might need them."

With his Stetson on and the night falling, she couldn't see his eyes. "Thanks, but you didn't have to bring them all this way."

"I didn't have to, but I did."

She wasn't certain what to say or do next. She just kind of hoped he wouldn't leave right away. "How's Sarge?"

"More settled. He told me all about a beautiful lady who read to him."

"He kept his eyes shut, so he probably meant Julia," she said.

"He knew you weren't Julia."

She wished she didn't blush so easily. "I enjoyed reading to him."

"Don't get lost in your studies over the weekend." Ben took a half a step toward her and his voice was low. "The whole idea of those two days is to do something fun or to take it easy."

She shrugged. "I'll have to think on that when I'm not up to my neck in work."

"Hopefully, you'll be able to figure it out soon."

She shook her head. "You sound like my mother."

"A wise woman. You should listen to her," he said, moving nearer. "I had to find out something from you that has been bothering me, and I want the truth."

Her face warmed. "Of course."

"If you don't want to be around me anymore, just tell me. Please."

"I don't understand," she said, hearing some unsteadiness in her voice.

"I just felt…the call I made to you before I left, you sounded as if you wanted to…" He shrugged. "You were backing up."

She felt her heart hitch. "Me, no, I thought…" She shook her head. "No, that wasn't the case. I just got confused."

He hesitated before framing her face with the heat of his hands, and kissed her. It wasn't fleeting or hesitant, but slow and warm, and she raised her arms to encircle his neck and get even closer to him. Another romantic notion she had never believed was real: the one about a kiss shaking someone's world. Yet everything shifted in her world to a new reality for her life at that moment.

Ben slowly eased away, his gaze on her as she opened her eyes. "That's why I brought the files all this way," he whispered. "I had to know, and I've waited too long to do what I should have done a week ago at the stables." He smiled. "But it was worth the wait." He stroked her cheek with his thumb then drew back. "Sleep well," he murmured as he turned and got into his truck.

Anna didn't move as she watched him leave. When he pulled onto the street and turned out of sight, she touched her tongue to her lips. Today had been strange, maddening, crazy, exciting, and had just ended wonderfully. Maybe she was starting to understand what it might feel like to fall in love.

ANNA WOKE EARLY on Saturday, and her first thought was about Ben and the kiss. A weight was off her shoulders knowing she'd been so wrong about things before he'd left for Cody. In the thin light of dawn creeping into her room, she looked at the ranch files sitting on a chair by the bed. She'd tried to go through them last night but had been so distracted by what happened with Ben, she'd given up. She'd settled for lying in bed and looking out the French doors at the moon and the stars in the night sky. Mostly, she'd thought about Ben coming all the way into town to kiss her.

The colors of dawn were sweeping across the early-morning sky, and she was restless. She glanced at her cell phone on the nightstand, which was flashing with a message that had come in late last night. It was from Burr.

Leo checking on Stag and Blanchard. We'll meet with Ben on Monday and hand it over to his team. Take it easy.

She sank back in the pillows and thought about what Ben had said. He was right. At least for a few hours, she'd have fun. She quickly got out of bed to dress in her ever-present jeans, a pink cabled sweater and her riding boots. She caught her hair up in a high ponytail, put on her jacket and stepped outside into the early-morning chill to head to her truck.

By the time she drove through the ranch gates and onto the service road leading to the stables, Anna didn't feel a bit guilty that she wasn't thinking about work or studying for the bar exam, just about riding in the clear morning. The only thing that would make it better would be to have Ben there with her.

Dwight was in the training ring working a small pinto. He waved to Anna as she got out of her truck and walked over to the gate. "Top of the mornin' to you," he said as he led the pinto toward her. "Looking for Punch?"

"Yes. I miss him."

"He missed you yesterday," the man said as he reached the gate.

Anna pulled back the barrier for him so he could exit with the small horse and then she followed him into the barn. "Is Ben already out this morning?" she asked as she headed to Punch's stall.

"Nope. Ain't seen him. Do you need help?" Dwight asked when he secured the pinto's reins to one of the grooming rings on the center post.

"Thanks, but you taught me well. I can get Punch ready."

"All right. Call if you need me," he said as he headed back outside.

She was up in the saddle and riding out the open rear doors of the stable in just under fifteen minutes. "I'm getting good at this," she said to the horse as she nudged him toward the north and the open grazing land.

When she reached the bladed road that ran to the original entrance to the ranch, she lifted her face to the sky. The world was pretty much perfect in that moment. The horse, the ride, the morning breaking—even the chill wasn't too bad. But it was the memory of the kiss last night that made her smile.

In the distance, she could see the cleared areas around the mess hall and bunkhouse, the two long buildings made of weathered logs topped with green-metal roofing. She still hadn't gone inside, but she wanted to, so she headed toward them. She stopped at the bunkhouse where the campers would spend their first night at camp.

She dropped the horse's reins, then climbed four steps onto the square deck and tried the door handle. The door swung back.

The long room ahead of her held numerous beds along each wall, all made up with brightly colored blankets and sheets. The words *Welcome to Hope* hung in huge wooden letters in primary colors on the wall in a sitting area with beanbag and canvas chairs near the entry.

"It looks good, doesn't it?"

Anna jumped and spun around to find Ben standing at the bottom of the front steps smiling up at her. "Wow, you scared me," she said breathlessly. Traveler was hitched to a post near Punch, yet she hadn't heard the horse or the man approach.

Ben came up the steps in two long strides. "Sorry," he said, still smiling. "So, what do you think of what's been done in there?"

"It's great. Love that sign on the wall."

"It's come a long way from the old bunkhouse."

His eyes held hers, shadowed from the morning sun slightly by the brim of his hat. His denim jacket was undone, and she kind of liked the vaguest suggestion of a beard shadowing his jaw.

"Dwight said you were out riding," he said. "I thought you were going to study over the weekend."

"No. I decided to listen to someone who said I should learn to have fun on the weekends. The closest I could come to fun today was a ride."

"So, is it fun?"

She definitely thought it was fun now that

he was there, but she wouldn't say that. "Yes, it is. Punch is fun to ride, and this ranch is just a great place to wander around. I actually think I'm learning to loosen up a bit."

"You're a fast learner," Ben said and came up to where she stood. "Are you heading back?"

"Not yet. I'm enjoying the scenery and the morning."

"Can I enjoy it with you?" he asked.

"Of course," she said, thankful she didn't have to ask him to stay for a while.

He crossed, sat on the wooden bench by the door and gave her a crooked smile. "Please, sit down."

She closed the door before she settled beside him and looked out at the view. It was breathtaking. The land rolled away toward the stables and hay barn in one direction and the main house in the other, but all were partially hidden by stands of trees. From where they sat, they could see over the lower trees and far away into the distance. "It's stunning," she said.

"Yes, it is," Ben murmured.

When she glanced at him, he seemed so at ease that she was thankful Burr and Leo had asked her to keep quiet about Finnegan and company until Monday. There would be enough time to worry about the attempted land grab then.

BEN HAD GONE down to the stables to try to get away from the house while he had a chance. He'd needed to think, to figure things out, and with Sarge finally calmed down and resting, he'd intended to go on a short ride. Then he'd seen Anna's truck by the stables, and Dwight had told him she'd left not more than ten minutes earlier, heading north.

Finding her in the doorway to the bunkhouse had made his day a whole lot better. She seemed to have that effect on him more often than not.

"You're so lucky to live out here," she said as she scanned the view.

"Believe me, I know." He didn't take his eyes off her. She was beautiful and smart, sexy when she had no idea she was, and she was so funny. At some point after the kiss, he had admitted to himself that he really liked her, and not in the casual way he'd been telling himself he did. With the other women he'd dated, he'd always had his exit strategy in place before he'd started anything, because it was a given that he would walk away sooner or later. A week, a month tops, and he'd be gone.

But with Anna, he kept thinking he might be able to justify staying longer than usual. For now, she was here, and he was here. It was that simple. And it plain amazed him how being close to her affected him.

"It has everything anyone could want," she murmured as she finally glanced at him.

Her eyes seemed bluer the way they had been at the stable after the wedding. If she stayed in Eclipse, he would do what he'd thought about earlier—coming back for Sarge—but he would also make time to be with her. "Yes, it does, doesn't it?"

She sighed softly. "The longer I'm here, I find more and more things that I didn't know I even wanted in my life."

Her words stunned him. She was like that to him; the longer he was with her, the more he found out about her, the more he realized he wanted more from her.

"This land is like forever. You could go away and in ten years," she said, "you could come back to this spot and it'll still be here.

The trees will be bigger, the stream could be dry, but you know once the water's there, it'll start humming again." Anna startled him asking a direct question without turning to him. "Where do you see yourself in ten years?"

He'd been taking life a day at a time both professionally and personally for what seemed like forever. As long as Sarge was here, he knew he'd be at the ranch. But after that, he'd go off into the world of contracts on his own. "Here, for sure while I'm needed, then I'll be here between contracts. I'll definitely be here for all the holidays and when the camp's open in the summers."

"I could have told you that you'd be here," Anna said as she looked at him with that soft smile he liked.

"I'm that easy to read?"

"Sometimes," she said. "Thank you for bringing the files last night."

He saw the slight flush to her skin. "I told you, I wanted to bring them." He reached for her hand and held it, liking the way she entwined her slender fingers with his. He also didn't want her to get on Punch and ride away too soon.

With their hands resting on his thigh, she

seemed to study him, as if trying to figure out what he was doing. Then she sighed and, for the first time in his life, Ben thought he just might understand what really caring for a woman felt like. Then again, he didn't know what anything was supposed to feel like in any kind of relationship. He just played each one by ear. All he knew was that he didn't want to let go of her hand right then.

"Where do you see yourself in ten years?" he asked. He thought her hand tightened slightly in his for a moment but wasn't certain.

"I hope I'll be in Eclipse working with Burr or watching him enjoy his retirement. He's become very important to me, like a second dad. I never expected that to happen, but I'm so glad it did."

He'd never expected to meet someone like Anna, but he was glad he had. "Where do you see yourself personally?"

"Well, I've had enough of nothing in my personal life, and you know about my lack of fun. I don't want that to be my future."

"What do you want?" Ben murmured.

The color was back in her cheeks. "I just want to be happy, wherever I am."

"What would make you happy?"

She shrugged. "Being in Eclipse, working with Burr and, don't laugh, having a happily-ever-after life."

He didn't laugh. "Not many people ever get their happily-ever-after."

"You don't think you will?"

"I'm not looking for it," he admitted.

"Why not?" she asked.

"Personally, with all my traveling, I don't have the time to build up a happy-ever-after scenario, and I'm keeping a promise to myself. That's important to me."

"That seems kind of sad, doesn't it?"

He didn't want to have this talk anymore. Not here. Not with Anna. Not now. "Life is what it is. You adjust and keep going. You don't look for something that might never happen."

She was silent then looked at him. "Do you really believe that?"

He shrugged. "Yes, I do."

"I've told you that I know very little about relationships, but it seems that having someone in your life like Sarge and Maggie did, or my parents did, would be wonderful. You'd have someone always there, someone always smiling when they see you come back after you've been gone. That sounds like happy-ever-after to me."

Anna certainly made him smile whenever he saw her appear. The moment at the wedding when he'd looked up and she'd been there had absolutely caught him off guard. "I'm sure you've had more than a few men smile when they saw you coming." He let go of her hand to softly brush her cheek with his fingertips. He felt her quiver faintly at the contact. "Unless you've been around men who are blind or stupid."

He expected a smile, but it didn't happen. "Maybe I was the stupid one," she said in a whisper.

"No, never," he breathed and took off his hat. He didn't want to talk about happily-ever-afters. He didn't want to talk any more about his life, which felt very empty most of the time. He leaned around her to set his hat on the bench and, as he drew back, he inhaled her warmth and that soft scent that seemed to be part of her.

Ben hesitated. He wasn't alone at the moment, and he didn't want to be. He saw something in her eyes, something that echoed in him. He leaned closer, brushed his thumb gently across her bottom lip and knew what he wanted.

His mouth met her softy parted lips and the contact felt like the culmination of what he'd felt start at the wedding. Now it was deepening into an intense longing for this woman that almost robbed him of his ability to breathe.

He started to ease back, to try to figure out what was happening, and he would have, if Anna hadn't shifted closer to him. Her lips brushed across his cheek as she buried her face in his neck, her warmth everywhere, and he knew that he'd never felt like this with anyone before. It excited him and confused him at the same time. He felt her heat around him, and the sweetness of her scent seemed to permeate everything. Their dance had been a mere hint at how she could affect him.

Her breaths sped up and all he knew was that he wanted her like this, in his arms, pushing back the world, letting him into a place he'd never even known existed before Anna had come into his life. He wanted time to stop, to keep her right there forever.

When he felt her tremble against him, he

pulled back and framed her face with his hands. Her lips were parted, her eyes slowly opening, and she whispered unsteadily, "I don't... I just..." Her tongue touched her lips as she breathed, a blush flooding her cheeks.

Ben watched uncertainty grow in her eyes, maybe confusion. "Maybe I'm moving too fast?"

"No—I mean, I don't think so. But I..." She closed her eyes tightly, exhaled and finally looked at him again. "I don't know. I just don't know, Ben."

She almost looked afraid now, and something hit him so hard he could barely move. She'd said she'd never had a relationship before. *Never.* He thought she'd meant she'd never had a serious relationship, one that could tie her down or complicate her life. It took him until that moment to make sense out of what she'd revealed bit by bit to him before.

He couldn't move, his hands still on the warm silkiness of her cheeks. When the truth hit him, he felt as if he was falling into emptiness. But one thing he'd learned in foster care was to never deny the truth. Pushing it away didn't make it any less real or any less painful. Anna's truth about being inexperienced in casual dating was as real as it got for him.

"Ben, I'm sorry," she breathed.

No, he was sorry, sorrier than he'd ever felt in his life. He was lost again yet couldn't break their contact. Not yet, because he knew that when he did, he'd never be this close to her again.

"You didn't do anything wrong," he managed to get out. "I pushed things, and I should have known you..." He swallowed. "You made it clear that you didn't have a messy romantic background." Her color deepened even more. "I'm the one who's sorry."

He knew she was looking for her happily-ever-after, and she deserved it. But he was the last person who could ever give it to her. No justifications could change him. He wouldn't let himself go any further. Oddly, he realized his reason for walking away went beyond his promise to himself. Another truth exploded in him. He simply cared far too much for Anna to mess up her life and hurt her.

"It's okay. It really is," she whispered unsteadily.

Nothing was okay, but he kept that to himself and lied. "I need to get back to the house," he said, making himself break their connection and stand to put some distance between them. "I told them I was just going on a short ride to think, and Julia needs me there."

"Oh…sure. Okay, yes…" she said without much conviction. "I—I should get back to studying."

"No, you keep riding. It's a beautiful day," he said as he looked up at the sweep of deep blue sky above them. He had to think, to try to adjust to what had just happened, but he didn't know how he would. He reached for his Stetson. As he put it on, all he knew for sure was that he wouldn't hurt Anna. Ever. "Julia needs to get some rest."

When she looked up at him, the confusion was still there, and he felt his heart drop. He watched her get to her feet and brush nervously at the wisps of hair that had escaped her ponytail. He didn't miss the unsteadiness in her hand as he turned away to leave. But she stopped him.

"Ben, wait. I'll ride back with you."

He glanced at her. "What about your fun?"

"I'm working on it," she said softly. "Believe it or not, I'm learning. Slowly but surely."

He'd read her so wrong, through his own

selfish prism. She was way out of his league, and he'd tried to build an emotional wall for his own protection. He'd been able to do that so easily as child, but now he almost couldn't. He shrugged, trying to act casual. "It's up to you."

She passed him, went down the steps and over to Punch. Picking up his reins, she hesitated then looped them around the saddle horn before she turned back to Ben, who was standing beside Traveler.

"What's really wrong?" she asked, her eyes narrowed as if she were having trouble even looking at him. "It can't be my inexperience. I mean, I never thought that was going to be a problem with anyone." She went right for the bottom line. "What really happened just now?"

He tried to brush her off. "You know, some things just can't work out."

She shook her head. "What does that mean?" She patted Punch on his rump as she took a step closer to Ben. When she moved, Punch jerked back and, before Ben knew what the horse was going to do, took off to the west.

"Punch! Punch!" Anna called, but he kept

going until he was around a curve in the road and out of sight. She turned to Ben, apparently as shocked as he was at the horse's running away. "I didn't do anything, did I?"

"You gave him a cue someway, I guess. He's probably halfway back to the stables by now."

"I hope so," she said on a sigh. "Can I hitch a ride back?"

There was no way he could ride all the way back to the stables with her behind him, holding on to him. He hesitated, about to tell her to take Traveler, give him to Dwight to trail him back so they could look for Punch. But he took too long and, instead of uncertainty in her eyes, there was anger.

"Forget it. I said I'd walk before, and I can. I like walking." And with that she started off to the south.

He hurried after her, touching her shoulder to stop her. "I'll walk."

"No thanks," she said and took off again.

"Whoa." Ben grabbed her upper arm to stop her before she'd taken a second step. "I'm sorry this all happened. I really am. And you can ride back." He'd stopped her by a huge log that had fallen to the ground a long time ago.

She pulled free of his hold, then spun around on him. "I'll walk."

He blew out a breath, knowing he had to be honest with Anna. Right then, he was quite certain she thought he was a total jerk. He probably was, but something in him wouldn't let her go without her understanding why he was doing what he had to do.

He motioned to the weathered log. "Sit down, and I'll tell you a truth that can't be changed."

She frowned at him, then silently moved to sink down onto the massive trunk of the fallen tree. Clasping her hands together, she stared down at them in her lap. When she kept silent, he sat beside her, making sure there was just enough space between them so he didn't inhale her soft scent each time he took a breath.

This was going to be harder than he'd thought it would be. But he'd do it.

ANNA SAT VERY STILL, closed her eyes, and wasn't at all sure she wanted an unchangeable truth about Ben. But she'd listen, then she'd leave and get back to being the person she'd been before he'd walked into her life.

"You're great. Really, really great," he began. "I apologize for letting things go this far."

She could barely make herself ask, "What do you mean?"

"I told you before that my life's not stable. There's travel, business, travel, more business. I'm not going to change. After Sarge…" He swallowed hard. "When he doesn't need me anymore, I'll get contracts again and go anywhere they need me. I think it's better for both of us if we just let whatever this is go."

"So, it's just, 'Oops, sorry, didn't mean that'?"

"No, that's not it."

"Then why did you…?" She couldn't finish the question. "I mean…you seemed to like me. I liked you and then you just stopped." Frustration all but choked her. "Why even start anything?"

"I thought…you know, whatever we could have would be like the other times in my life. But things could get complicated and it would never have worked."

Her jaw clenched as she finally looked at Ben. "How could you know that?"

He sat forward, his hands pressed to his knees, his eyes downcast again as he answered her. "Because you'll want a happily-ever-after sooner or later."

She blinked at that. "What? Yes, of course I want that sooner or later."

His dark eyes met hers as he straightened and she could see the tension in them as he asked, "What would that involve besides someone smiling when you show up?"

She shrugged. "I don't know. Being where I want to be, with someone I love who could love me."

"You wouldn't want anything more than that?"

She blew out a breath. "Okay, I want cats, dogs, more horses and a ranch where my kids could ride all day if they wanted to. What difference does that make?"

"I'm going to be blunt."

"Please do be blunt," she said with heavy sarcasm.

She saw him flinch at her tone of voice, and she hated that, but kept silent until he said, "I don't want kids. That's part of my promise to myself. I'll never bring a child like I was into this world."

Anna was stunned. The world started to tip on its axis, and she knew she was going to fall off. "What? Y-you… How can you not want kids?" That made no sense to her.

"I love kids. Everything I do is for kids. But I told you about my miserable early life and my biological parents. Their marriage produced a kid who hurt people just because he could, who took what he wanted, no matter who had it, and hated good people with a viciousness that was unreal."

"I know, you told me, but—"

"Anna." He cut her off, his eyes darkly intense, his voice rough. "I will never bring a child into this world. You were right. I'm breaking that cycle. I promised myself a long time ago, no marriage, no kids. I'd just concentrate on helping the lost kids already in the system."

His words made her feel sick to her stomach. "Ben, you are who you are now, not what your parents were."

"I know my own truth, Anna." He exhaled on a hissing breath. "I can't take a chance of a kid that damaged coming into the world because of me. So, I promised myself I'd never get that far with anyone."

She was clasping her hands together so tightly they ached. Whether he wanted her or not, she hurt for the box he'd pushed himself into. He was wrong, so wrong, and he couldn't see it. "Ben, you can't believe that."

"I do," he bit out. "I'm telling you the truth, the whole truth. I can't—and won't—draw you into my life, then leave you broken when it all falls apart."

"No, the truth is that all of that stopped for you when you got here, when you had Sarge and Maggie caring about you, seeing who you were deep inside, pushing you to find the best in yourself. And you've found that by helping kids heading for that cliff you were aiming at. Sarge and Maggie believed in you, and if they truly had a gift, it was in being able to see the value of the child behind the hurt and anger and fear."

He buried his face in his hands as he hunched forward, his elbows on his knees. She saw his shoulders move with each rough breath he took, and her heart ached for him. "Please, Ben. Don't do this. You're everything they thought you could be and so much more."

He slowly took off his hat and held it by the brim with both hands. Then he met her eyes and she saw a deep sadness there. "You needed to know. It's done. I wish for you to find your happy-ever-after."

Her hands almost felt numb now. "So, you've decided what's best for me? That's what this was all about. If I was willing to have a—what?—an affair with you then smile and walk away in a week or a month, that would have been all you asked to stick around?"

His expression tightened at her words, and he simply shrugged it all away.

Anna couldn't get any words out. She'd always dreamed of meeting that one person, a forever person meant for her. She wanted that. Ben was right, but she never thought she'd finally fall in love with someone who didn't see forever ahead of them. Love. Her stomach churned. She loved him, and there was no future for them at all.

Silently, Ben stood and looked down at her, his hands crushing the brim of his hat. It gave her no pleasure to see unhappiness in his eyes. "Forget about me, Anna."

She stood to face him and he took a step back to avoid any contact. "I wish I could," she whispered.

"You have to. You'll find someone good

and get into a solid happily-ever-after relationship."

She'd had enough and seethed. "Stop it. I don't need your platitudes. That's pathetic. I'm not desperate. I just... I read you all wrong." She bit her lip. "Never mind."

"I just want you to have whatever it takes for you to be happy."

"You don't have a clue what would make me happy, Ben, not a clue. So, I'll tell you a blunt truth about me. Until right now, I thought having you would make me happy." She'd said it and there was no taking it back. She didn't want to. "That's all I've wanted since you walked into Burr's office to meet me that first day."

She didn't wait for his response but turned away, not about to beg for what he'd never give her. She headed off to the south, needing distance from Ben and the horrible pain she felt right then. But Ben was right there beside her.

"Are you okay?" he asked.

She bit her bottom lip again, shook her head and kept walking.

"Anna," Ben said as he kept pace with her. "You ride Traveler back, and I'll walk." She kept her eyes down and didn't miss a step. "Come on," he said. "It's a long way back. Be reasonable."

That stopped her dead, and she turned to look right at him. "Me be reasonable? You're right, I'm being unreasonable. Me, Anna Watters. I've been jumping so far out of my comfort zone since I came here that I finally did a face-plant."

"I'm sorry," he murmured. "But I'm in this alone."

She cocked her head to one side. "I think that's the saddest thing I've ever heard," she said and started off again.

When she dared to look back, Ben was standing, watching her, then he turned and went to where he'd left Traveler. Thankfully, he rode off to the west and the high country.

She kept going, feeling sick, remembering thinking that Ben was charming. Now she didn't know much about him, except that he was out of her life. She really had to get back to the person she had been before coming here and meeting Ben. She'd been almost destructively impulsive and stupid, knowing why she'd come to Eclipse but veering away from that purpose to get tangled up with a man she'd never have. She wouldn't make that mistake again. As soon as she knew Punch was safe, she'd find a place to board the horse. Then she'd never have to come back to the ranch again.

DWIGHT WAS BRUSHING Punch when she stepped into the stables, then pointed out that she should never loop the reins over the saddle horn. "You gave him the freedom to do what he wanted to," the man explained before she headed to her truck. As soon as she drove out the gates at the county road, the tears came.

But by the time she pulled up in front of the office, she was simply numb. Burr wasn't there so she went in to distract herself with studying. She couldn't keep thinking what she was thinking. She had to focus on preparing for Monday when she'd have to see Ben one last time.

When Anna finally headed back to the B and B around five o'clock, she went up to her room and didn't leave it for the rest of the weekend.

On Sunday evening, she spotted the two ranch files Ben had brought for her before her world had fallen apart. She had barely looked at them, and she couldn't make herself read them now. So she stacked the two files on the small bench by the door and decided to ignore them until it was time to return them to the ranch.

Just before midnight on Sunday, Anna was in the poster bed staring out the French doors at a three-quarter moon hanging high above in the star-scattered night sky. She sank back into the pillows piled against the headboard and waited for dawn, not expecting to sleep at all. But the next thing she knew, she was waking up and the clock by her bed read six o'clock.

Anna looked around the room and saw a whole lot of nothing. She wanted out of there. She dressed in jeans and a plain hunter-green flannel shirt, then put on her boots. She twisted her hair into a low knot before grabbing her new jacket, phone and keys, and stepping out the door.

# CHAPTER THIRTEEN

ANNA CRUISED THROUGH town in the truck without seeing another car in either direction. Everything was locked up tight. Once she was at the office and inside, she started fresh coffee, then sat in front of her computer, ready to do some studying to divert her attention.

But instead of Wyoming criminal law essays coming up on her monitor, the plot map that showed the Eclipse Ridge Ranch parcel with the boundaries defined took center stage.

She moved her mouse to close the file, but something made her hesitate. Something seemed off, and she couldn't put her finger on it.

She stared at the map, the same one she'd looked at after Finnegan and Lanier had left it open on the table in the Annex basement. She leaned closer to the monitor, noticed a tag on the bottom of the map and zoomed in to read it. The total acreage for the Eclipse Ridge Ranch was printed out: *5,711.2 acres.*

Burr and Ben had both said the ranch was over six thousand acres. Maybe Ben had given a generous rounding off, but she didn't think Burr would do that. He was a stickler for exact figures.

She pulled up another map that showed the ranch again, but with tags on the land bordering the ranch and the ranch's acreage. The tag for Eclipse was faded and positioned at a jagged boundary by the section on the northwest upper corner. She leaned in closer to the monitor, trying to read the tag, and saw that it noted 706.7 acres. That didn't make any sense. She'd been assuming that was part of the main ranch land, not a separate entity.

Anna studied it a little more and then looked up the plot number online at the county site and found it was a landlocked section of government-protected property. She checked and double-checked, but everything she found backed that up.

She printed out the first map and followed the boundary with a red pen to define it. When she'd finished, she knew that the smaller section of land had unbelievably irregular boundaries that looked as if it held most of the land area where the camp was being laid out. She found the gorge and lake, and all the water spots and windmills Ben had pointed out to her on one of their rides.

She went onto the county site again, traced the tract number and saw that it had never been approved for private use going back as far as she could find. She sat back in her chair, feeling nauseous. She thought she'd found what Finnegan and Lanier had been hunting for. If she was right, it broke her heart.

"Hey," Burr said, and Anna almost jumped out of her chair.

When she turned, he was in the doorway just taking off his jacket. "I came in early, but you..." He frowned as he stepped into her office. "Hey, what's wrong?"

She shrugged, unable to think of what to say. She finally motioned to the monitor. "I think I found the missing piece of the puzzle that Finnegan and Lanier are looking for."

Burr stared at her, then pulled a chair over and sat down hard on it. "What are you talking about?"

Anna tried to explain it to him, a simple error on her part, the error of not seeing

something she should have. When she finished, the lines bracketing Burr's eyes and
mouth seemed deeper. "Th-that's… That's…"
He couldn't finish.

She took a tight breath. "I don't think it's
their land, Burr. It might never have been.
That whole section, seven hundred plus acres,
it's the core of the campsites. Worse yet, in
the paperwork, it shows six dried wells on
the legitimate ranchland. Ben showed me that
they'd been sealed. With those dry, almost
all their present water supply is coming from
that small parcel and it's the lifeblood of the
ranch."

Burr murmured to himself. "I honestly
never thought something this damaging
would come up."

"The rest of the land is Sarge's to keep forever, but if the water goes, the camping sites
are gone, and it's going to destroy the camp
and any chance of even working that land.
Even if they figure out how to do it on what's
left of the ranch, Sarge will never understand
it by the time they are able to open the camp.
Worse yet, this is the map that Finnegan and
Lanier were looking at and taking pictures of
for some presentation.

"What do we do if it's not their land?" she asked Burr, desperate for him to have an answer that could work.

"We show Leo and explain it to him. Then we get this all to Ben and the others. Let me call Leo. I'll be right back."

She sat there in the silence, waiting.

When Burr returned, he looked even grimmer than when he'd left. "Leo believes it's federal land, and it's lost to the ranch. So is the water supply. He's checking something and going to call me back so we can get a meeting right away."

She wanted to forget she ever saw the flaw on the map, but she knew what her dad would say if he was there with her. *The truth hurts but lies destroy.* He was right, and she knew it. "The family needs to know."

The landline rang and Burr grabbed it. "Yes, okay," he said. "Nine o'clock. Got it." When he hung up, he looked shaken. "Leo confirmed the small acreage with an engineer he trusts. It's government land. He's coming right over and wants to get to the ranch by nine."

"I shouldn't have missed it, Burr. I was distracted, not focusing enough." She exhaled roughly. "Stupid," she muttered.

"You found it, that's what counts. If we're lucky, Ben and the others will be on the offense, not the defense."

He was right and, after all, she had made a promise to Ben. "I'll call to let Ben know we're coming."

When Burr stepped out, Anna picked up her cell and put in the call.

Ben's cell phone rang twice before she heard his voice. "Anna?"

She hated the unsteadiness in her voice when she said, "I need to talk to you."

"Why?"

She almost flinched at the sound of the single word. "I told you I'd let you know right away if I found anything."

There was dead silence on the line then she heard Ben suck in air. "How bad is it?"

"We'll be at the ranch at nine," she said, hit End and called out to Burr. When he came into her office, she said, "I called Ben."

"Leo's on his way," he said as he moved closer to her chair.

She looked up at him. "What a mess," she whispered.

Burr crouched in front of her. "Don't be so hard on yourself. This is all about protecting Sarge and his legacy, the camp. You've done a very good thing to find that."

"I hope so," she said.

Burr frowned. "I know this is terrible news, but I thought you'd be feeling good about cutting off Finnegan and Lanier at the pass."

"I am," she said with only partial truth. She hated what was ahead, but maybe it would be a form of closure that she needed.

BEN STOOD ON the top step of the porch at nine o'clock, watching the driveway. Finally, Burr's huge truck come into view as it hit the rise and Ben stayed very still as it slowed to park at the foot of the steps. Anna's truck pulled in behind it.

Burr stepped out of the driver's side and the mayor exited from the passenger's side. Burr nodded to Ben, reached into the truck and took out a long tube and a large briefcase.

The lawyer and Leo mounted the stairs and stepped up to him. Burr hesitated then said, "Sorry about this, but you'll need to get it to the attorneys at the Foundation."

Ben's chest felt tight. "It's serious?"

"Very," Burr said as he and Leo walked toward the open door to enter the house.

Ben turned and Anna was there. Eyes down, she approached the steps, but then stopped and looked up at him. He'd missed her and it had only been a couple of days. She was wearing that useless suede jacket and faded jeans. She hesitated, as if thinking of turning around and leaving, then finally took the steps slowly up to face him. She looked tired and sad. "I'm so sorry," she murmured before going into the house.

The meeting was at the large dining table. Burr, Leo and Anna on one side, Ben alone on the other. Neither Jake nor Seth could be reached.

Burr explained what they'd found, showed Ben the map and the paperwork for taxes on the small parcel, and then sat back. "I think we need to get on a conference call with Seattle as soon as possible."

Ben felt numb and avoided looking at Anna, because when he did, it hurt too much. The whole thing with the ranch hurt, too much. It wasn't until Burr and Leo stood to go visit with Sarge for a few minutes that Ben finally spoke directly to her.

"So, it's really bad, with the water and all. I guess I owe you for offering to look into things here."

She blinked and he noticed that her eyes were more gray than blue. "I'm sorry. I didn't expect to actually find anything major, just the crossed t's and the dotted i's. Little things. But…" She bit her lip. "Norman B. Good isn't as good as he thought he was. He might even have taken bribes to grease the wheels for the purchase of the ranch south of town. But Finnegan and Lanier are the enemy. Hateful people."

He was taken back by that statement. "You've met them?"

"Yes, sort of, when they were checking out the maps and tax records for the ranch at the Annex."

"You really did get involved."

She shifted nervously in her chair and he was pretty sure she wanted to be anywhere but there with him. "You know, Burr and Leo don't need me for that call to Seattle." She stood. "Tell Burr that I'll go back and hold the fort down at the office while he does what he needs to do out here."

Ben got to his feet as she turned to leave. "Anna?"

She glanced across the table at him. "I don't know how to thank you for...for doing what you did. At least the attorneys can get going on fighting for the land."

"Yes, they can," she said. "Again, I'm so sorry." With that she walked across the great room and into the foyer. The sound of the door opening and then closing ended everything.

WHEN BURR CAME back to the office after the trip to the ranch, he didn't mention Ben, just said that the family hoped the town wouldn't find out until they understood what was going to happen. But three days later, the small-town gossip chain proved to be mighty when put into action. Everyone seemed to know everything about the ranch being in jeopardy.

When the landline rang, Anna reached for it, but Burr got to it first. "Law Offices of Addison and Watters. Burr speaking." He listened then said, "Of course, I understand." He listened some more. "No, I can't comment on it." He listened again then responded, "Yes, absolutely, I will."

He hung up and looked at Anna. "Well, that was Ray Barnes. He runs Eclipse Gems & Stars down by Elaine's, and he's an old friend of Sarge's."

She'd expected blowback sooner or later, after news of the developers going after the ranch became known and the town found out about her part in discovering the key to it. "It's just human to want to blame someone, and if it helps, I can take it."

"Anna, Ray called to say you did what you had to do, and they're praying for it all to work out for the best. He's offered to help Sarge any way he can, although I'm not certain he can do much except maybe give up a precious stone to put into a ring."

She stared up at Burr, realizing he was trying to kid and lighten up the mood. "What?"

"Nothing. Just a terrible joke."

She exhaled. "I'm sorry. I'm the outsider and I don't want anyone else blamed for the mess."

"This isn't a blame game, Anna. I told you these are good people, and they know you're a good person, too." He shook his head. "I almost forgot. I ran into Henry at Elaine's, and he said to tell you that the trailer hitch is installed. He'll drop your truck off this afternoon. Also, Lou Bradley, the head attorney from Seattle, called me on my way back. He's arranged an emergency court hearing in Cheyenne next Wednesday. He pushed hard for it, especially since Finnegan and company seem to know everything now."

"I'm sorry to hear that," she said and imagined William Finnegan doing a victory dance. It was an ugly mental image.

The front door opened, followed by a voice she hadn't realized how much she'd missed hearing until right then. "Hey, Burr, have you got some time to talk?" Ben called.

Burr went to the open door and nodded. "Of course, Ben. Go on into my office."

Anna tensed as Burr headed off. Ben came into view and glanced her way. He looked shocked, but there was no smile like the one at the wedding when he'd been surprised to see her. Then he was gone.

Burr's office door shut a moment later. A split-second glance from Ben was all she needed to admit that any effort she'd been making to convince herself that she couldn't love Ben, not after knowing him such a short time and after the way he acted, had been a waste. She loved him, and she knew she probably always would, even though he didn't want her.

BEN HAD ONLY come in to see Burr because Anna's truck hadn't been parked outside the office. He'd thought she wasn't there. He'd been wrong. There she was and, for a fleeting moment, her eyes had met his as he'd kept walking. But the image of her wearing a sky blue sweater and looking as startled as he'd been had hurt. He missed her and he had to work harder on not thinking about her so much.

Burr closed the door and motioned him to a seat across the desk from him. "So, what do we need to talk about?" Burr settled in his chair.

Ben didn't know where to start, so he just plunged in. "It's about Anna."

That's as far as he got. Burr leaned forward and pressed his hands flat on the desktop. "Son, stop right there," he said, not unkindly at all, just firmly.

"Burr, I—"

"She did what she had to do."

Ben sat back. "Of course she did." He didn't

want Anna to suffer for only doing what she'd promised him she would. "I need to ask you a favor, but I don't know if I should."

"There's only one way to find out," Burr said.

"Okay, Anna and I... We became pretty good friends, but things changed, and not because of the ranch situation. It was all my doing. I can't fix it, and I won't be seeing her again, but I would appreciate it if you'd let me know how she's doing from time to time or if she needs help of any kind?" After all she'd done for him and his family, he found it hard not to care about how she was going on with her life.

Burr's eyes narrowed as he sat forward again. "I knew something happened between the two of you, even though she's not talking about it. So why don't you fill me in on what you did to her?"

Anna had said she was starting to think of Burr as a second father, and the man seemed to be very protective of her. "I told her why we can't get involved—not with my work, and Sarge, and other things—and I didn't want it to go too far. I hurt her, and I regret that more than I can say, but it's done and can't be changed."

Burr studied him intently then asked bluntly, "Do you love her?"

Ben exhaled, looking away from the man across from him as his thoughts jumbled in his mind. He didn't know about love, but he knew he cared more about her than he had for any woman who had been in his life before her. He stood. "I should go. I just wanted to make sure she's all right."

"She's not all right, Ben, but I hope she will be." Burr rocked back in his chair. "If I see you out and about, and you ask about Anna, I'll tell you what I can."

That was all he could ask for.

ANNA ONLY SAW Ben twice in the days leading up to the court hearing in Cheyenne. Both times had been on the street, her in her truck and him walking. The first time she spotted him, he was with Boone near the general store. The second time, he'd been heading into Elaine's with Tripp.

She hadn't expected the chance sightings to hurt so much, so she'd determined to stop looking. She still went to ride Punch in the early mornings, never going near the house or the other structures. Traveler was always in his stall. Ben was nowhere around.

When she got ready to go to the office at six o'clock on the morning of the hearing, she dressed the way she had in Chicago. She chose to wear her suede jacket again, along with black dress pants, low heels and a white, tailored shirt. Her hair was skimmed back from her face in a simple low twist.

She started for the door but paused when she saw the two files Ben had brought to the carriage house on that Friday night. They were still sitting on the bench by the door. The Seattle attorneys had asked for the private files and had wanted all of them. She'd left them there to take with her into town and had walked right past them for the past two days without even glancing at them. She retrieved the files and put them in her leather shoulder bag, then headed out to the truck. She'd didn't know if there was anything in the files that might help, but she'd hand them to the attorneys at the courthouse and let them figure it out.

Once she was at the office in front of her computer, she stared at the blank monitor.

Nerves were twisting her into knots, and she wished Burr would hurry up and get there. She got up and went to the small refrigerator they used for drinks and snacks, but only found one power bar and two bottles of water. She took the bar and a bottle, then went back to sit by the computer.

As she tore the bar open, she eyed her leather shoulder bag, the edges of the file folders jutting from the open top. All those files did was remind her of too much, especially the lingering emptiness she felt so often lately. She tossed her bar onto the desk and reached for the bag to move the files out of her sight, but when she glimpsed the tab of the top one, she stopped and stared down at it. It was simply labeled *Water*.

*The one thing Sarge and Maggie didn't have years ago...*

She opened the folder. It held receipts and manuals for things like augurs, well casings, six pumps and piping, along with parts for windmills. They had all been purchased about thirty-five years ago. She sorted through it, page by page, then saw the receipts for existing wells tested and re-drilled to deeper levels to find better water streams.

She didn't know a lot about wells, but when she read a report on the first dry well, she understood how the testing had turned out.

Negative. No sustainable streams found. Recommend sealing and tagging.

She checked another report. The same outcome. She had no doubt the four other similar pages would have the same conclusions. Most of the water streams on the ranch had dried up years ago. She couldn't even imagine the hurt inflicted on Sarge and Maggie knowing their home could be destroyed because of something as basic as the lack of water.

She almost closed the file, then spotted more papers stuffed in the side pocket of the folder. She took them out and sorted through four more pages of Sarge's search for water. He'd even hired a person who did water dousing, also known as divining, using a stripped V-shaped branch made from the trees on the land. They'd found nothing. The last piece of paper was different from the others, heavier, more yellowed and folded once. She pulled it out, opened it, and her heart started to race.

Anna read the single page, then reread it. She

was still sitting there with the paper in her hand when she heard Burr come into the office a few minutes later. She turned as he approached her. "Are you ready to hit the road?" he asked. When Anna didn't respond, he frowned. "Hey, are you okay? You do not have to be there today, if you can't do it. I mean that."

"The attorney's assistant asked for any old files from the ranch, and I was supposed to get the ones I borrowed from the ranch files to him. I plain forgot until I saw them at Gabby's this morning. I was going to take them with me, and hand them over at the courthouse." Then she told him what she'd found. "Sarge and Maggie were watching the ranch die. I thought he'd maybe gone on to the government out of desperation to dig wells that no one would ever know existed. He didn't."

She held out the paper to him, and as he scanned it, she said, "Burr, it was all about the water. It always was." Anna felt a joy she thought she'd never feel again. They'd won! And yet… "I thought I'd found everything connected to the land, all the filings and the taxes from year one. I was wrong again, and I caused pure misery for everyone who loves Sarge."

Burr hushed her, but never took his eyes off the paper in his hands as he slowly reread a grant deed for 706.7 acres of land on the northwest side of the ranch. It had been presented to James Arthur Caine and Margaret Susan Caine. The official stamp was dated fifteen years after the original land purchase. If it was legitimate, the landlocked government parcel had actually been Sarge's property for about thirty-five years.

At the bottom of the single page, beside an embossed stamp from a notary, there was a handwritten note in fading ink. Burr read that out loud in a less than steady voice. "'Please accept this gift for all that you and Maggie have done and are going to do for youths who have no one to care. I do trust that the land with its water rights will help you in your mission of saving one child at a time. God bless you both.'" It was signed by the then governor of Wyoming.

As Burr finished reading, his voice broke, and he slowly shook his head. "Anna, this…" She saw him swallow hard before he looked down at her. He might never cry, but he looked close to it at that moment.

"It's real, isn't it? It was all about the water

rights, so he and Maggie could keep the ranch and keep helping kids."

"Yes," he breathed. "We need to get this to Lou Bradley quickly."

"Call the ranch."

He shook his head. "They changed plans and went to Cheyenne last night to be ready for the hearing today."

Anna's heart was racing. "Okay, you call Bradley and fill him in. How long is the ride down to the courthouse?"

"Maybe five hours."

"Okay, let's go," she said, gathering up her things while Burr slipped the grant deed into an envelope and fastened the seal.

WHEN BURR AND ANNA entered the two-story courthouse, they were met at the security area by the head attorney for the foundation, Lou Bradley. Greetings were short as they moved through the security scanning then they headed up to the room where the hearing was being held on the second floor. As they stepped off the elevator, Bradley—a short man in a very expensive gray suit—led the way into the hearing room, told them to sit down and that he'd be right back.

Burr and Anna stood at the back of the room that was divided by a railing separating spectators from the bailiff, the clerks and the judge. Anna recognized quite a few people from Eclipse, then glanced to her left at the second row from the back. William Finnegan was sitting by himself.

Then Bradley was back, the judge was seated, and it took less than five minutes for her to declare the deed to be original and that the land was James Caine's property, along with the water rights. With a knock of her gavel, it was all over.

Anna had almost been holding her breath until that moment, then she turned and hugged Burr.

"Kiddo, you did it," he murmured in her ear. "One other thing, Norman B. Good handed in his resignation yesterday. Leo told me to let you know."

She looked over his shoulder at Finnegan, who had just spotted her, and she grinned, finally doing a modified fist pump for his benefit. She thought she read his lips, then decided she didn't care what he called her. Slipping her arm in Burr's, she hurried out of the hearing room. "Burr, where is the family?"

"I don't know."

Bradley was there, coming up behind them, and his hand with its diamond-encrusted pinky ring rested on Anna's shoulder. "Ms. Watters, if you ever need a change of scenery, I would be proud to have you join our firm."

"Thanks, but I'm pretty happy where I am," she said, and Burr grinned at her. "Where's the family?" she asked the attorney.

"Once they knew the hearing was just a formality, they left for home." He held the large envelope out to Anna. "I promised I would give this back to you and Mr. Addison to take out to the ranch when you get home. They're really anxious to see the original for themselves."

Burr nudged Anna. "Let's get out of here, or we'll be inundated with lunch offers and people wanting to celebrate."

Anna followed Burr to the staircase and outside. Once settled in his truck, they set off for Eclipse.

When they arrived back in town, Anna asked Burr to drop her at the office so she could pick up her truck and drive herself to Gabby's. She felt drained and, honestly, didn't know how she'd do around everyone who'd be at the ranch.

She opened the door to get out of Burr's truck. "Gabby told me that there would be an eclipse tomorrow morning, early, and there's a great observation deck her grandfather built on the carriage house roof. I've never seen a full eclipse. So I think I'll rest, then watch it."

"Enjoy it," Burr said. "I'll get the deed out to the ranch."

"Tell everyone congratulations from me."

BY SEVEN O'CLOCK that evening, Sarge was sleeping in his room after he'd finally been told about the camp and the water rights. He'd really understood, and the joy on his face had been stunning. It made everything they'd gone through worth it. The others lingered in the great room, talking about the past and the future, while Ben sat silently with them, facing the stark reality that his future was set. He'd made sure of that.

Jake was with Libby on the couch. Seth and Quinn were playing Go Fish with Tripp, using the large ottoman for their table. He sat back, watching them, so thankful for his family, he couldn't put it into words. Then he heard someone drive up out front. "That must be Burr and Anna," he said and rose to greet them.

When he opened the front door, Burr was at the top of the step, an envelope in his hand that he held up for Ben to see. "Here it is. The real deed."

Ben felt a second wave of relief, the same as the first one he'd felt when Bradley had told them about Burr's locating the deed. "I don't know how to thank you for finding it."

"I didn't find it. Anna did."

He hadn't expected that. "What?"

Burr explained about the file, telling him what had been going on before the governor of the day had deeded the land to Sarge and Maggie. "So, it's all Sarge's. Every square inch of land and every drop of water."

Ben looked beyond Burr, but there was no Anna coming up the stairs. "Isn't Anna with you?"

"No," he said. "She's resting so she'll be awake to see the eclipse from the deck above the carriage house tonight."

"Is she okay?"

"Let's just say, I hope whatever reason you did what you did to her was worth it to you.

Honestly, I don't like anyone hurting her like you did."

The blow from Burr's words was low and direct. And Ben deserved it. "I had to do it, Burr."

"Then I wish *you* luck," Burr said, moving past him and into the house.

Ben had done the right thing, maybe not the way he should have, but he'd made sure he'd never hurt Anna again. He'd kept his promise to himself, but he wondered what price he'd pay in the future.

## CHAPTER FOURTEEN

At two o'clock in the morning, Anna was on the viewing deck above her room at the carriage house as the eclipse began. The moon barely showed a sliver of the earth's shadow on one edge. She had bundled up in jeans, a sweater, her red jacket and her boots, along with the pink wool throw off the bed to cover her legs. It was her first real eclipse, and she was watching it alone.

She stared up into the sky and saw dark clouds rolling in from the east. If they got any closer, she knew she wouldn't see the eclipse. If it didn't happen, it didn't happen. Life would keep going. Hers would keep going in Eclipse. It was home to her now, something she hadn't expected, but she knew this was where she was supposed to be.

She heard the creak of the ladder that stood right next to the door to her room. It was the only access point to the viewing deck from below. Another creak sounded and she turned, thinking Gabby must have decided to come up to watch the eclipse with her. But Gabby wasn't there. It was Ben stepping up onto the deck. She knew he saw her immediately, but he didn't say a word, just stood there motionless for an achingly long moment. Then he came toward her and sat on the viewing chair next to hers.

She didn't want him there. She didn't want him to be inches away from her. She didn't want to see his profile, the set of his shoulders under his denim jacket. And she didn't want to see him take off his Stetson and set it on his thigh crown-down. It all hurt too much.

Anna turned away to look up at the moon being blurred by the earth's shadow creeping in from the edge. "What are you doing here?" she asked. She sensed him shrug and then shift in his chair. Forcing herself to look at him, his impact on her only intensified.

"I needed to say something to you," Ben finally answered.

What she wanted was for him to leave her alone. "I think you've already said enough. I'm a fast learner."

Ben ignored that. "Burr said you found the deed."

"It was in one of the files I spilled on the floor in the office that day, the one marked *Water*. Since the land grant was all about the water rights, Sarge kept it with the receipts he had for setting up the new wells."

She heard him take a rough breath. "I needed to thank you," he said in a low voice. "It's over and done, and you made that happen. No one can challenge that land now." He stood, looked down at her and said, "If you ever need anything, we owe you more than we can ever repay."

Anna watched him turn away as he put his hat on and headed for the ladder. "Ben?"

He stopped at the sound of his name and turned but didn't walk over to her. "I have to get back, but I just wanted to say that to you. I owed you that much."

Frustration almost choked her, and words came to her that she had no idea she'd utter to him. "You know, you're a coward."

She heard his sharp gasp. "What?"

"You have this idea in your mind that you are not worthy of anything. No kids, no marriage, and especially that you're not lovable."

She stunned herself saying that, but she knew it was what she felt. "So, you do a good thing for kids in the system, you try to fix them, the way Maggie and Sarge wanted to fix you. Then you move on to another child, and another and another, and in the end you're alone."

"You don't know what you're talking about. You, with your perfect childhood, how could you know?"

She pushed up from her chair and took a step closer to him. "My dad died when I was thirteen. I know what bad is in life. I watch my mom, who's almost lost without him. I know about that. I miss him every day, every single day. Then I come out here and I lose my mind and almost fall in love with you. I know what I'm talking about." She took a shaky breath. "But you know what? I give up. You can wallow in your life and feel virtuous."

"I'm not wallowing, Anna. I'm facing reality—my reality."

"That's it." She quickly moved past him, climbed down the ladder, felt the porch under her feet, then crossed to go into her room and lock the door behind her.

She couldn't even cry. It was done. Really done. She went to the bed and fell back into the pillows. She was nothing right then, just empty.

Then she heard Ben descending the ladder, and mentally followed his progress rung by rung, his feet finally hitting the porch floor. There were steps on the landing that were followed by a soft rap on her door. "Anna?"

She heard him test the doorknob and then there was silence before he knocked again. "Please, open the door."

She closed her eyes tightly and managed to speak in a surprisingly unemotional voice. "Ben, go away. I'm here to pass the bar exam, build my career and work with Burr. That's what my life is going to be. I can't be your cheerleader when you don't believe in yourself. You do what you have to do with your life, but leave me alone."

BEN STOOD THERE as darkness fell when the eclipse was complete. He just stared at the door.

As he replayed Anna's words, he experienced a unique misery he'd only felt when he was a child. It was that sense of total loss every time he was put into the system and every time he was switched to another foster facility or sent back to juvenile court. Even in the system, they'd just wanted him to go away. Anna had joined that group, and he'd forced her there.

He pressed a hand flat on the door and leaned his forehead against the cold wood. As he felt the unyielding barrier and the deep chill in the contact, he realized right then that Anna Watters was the only woman he had ever truly wanted to keep in his life.

He stood back and reached into his jacket pocket for his cell. He felt desperate to make sense out of his life, a life that had morphed into something he didn't even recognize anymore. He found Anna's number, hit the Message icon and typed a text to her, asking her to let him explain. He hesitated then sent it. The first rays of moonlight were returning as the eclipse waned. Ben sat on the top step by Anna's door, his hat in his hands, waiting for a reply or for the door to open.

When the moonlight was fully revealed again, he stopped himself from pounding on the door. He'd lost everything, and it was his own doing.

As he stood to leave, he heard the click of the lock and the door swung back. He moved closer to look inside. Anna was there, standing in the soft glow of a bedside lamp. Her hair was down, and she was wearing a shirt of some sort that fell to her knees. How could he have ever thought he could live without her in his life?

"I...I thought you'd gone," she said so softly he could barely hear it.

"I couldn't. I wanted to know if you read my text."

She shook her head and her long hair drifted around her shoulders. "I didn't at first. You'd said more than enough. So had I."

He'd never felt so desperate in his life. "Please, just listen. Then I'll leave, if you want me to."

He heard her exhale softly. "Okay." She motioned to him. "Close the door. It's freezing."

He stepped in, swung the door shut and faced her in the soft shadows of the room.

Anna hesitated, turned, walked over to the bed and reached for her phone on the side table. She went to the foot of the bed and sank down on a large flat-topped trunk against the footboard. She was silent, just staring down at the phone in her hands.

Ben moved closer, saw a stool to one side and grabbed it so he could sit and face her. He took off his hat and gripped the brim in his hands as he waited for her to say something. When she just sat there staring at her phone, he decided to just tell her the naked truth. "I figured out a few things during the eclipse after you locked yourself in here. I can't ignore them any longer. I don't want to."

She didn't respond.

"Anna, I've never met any woman before who I wanted to stay in my life, to do anything even close to forever with. Before you, I walked away from all of them."

His words weren't thought out as they fell between them. It was his truth, and he was ashamed of how arrogant and selfish he'd been in the past. But he didn't stop. "Then you were there, and I thought it would be fun to be around you, nothing serious, just to enjoy time with you, like I did with the others."

He heard her take a sharp breath, and he was afraid she was going to get up and ask him to leave. He kept himself from reaching out for her. "I'm sorry, but the thing is, I thought I was letting you go for your sake, being honorable for once. I know now it was for my sake. It terrified me when I finally realized you are the only one I want to be with."

She closed her eyes tightly but still stayed silent.

"I was afraid to need someone, Anna, really afraid, because just about anyone I've needed in my life has abandoned me, except Maggie, Sarge, Jake and Seth. Easier not to need anyone else than to go through that again. So, I had my justification for being the one to leave. Then I realized you wanted everything I was running from." He sucked in air. "I forced you to do what I was terrified you'd do...walk away from me."

She released a shuddering sigh then opened her eyes.

"I haven't told you the most important thing."

Then he said something so profound, yet so foreign to him, that it literally shocked him. "I love you." They were such simple words, but just saying them out loud to Anna brought a monumental change in him. It freed him in some way he couldn't begin to explain.

"No, no," she whispered. "I can't do temporary. I wish I could. I wish that more than you'll ever know." She swallowed as she shook her head. "No, I've gone my whole life not even thinking I was in love, not looking for it, then I thought I'd found it, and it's… it's broken."

He tossed his hat onto her bed then sat down beside Anna on the trunk. He took a chance just touching her cheek, feeling her silky skin under his fingers. "I've been the one broken—until you were there, the piece missing in my life, the most important part of me. You make me whole, and I can't lose that. I can't lose you, Anna. I can't." He hesitantly leaned closer then kissed her, a bare brush of his lips across hers. "Please," he whispered as he drew back enough to look into her eyes. "I love you."

"How much do you love me?" she asked in an unsteady whisper.

That took him aback. He had no idea how to explain what he felt for her, much less how to quantify it. "I just love you, everything about you. Your dimples that match, your eyes when they change color from gray to blue. The way you kiss that stupid horse on the nose and get excited about a humming waterfall. I love that you read to Sarge and almost can't say the name Paul. I love the way you eat ribs with a knife and fork, and laugh at things that are just plain crazy, and the way you care about people."

Her eyes searched his face and she looked ready to cry. "I love you, too. I do," she whispered unsteadily. "But I'm doing forever and only doing it once in my life."

"Just tell me what you want."

"I want you with no conditions attached, no restrictions, no places we can't go with each other or for each other." She sniffed but ignored a tear that slipped silently down her cheek. He smoothed it away with his thumb, surprised to see how unsteady his hand was. "This is all totally new to me. I've never, ever… I mean, I've never been in love, but I know I can't live with limits on loving you or you loving me. I don't care if you travel a lot. I love what you do, and I'll be with you, but don't tell me that there's a part of you that I can't ever have."

He knew exactly where she was going and his heart began to race. "Kids. Anna, I don't know—"

She touched his lips with her forefinger, stopping what he'd begun to say. "Ben, I do know. You're the kindest, most caring man I have ever met in my life. You are truly re-markable. Any child you loved would be just as remarkable, because you'd believe in them and be there for them.

"It's not whether they would be your bi-ological child or your adopted child, they'd simply be your child, the way you'll always be Maggie and Sarge's son. Just the way Tripp is Seth and Quinn's son. Maggie and Sarge saved your life. That's what you could do for any child of yours."

Looking into her eyes, he knew it had never really been about him having children or not having children, but about that fear of being left. Now he was in love for the first time and he knew it would be forever. A weight he'd carried all his life was lifting as that scared little boy seemed to slip away.

He pulled Anna into his arms. She was ev-erything to him. Her presence and her touch took away all the nothingness in his life. It filled all his emptiness. Words came without any hesitation. "I love you enough to trust you completely and make our life together the best happily-ever-after life, with kids and dogs and cats and horses. Any way it happens." He was feeling brave now. "Anything else?"

"I just want the best life together with you forever," she said and kissed him, a connection so complete that his past was gone. He had his present and his future in his arms, and he wasn't letting her go. He'd finally broken out of the shadows and his only promise was to make Anna happy for the rest of their lives.

DAWN WAS STILL an hour away when Ben and Anna drove onto the ranch. Julia had told Ben that Sarge was okay when he'd called to check in, but he was asking to see Ben. He wanted to see Sarge, too. So, they went together into the ranch house and Julia was there. "Oh, were you two out eclipse watching?"

Ben slipped off his jacket and boots while Anna did the same, then he stood and smiled at her. "Yes, we certainly were, and it was beautiful. Go and get some sleep, Julia. We'll take care of Sarge."

She looked from Ben to Anna quizzically and nodded. "Thanks," she said and headed to her room.

Ben took Anna's hand, kissed her quickly,

then went in to see Sarge. He was sitting at an incline on the bed, the blue blanket pulled up to his waist, and he was looking annoyed. When he saw Ben and Anna, he smiled. "Well, well, well, if it isn't the pretty lawyer. Hello, there." It didn't seem to make a difference to Sarge that it was kind of the middle of the night.

"Anna came with me to visit with you for a while," Ben said as they took the chairs by the bed. He caught her hand with his and smiled at Sarge. "You're looking spiffy."

Sarge rolled his eyes then looked at Anna for a long moment. "Say, are you living here now?"

"No. I live in town, but I just love this ranch. It's incredible, and I think it would be a perfect place to live."

Ben squeezed her hand and met her blue eyes for a moment. "It's perfect now," he murmured.

Anna smiled and looked back at Sarge. "I bet it was one of your best days ever when you bought this land."

His faded blue eyes met hers. "Yeah, it was, but that was a long time ago." His gaze went to the picture still propped on the chair by the bed. "An even better day was when Maggie came with me to the cabin, then we moved down here."

"That had to be very special," she said.

Ben watched the two most important people in his life talking. It felt right, so right.

"Oh yes." Sarge sighed. "But there were other special times." Then out of the blue he said, "When we got that letter, you know, we'd been in bad times with the wells going dry. Maggie cried when she read the letter to me, but she was real happy, too. She did that sometimes, cry when she was really happy."

Ben leaned closer to slip his arm around Anna's shoulders, so thankful she was there with him. "What letter was it?" he asked.

Sarge was very quiet, just stared up at the ceiling for what seemed forever before he finally cast a narrowed glance at Anna. "It was an invite from the governor to go and visit him, and that's where he gave it to us." He chuckled huskily. "I didn't even vote for him, you know, but he was a real good guy."

Anna asked, "What did he give you?"

Sarge looked at her. "The governor said he'd heard that our wells were drying up, and he wanted to keep the ranch open so the boys would be able to go swimming." He laughed again. "That old tire swing broke a lot, but it was good fun. Maggie got the first ride to test it, and she jumped right into the lake, didn't she, son? She was pretty brave, huh?"

Ben could hardly answer around the tightness in his throat. "Yes…she was very brave," he said.

Anna rested her head on Ben's shoulder. "She sounds remarkable."

Sarge had a wistful smile and there was not a trace of sadness in his eyes now. He was clearly remembering good times. "So remarkable," he breathed. "But I never did it, even when Maggie tried to get me to do it." He looked at Ben. "You boys were clapping and chanting my name, but I didn't get on that swing. I was too smart for that."

"You don't know what you missed," Ben said.

He met his eyes. "Yeah, you're right. I wish I'd done it, you know. Just one time. Maggie would have loved that."

"Yes, she would have," Ben said.

Sarge exhaled and seemed to settle more comfortably into his bed. "We had steak with the governor." His voice was low. "Maggie got daisies." He sighed. "Her favorite flower."

Ben had always wondered how Sarge had found the love of his life and they'd been so happy together. But now, he felt as if he was just starting on that journey with Anna. "That's why she planted them up at the cabin."

"They made her happy...so happy." Sarge's eyes slowly closed as he whispered, "She had that smile...that beautiful smile. I loved that smile...so much."

Ben glanced at Anna, who was wiping at her eyes as she watched Sarge ease into sleep. He leaned closer to Anna's ear. "He remembers," he said softly.

"But the swing had to be up long before you came here. How did you know about it?" Anna asked in a quiet voice.

"Actually, Sarge didn't put the tire swing up until the first summer I was here. It was really hot, and Maggie wanted it. I guess he was remembering good times and ran them all together."

He kissed Anna's cheek, feeling a peace he wasn't sure he'd ever felt in his life. "I love you," he breathed.

Out of nowhere Sarge said in a low voice, "I told you, Anna. Ben's a keeper."

Anna grinned at Ben, and the dimples were there. "Yes, he certainly is a forever kind of guy."

## *EPILOGUE*

THE BUS WITH the campers pulled through the gates and under the arch that read *Sarge's Hope* at eight o'clock in the morning the Saturday after the Fourth of July. The boys, between twelve and fifteen years of age, had come from three facilities in the southern end of the state. Dwight rode a horse alongside the bus as it made its way along the bladed road, past the old cabin and on to the parking area by the registration center and the mess hall.

As the bus came to a stop, Ben and Anna were there, waiting with the staff, for the doors to open. They were both wearing jeans and camp T-shirts along with riding boots on the warm sunny day. Anna could feel Ben's excitement, and it echoed within her.

Sarge was also there, waiting at the reception center. Jake and Libby had driven him down at the last minute, and Cal and Julia had readied him on a bench by the doors where the boys would register. He was smiling from ear to ear, watching as the campers disembarked one after the other. They stood in awe looking around.

Anna leaned closer to Ben. "This is it, sweetheart, the first feet-on-the-ground."

He hugged her tightly to his side. "I'm getting nervous."

"Why? It's all set, and everything's perfect."

"But the boys, what if they—?"

She turned to him. "Burr told me you can't add an inch to your height by worrying about being short."

"That's profound," he said with a slight smile.

"I thought so." She watched as the group leaders showed the boys where to line up while they checked their names and noted where they'd come from. "The staff you put together is great. They aren't babysitters and they can help the kids emotionally and physically," she said.

Ben scanned the group and leaned toward Anna. "See that boy over there with his hair shaved high on each side, maybe thirteen or so?"

She saw the boy he was talking about,

a skinny kid who hung back from the others. He looked bored to death. Or disgusted. Maybe both. "He doesn't look excited, does he?"

"I'll be right back," Ben said as he headed in the boy's direction. She watched the man she would marry in September stop by the boy as the group leaders explained about the horses. Ben leaned over and said something that brought a frown to the boy's face. But Ben nodded and smiled. The kid wasn't smiling.

She looked over at Seth and Quinn, with Tripp staying close to them, and at Jake and Libby, who were helping the team leaders get things in order. Then Anna glanced at Sarge, who seemed focused on Ben and the boy. He never looked away until Ben patted the kid on the shoulder before coming back to Anna.

"What happened?" she asked.

"I recognized him."

"You knew him before?"

"No, but he's just like I was. You know what he said to me when I tried to talk to him? He said that it smelled around here."

Anna smiled. "You did say that yourself."

"Yeah, and he said that he wished he hadn't come."

"He's only here for a week, Ben. He might never like it."

He looked right at her. "He might not, but I'm not writing him off."

She slipped her hand into his and laced their fingers. She loved him so much. She also knew that his decision to take over the administration of the camp through the Foundation as an on-the-ground director was a perfect one. "I think he'll be just fine with you around," she said softly.

Ben squeezed her hand as he glanced over at Sarge. Anna watched the two men look at each other, catching Sarge's nod and smile. Anna could tell for that moment in time, the man understood everything and approved.

Seth and Quinn went to Sarge and sat to his left while Tripp sat on the older man's lap. He and his grandpa were great friends.

Jake and Libby walked over to join the others.

Sarge looked up and said something to Libby, who instinctively touched her stomach. Her pregnancy was just starting to show. It had brought a lot of joy to Sarge when they'd told him at Jake's birthday party on the Fourth of July that their baby was a little girl, and her name was to be Margaret Liberty Bishop. Sarge had been thrilled that Seth and Quinn had brought Tripp into his life, a grandson, and now he was going to be a grandfather to a little girl named Maggie.

Ben leaned closer to Anna. "Did you see who just arrived?" He pointed to a truck pulling in behind the bus.

Burr got out. Spotting Anna, he waved and went around to open the door for his passenger. Elaine stepped out and the two of them headed for Ben and Anna, already wearing their camp T-shirts.

"This is fantastic!" Burr said as they neared. Even though he and Elaine had been dating for a couple of months now, they still acted like teenagers.

Burr hugged Anna and whispered in her ear, "You made this happen. I'm very proud of you."

That meant so much to her. "Thank you."

"Right now, it seems I've been volunteered to help the mess cook provide food for this crowd." Burr glanced in Sarge's direction.

"Now, that's a sight to behold. I haven't seen him look so happy in a very long while."

Anna had thought the same thing, as if having a bright future unfolding in front of him had given Sarge a second wind. She hoped it lasted for a long time, or at least until he held his granddaughter in his arms around Christmas.

Most of the new arrivals were now scattering off with their team leaders, and horses were being led to the practice area for the campers to be rated and assigned a ride.

As they watched, someone shouted Ben's name and they both turned their eyes toward the source. Sarge was waving at them. "Come on, get over here, son!" Sarge called out.

"Coming," Ben called back. Taking Anna by her hand, they made their way over.

As Anna and Ben joined the others gathered around Sarge, Sarge motioned to the photographer. "He's gonna take a family photo with my boys and their ladies."

"And me, Grandpa!" Tripp said quickly.

Sarge laughed. "Absolutely, with my grandson, too."

Ben and Anna went to stand behind Sarge,

and Ben put his arm around her then rested his free hand on Sarge's shoulder.

Anna heard Sarge whisper, "Maggie, our boys did it."

When the photographer snapped the last shot, Jake, Seth and Ben were looking at their father and smiling.

* * * * *

# Get 4 FREE REWARDS!

**We'll send you 2 FREE Books plus 2 FREE Mystery Gifts.**

**Love Inspired** books feature uplifting stories where faith helps guide you through life's challenges and discover the promise of a new beginning.

**FREE** Value Over **$20**

# HARLEQUIN SELECTS COLLECTION

**19 FREE BOOKS IN ALL!**

RaeAnne Thayne — A COLD CREEK HOMECOMING

LINDA LAEL MILLER — SIERRA'S HOMECOMING

B.J. DANIELS — MOUNTAIN SHERIFF

### From Robyn Carr to RaeAnne Thayne to Linda Lael Miller and Sherryl Woods we promise (actually, GUARANTEE!) each author in the Harlequin Selects collection has seen their name on the *New York Times* or *USA TODAY* bestseller lists!

**YES!** Please send me the **Harlequin Selects Collection**. This collection begins with 3 FREE books and 2 FREE gifts in the first shipment. Along with my 3 free books, I'll also get 4 more books from the Harlequin Selects Collection, which I may either return and owe nothing or keep for the low price of $24.14 U.S./$28.82 CAN. each plus $2.99 U.S./$7.49 CAN. for shipping and handling per shipment*.If I decide to continue, I will get 6 or 7 more books (about once a month for 7 months) but will only need to pay for 4. That means 2 or 3 books in every shipment will be FREE! If I decide to keep the entire collection, I'll have paid for only 32 books because 19 were FREE! I understand that accepting the 3 free books and gifts places me under no obligation to buy anything. I can always return a shipment and cancel at any time. My free books and gifts are mine to keep no matter what I decide.

☐ 262 HCN 5576          ☐ 462 HCN 5576

Name (please print)

Address                                                                   Apt. #

City                              State/Province                    Zip/Postal Code

### Mail to the **Harlequin Reader Service:**
**IN U.S.A.:** P.O. Box 1341, Buffalo, NY 14240-8531
**IN CANADA:** P.O. Box 603, Fort Erie, Ontario L2A 5X3

50BOOKHS22R